WINTER'S WEB

WINTER BLACK SERIES: BOOK SEVEN

MARY STONE

To my husband.
Thank you for taking care of our home and its many inhabitants
while I follow this silly dream of mine.

DESCRIPTION

Human webs are the deadliest...

When Ryan O'Connelly—the unwilling accomplice of a bank robber turned mass murderer—slipped out of the FBI's grasp, no one expected to hear from him again, much less of his own volition. But when he shows up at the FBI's doorstep after almost a year of successful evasion, he has information to point Special Agent Winter Black in the direction of a brutal serial killer.

As Ryan takes the team into the deep, dark web of sinister secrets, Winter receives an even more disturbing message from her brother than the last. She can feel him out there...watching, waiting.

Lucky for Winter, she isn't afraid of spiders. She's only afraid when the spider disappears.

Book seven of Mary Stone's addictive Winter Black Series, Winter's Web, exposes what goes on behind closed doors and the web of lies and deadly truths we ignore to protect the ones we love.

1

As Nathaniel Arkwell stepped out of the garage and eased the door closed behind himself, he noticed right away that the house was far quieter than usual. Turning the deadbolt back into place, he glanced around the mudroom, taking in the bench, the few pairs of shoes beneath it, and the jackets that hung from hooks on the other side.

The space was immaculate. Even the black chalkboard above the bench had been recently wiped clean. Nathaniel's daughter, Maddie, had made the board over the summer to help her remember important school functions.

The knack for organization was a trait she'd inherited from him. In all Maddie's seventeen years of life, Nathaniel could count on one hand the number of times he'd had to remind her to clean her room. More often than not, her bedroom was every bit as tidy as his home office.

He was grateful for the common ground he and Maddie had discovered as she grew older. They maintained an open dialogue about everything from her senior geology class to the navigation of the high school social scene.

However, a knack for cleanliness was virtually the only

thing Nathaniel and his college-aged son had in common. In the eleven years since Katrina Arkwell—Nathaniel's beloved wife and the mother of his children—died, the gap between him and Cameron had only widened. He'd made a valiant effort to bridge the veritable canyon between them, but to no avail.

The thought coaxed a sigh from his lips. Sometimes, he thought Katrina had been the only thing that kept his son tethered to the real world.

With one foot, Nathaniel shoved both shiny black dress shoes beneath the bench before he made his way through the hall and into the spacious kitchen.

A tinge of light was visible through the picture windows at the other end of the room. The splash of color was all that remained of the sun's rays. For the third night in a row, he hadn't gotten home from work until after the sun had disappeared below the horizon.

Like the mudroom, the kitchen was spotless. The house-cleaning staff had already left for the day, and apparently, no one had been through the house since. If Cameron or Maddie had used the kitchen, there would be evidence of their pit stop. As neat as they were, there would be, at the very least, the faint smell of pizza or tacos. Maddie had recently discovered a love for onions, so Nathaniel was certain he'd still be able to smell her last meal.

No, he already knew that neither of his children were home. He couldn't stop yet another sigh, this one in relief, at the knowledge. He loved his children, but quiet wasn't a privilege he often received.

Cameron attended classes at Virginia Commonwealth University and Maddie was a high school senior, but their days off tended to correspond with one another. Tomorrow was a weekday, but neither of them had class, Nathaniel remembered. Maddie sent him a text earlier in the day to ask if she could stay overnight with a friend, and he'd given her his blessing.

And with Cameron? Well, who knew. Nathaniel could only hope he was at a kegger or a bar. Some place conducive to the activities of a normal college kid.

Nathaniel strode through the kitchen and the breakfast area, his stocking feet little more than a whisper of sound. He shrugged off his messenger bag as he headed past the great room and to the base of the staircase. Aside from the usual recessed lights and a floor lamp, no other fixtures had been turned on.

Feeling much older than his forty-four years, he ascended to the open loft of the second floor. From the raised vantage point, he took one last look over the living area and what he could see of the kitchen and breakfast room. Still, there was no movement.

Though he had no reason to think danger awaited him on the second floor of the house, the hairs on the back of his neck rose to attention at the unsettling quiet.

Clenching his jaw, he gave himself a mental shake, hoping to rid himself of the sudden bout of paranoia. The outside of the house was monitored twenty-four-seven via a system of security cameras and motion sensor lights. Inside, the alarm system came with around the clock backup support of one of the city's best regarded personal security firms.

Well, if there were no children or employees who needed his attention, he might as well take the opportunity to get a head start on some work.

In part because the house was so clean, and in part because he'd just been in his office that afternoon, Nathaniel noticed the envelope as soon as he flicked the switch that brought the floor lamp in the corner to life.

There, in the center of the polished mahogany corner desk set a nondescript white envelope. His first thought was that Maddie had surprised him with one of the charms she'd taught herself to make. But as he drew nearer, he knew the handwriting wasn't Maddie's.

The handwriting belonged to his son.

Nathaniel wasn't convinced that Cameron was a bad kid, but the boy was...odd. He portrayed himself much differently to his classmates and even his sister than he did to his father. To them, Cameron was a normal, twenty-two-year-old undergraduate student.

But to Nathaniel, he was someone else entirely.

Nathaniel was allergic to cats, and after an attempt to bring in a guinea pig for Maddie when she was eight, Nathaniel was finally grateful for the allergy. Porky the guinea pig went missing a couple weeks after Maddie brought him home.

At first, Nathaniel just assumed that his eight-year-old daughter had left the door to the cage unlocked, and Porky made a run for freedom. As far as he'd been concerned at the time, the loss was a normal part of growing up and learning responsibility. He hadn't been harsh with Maddie when he sat her down to discuss the guinea pig's absence, but she was still adamant that she'd been diligent in looking after her pet.

The days turned into weeks and the weeks into months, but there was still no sign of Porky.

Then, that spring, their longtime housekeeper, Martha, had been digging in the garden to tend to her yearly vegetable patch. The remains were highly decomposed at that point, but Martha pulled Nathaniel aside to show him the body not long after she found it. Nathaniel had never excelled at anatomy or possessed any other medical expertise, but even he could tell that Porky had been ripped to pieces before the poor thing was buried.

A coyote, maybe. Or a cat. He'd assured the woman that

Porky had been attacked by a wild animal, nothing more. It was just something that happened.

Porky was the first, but the guinea pig was far from the last.

Eventually, after Martha caught Cameron dissecting a small dog, she put in her two weeks' notice, and Nathaniel had given her a huge severance bribe to ensure she kept her mouth closed regarding the incident. There had been posters all around the neighborhood for weeks after the incident, each offering a cash reward for an update on the pup's whereabouts. Each time Nathaniel saw one, he felt physically ill.

Even then, he'd convinced himself that Cameron's fascination with the inner workings of living creatures was normal. Maybe Cameron would become a doctor or a surgeon, maybe that was why he'd taken to chopping up small animals.

But somewhere in the back of his mind, he'd known.

After Porky, Nathaniel didn't permit any more pets. He'd caved and gotten Maddie an aquarium a year ago, but he figured fish were a safe enough option.

Leaning his messenger bag against the side of the desk, Nathaniel dropped down to sit in the leather office chair. As he picked up the envelope, a small object shifted inside.

Though he expected a slip of paper to explain the contents, the only item sealed within was a cheap plastic flash drive.

As he dropped the device into his palm, his mouth suddenly felt like it was stuffed with cotton balls. Swallowing against the unpleasant dryness, he reluctantly opened his laptop and pressed a button to bring the screen to life.

There was only one file on the drive. A video.

Nathaniel raked a shaky hand through his hair as he opened the file.

When he spotted the length, his eyes widened. Four hours?

As he gritted his teeth, he leaned in closer to squint at the screen. The camera had been placed high up in a corner of the dim room, either mounted to the wall or atop a shelf. Aside from a twin-sized bed against the far wall, a wooden chair, and an end table, the space was unadorned. He thought he saw the shape of a person tucked beneath the blankets, but the area was cloaked in shadows, and he couldn't be sure.

He hovered an index finger above the trackpad, clenching and unclenching his jaw as he willed himself to press play.

For the first few moments, he thought the video wasn't a video at all. He did such a thorough job convincing himself that the image was a still that he almost leapt out of his seat when the shadows along the bed shifted.

A young woman sat upright, her movements hurried as she flung off the dark comforter. Her head snapped from side to side, but the recording had been made with no audio. Though Nathaniel could see that she was speaking, he couldn't hear anything aside from the uneasy stillness of the empty house around him.

He didn't recognize the room, didn't recognize the girl, the furniture, none of it.

Nathaniel took in a sharp breath as the young woman climbed out of bed.

One of her ankles was shackled. Wherever she was, she had been chained to a wall.

Mouth agape, he watched in stunned silence as she made her way around the room to inspect the walls and the floor. Either she didn't notice the camera, or the device had been hidden.

As Nathaniel caught a glimpse of her panicked expression, he hoped that this was some sort of film project—some artsy representation of human trafficking or the start of a homemade horror movie. As long as everyone involved was consenting, he didn't care what the video was.

But the more he looked at her terrified countenance, the more and more certain he became that she wasn't in that room of her own volition.

It was a film project. It had to be.

Cameron rarely discussed his school courses with Nathaniel. He must have enrolled in an elective film class to satisfy a general education requirement.

That's what this was. He was sure of it.

No matter how convincing his rationalization, Nathaniel couldn't fight off the tightness in his throat as he watched the blonde woman tuck her knees up to her chin at the foot of the bed.

As much as he wanted to know what else the video might have captured, he couldn't sit and watch the girl's frightened movements for four whole hours. After a steadying breath, he tapped the fast-forward button.

She didn't move from the bed until the half-hour mark, and even then, she was back on the mattress within ten minutes. At the accelerated pace, he could almost trick himself into thinking her movements were no longer frightened or panicked.

The two-hour mark passed, then three, then four, and still no change. Just as he was sure the entire video was merely footage of the young woman in the dim room, the screen flashed to black.

With a sharp intake of breath, Nathaniel tapped the touchpad again to bring the pace back to normal.

When the black screen flipped back to the video of the room, the space was bathed in the bright glow of what Nathaniel assumed were stage lights.

The woman was no longer alone.

There was only enough of the man's skin visible to

confirm that he was Caucasian, but otherwise, he was clad in black from head to toe. Even the eyeholes of his ski mask were covered with a pair of dark sunglasses.

As the man approached his captive huddled on the concrete floor, Nathaniel could hear little over the pounding of his pulse. Bile stung the back of his throat, but he couldn't so much as will himself to swallow. All his attention, all his energy, everything he had was fixed on the event unfolding on his computer screen.

The stage lights glinted off the tear streaking down her flushed cheeks as the woman scrambled away from the man's advance.

Her effort was futile. She'd backed into a corner. There was no escape.

As swift as a venomous snake, the man snapped one arm out and clamped a gloved hand around her throat.

She shouted and tried to shove him away, but the attempted rebuff was in vain.

Nathaniel didn't know what to expect next. He didn't know who the man was, and despite the close vantage point, he still didn't recognize the girl.

It's a film project, he reminded himself.

A film project.

Silver flashed beneath the bright lights as the man produced a butcher knife from behind his back. With the same unnerving quickness, he pressed the blade to her throat.

There was no audio, but Nathaniel could clearly make out the word "please" as she pressed herself farther into the corner. Unperturbed, the man clamped a gloved hand over her mouth, shoved her head back, and dragged the knife across her throat.

"Jesus Christ!" Nathaniel exclaimed, jumping back from

the laptop so hard and fast that his chair crashed into the wall.

Blood. So much blood.

As her head lolled and her lifeless blue eyes turned toward the camera, Nathaniel closed his own.

It was a film project. It was a homemade horror movie, and the blonde was a damn good actress. Fake blood could be purchased by the gallons. Prosthetics used to mimic wounds of every size.

Yes.

That was it. That was the only possible explanation.

A film project.

It had to be.

2

Before he pressed the enter key to initiate the video call, Ryan O'Connelly raked a hand through his hair and sighed. For almost an entire year, he'd crept through life in the shadows. The darkness had become his new normal, anonymity his new mode of operation. If he kept his head down and stuck to the shadows, he had a chance to avoid detection by either the Federal Bureau of Investigation or any of the law enforcement agencies that'd be happy to take him down.

He was used to life on the run, but he was used to worrying about one person and one person only. Himself.

But now, he wasn't alone anymore.

Less than a week after the ordeal with Heidi Presley—a certifiable psychopath who'd left a trail of bodies in her wake as she went around the country to recreate a series of legendary heists—Ryan had received a desperate message from his little sister. That had been nine months before. At the time, Ryan had been able to get his sister and her children to safety. But to what end? So that they could fear that each knock on the door would be the law coming to get them?

They'd lived in fear long enough.

It needed to be over.

He and his sister had grown up in abject poverty in the heart of Chicago, and they'd both been subjected to the violent whims of their uncle. The man was a drunk and a slob, but in all honesty, those were his two most redeeming qualities.

For the time they'd grown up together, he and Lil had been inseparable. He'd watched her back, and she'd watched his. Ryan had thrown himself in their uncle's line of fire to protect his sister more times than he cared to count, but after the bastard almost killed him when he was just a sophomore in high school, he left. He didn't tell his friends, didn't tell his sister, didn't tell a single soul. At just fifteen years old, he limped out the door, swearing to return when he was able.

When he did return months later, the shitty little apartment was filled with new tenants. Lillian was gone.

It had taken him more than two years to find her again, and when he'd finally found the courage to face her, she'd punched him in the face.

He'd taken the hit like a man, knowing he'd deserved it and more, but when he begged her to go with him, she'd refused. She had been about to turn seventeen, and she claimed that she was in love with a man nine years her senior. He'd keep her safe, she'd told him.

Unlike my brother.

Lillian hadn't said the words, but he'd felt the weight of them, nonetheless.

At the time, Ryan had taken the refusal as a personal slight. He'd tried, and he convinced himself that he had done all he could.

When she still said no after he'd asked a third time, he did what he had to do.

He left before his uncle could catch on to his presence.

For the second time, he left Lillian without so much as a glimmer of hope.

He'd been scared—scared of his uncle, scared of who Lillian had become while he was gone, scared of being forced back into that lifestyle. He was enough of an adult now that he could admit to the fright.

Now, fifteen years later, he knew she'd done whatever was needed to survive. But back then, her refusal stung like a slap in the face. He hadn't been at her wedding that took place just a few days after she'd turned eighteen years old. He also hadn't been there when her husband died a few years later. It wasn't until she was married a second time and became pregnant that they'd spoken again. She was a few months pregnant at the time, and despite the distance that had come between them, she proudly made him the godfather of her first child, a little girl.

When he got Lillian's panicked call a week after Heidi Presley's reign of terror finally ended, he'd been determined not to leave her behind like he had when they were teenagers. Just as Ryan had sworn to himself years ago, he didn't hesitate. He didn't cast judgment. He just helped her.

The most dangerous time in an abusive relationship—the time when the victim was the most at risk to be killed by their abuser—was when they were leaving. Unlike fifteen years earlier, Ryan was there for the long haul.

Lillian was safe now, and he'd make sure it stayed that way.

Flexing the fingers of one hand, he pulled himself out of the reverie and tapped the enter key. He'd already sent her a text to give her a heads-up for the video call, and she answered before the second ring had finished.

With a slight smile, she pushed the strands of dark hair from her eyes as she offered a quick wave. "Hey, bro. How's it going?"

He laughed for the first time in what felt like a thousand years. "Bro? What, are we in a frat now?"

Her pale blue eyes were brighter as she laughed, and for a moment, the shadows of weariness didn't seem so pronounced. "If we were, we'd have to come up with a secret handshake."

Some of her mirth found its way to his face as he chuckled. "No doubt. Are Evan and Erin in there with you?"

Glancing to somewhere offscreen, she shook her head. "No. They're watching *Pokémon*. You were right, by the way. They're hooked. I bought them each a stuffed Pokémon when we went to the store after school this afternoon. Erin got a little cat, and Evan got a little turtle." She swung her legs off the edge of the bed and walked off screen. A few seconds later, he heard the soft click of a door closing.

Ryan had to make a conscious effort to keep the strain from his smile when she returned, sitting back down on the bed. Lil, Evan, and Erin had settled in Omaha, Nebraska, and Ryan was clear out in Virginia. So far, his time on the East Coast had been lonely. It didn't help that he was stalked by a pervasive worry that Lil's abusive ex, James Lowell, would locate the three of them. At least if Ryan was there, he could do something about it.

Even though Ryan's so-called work took him all around the globe, he had made a point to try to keep in contact with his sister after she'd given birth to Erin. But with each passing month, he'd felt like a riptide was pulling Lillian farther and farther away from him.

Those last few times he'd traveled to Chicago to visit his niece and nephew, Ryan hadn't missed the concealer Lillian used to cover the bruises on her arms.

It was a misunderstanding, she'd told him. A one-off. James had been laid off from his long-time position as a welder, and they were stressed. Lil was enrolled in community college classes for the upcoming semester, but they had to put the plans on hold so she could get a full-time job to help support them until James found another position.

Her explanation had been so hopeful and genuine that Ryan believed it. Only months later, long after the late-night conversation, did he realize that the line was the same used by countless other victims of abuse around the world.

Lil's voice snapped him out of the glum thoughts. "I can't believe kids are still into that stuff. I mean, *Pokémon* was popular when we were in school, right?"

He tried to appear thoughtful as he scratched his chin. "I suppose so, yeah. I remember kids trading the cards during lunch hour. I think it missed me by a couple years, though."

She spread her hands in a show of pensiveness as she took her seat. "It's never too late."

"I'll have to start my own Pokémon collection the next time we're all together." Even as he smiled, he didn't miss the shadow that passed over her face.

"I'm guessing that's what you wanted to talk about?" Her voice had grown quiet as her blue eyes flicked back and forth between the door and the webcam.

He nodded slowly. "Yeah. It is."

The shadow of concern had darkened, and she looked like she hadn't slept for a full forty-eight hours. "You saw that poor girl in the video. You saw her eyes. I know it's been a long time, but Jesus, Ryan." She paused to rub her forehead. "We've seen someone die before. And...and her eyes. Those were dead eyes. There's no actor who could fake that."

Ryan'd been hesitant to bring up the disturbing videos to his sister at first, but he couldn't get the nagging guilt out of his head and had needed to talk to someone about it.

Someone he could trust. Besides, Lil had been in the midst of getting her criminal justice degree when her first husband died, with a goal of becoming a forensic investigator when she graduated. His sister loved crime investigation shows and read CSI novels by the dozens.

Plus, she was right. They'd both seen dead bodies before. Their mother's drug overdose. Their father's suicide. How could people do something like that with their children in the house?

At first, Ryan had tried to pretend that he hadn't seen the video, but after only a couple days, he'd broken down and explained to his sister what he'd found. He hadn't wanted to burden her with the knowledge, but these days, she was his only friend.

Clenching his jaw, he nodded again. "I know. And I know where I found it. That website, it's a dumping ground for twisted people like Ted Bundy and that old bastard from out here in Virginia, Douglas Kilroy. It's where those pricks go to kill time. None of the videos on there are fake. Whoever that girl was, she's dead. And whoever that guy dressed in black was, he killed her."

Lil combed the stray strands of hair away from her forehead as she sighed. "Look, I know that plan I came up with is a long shot. I know that the FBI's been after you for a while now, and taking this thing to them to try to get back in their good graces, or at least to get off their shit list, probably isn't even possible. I know there's a real chance that none of this will work out, but..." As her voice cracked, she brushed the tears away from her tired eyes.

He hated how much of Lil's self-worth that bastard had taken from her. Abusive pricks were all the same like that. They wanted their victims to sever all ties to family and friends, to be completely dependent on them.

If Ryan was there right now, he could give Lil a hug and a

bit of reassurance. But he couldn't be there. He couldn't risk putting Lil, Evan, and Erin in the FBI's crosshairs. If the bureau found them, they'd charge Lil with harboring a fugitive or whatever other nonsense violation they could concoct.

As it stood, she was already on shaky legal ground that had little to do with him.

Lillian had been awarded custody of Erin and Evan, but the door was still open for their father to sue for visitation in spite of the abuse charges and restraining orders she'd filed against him. Winning sole custody and completely cutting one parent out of a child's life was a difficult legal feat, even if the parent in question had been accused of violence.

Ryan ground his teeth together. The stupid law had placed his sister precisely between a rock and a hard place. She'd had little doubt that the bastard would kill her if she stayed put in Chicago. Fleeing and not appearing in court meant facing charges ranging from a custody violation to kidnapping.

With very little choice left and with Ryan's help, she dropped off the face of the planet and changed all their surnames.

But they still weren't completely safe.

If the Feds caught Ryan with Lil, then they'd send Evan and Erin back to their asshole father. And while Ryan was more than willing to risk his own safety in the pursuit of a better quality of life, he wasn't willing to risk the safety of the only family he had left.

Not again.

Never again.

Ryan shook his head. "No, Lil. Don't say that. You're right. I mean, I came here to make some money off these rich arseholes, but you're right. If that video is the kind of twisted stuff they're into, then someone needs to do something about it. And right now, it seems like I'm the only one who cares enough to do it."

With a light sniffle, she wiped her eyes with the sleeve of her shirt. "It's the bystander effect."

He ran through his mental dictionary and came up blank. "What's that?"

She leaned closer to the screen. "When there are a lot of people around during an emergency, there's a lot lower likelihood that any one of them will do something to help. They just assume the person beside them will jump in, or that someone else will see what's happening and help. I learned about it in my intro to psych class a few years ago. The more people who are there, the less likely any one of them is to do something."

Ryan shoved a hand through his hair and heaved a sigh. "Jaysus. Yeah, I guess so. Sure seems like it here."

A week ago, his contact in a group of Virginia's wealthy elite—a middle-aged widow whose husband had been a prominent member of the group—had come to him with a rumor she'd heard around their secretive club. According to that rumor, one of the members had a penchant for taking out their ire on a certain subset of the population—prostitutes.

Just like Ted Bundy and the Cleveland Strangler, the man preyed on the most vulnerable members of society.

His contact's seat in the so-called secret club was largely honorary. Though her deceased husband was a founding member of the group, Mrs. N had never taken much of an interest in their activities. She'd shown up to the events with her husband, but otherwise, she'd steered clear of the other members.

To her credit, Mrs. N kept up a convincing façade of indifference when they were at dinners or other social events. The men and women with whom they met were all the same. Wealthy and powerful. And as a public figure herself, Mrs. N couldn't risk inviting their wrath.

Ryan cleared his throat and returned his attention to the laptop. "You're right. Someone needs to do something, and this is the best chance I've got at clearing my name with the Feds."

After a jaunt down to the dark underbelly of the world wide web, Ryan found an entire forum dedicated to the voyeuristic pursuits of stalkers all around the globe. They swapped information, shared photos, helped one another plan, all of it.

And there, he found the video of a blonde woman. Watched in horror as her throat was slit, her blood pooling all around her.

He'd seen firsthand the damage a psychopath could inflict if they were left unchecked. Heidi's brutality was still fresh in Ryan's mind, and he wasn't sure he could cope with the guilt of knowing he could have prevented any more innocent deaths.

It was Lil's turn to sigh. "Why does it have to be you, though? Why did this Mrs. N woman have to tell you about it? Shouldn't she have been the one to go to the cops?"

He bit back a groan. "She's a state senator. She's got an image to uphold, and apparently, even though she's got a little bit of a conscience, she doesn't have enough of one to risk her career and her cushy life. You want my guess about why she told me and not someone else in that group?"

Lil nodded.

Ryan shifted in his seat. "Because she personally knows all those other people, and she knows better than to try to talk to any of them. She wasn't about to tell any of them that she thought one of their ranks was kidnapping and murdering prostitutes at the edge of town. Wasn't about to tell them that her prostitute sister was scared because some of the women had been disappearing."

Lillian's expression darkened. "She probably doesn't even want them to know that she has a sister, does she? My god, those people are all the same, aren't they?"

Ryan finally let out a weary breath. "They are. And apparently, a lifelong thief has more of a conscience than any of those arseholes. Even the ones that actually have a conscience to speak of."

With a quiet snort, Lil shook her head. "Apparently. You're going to do it, then? You're going to the FBI?"

If the fear in Mrs. N's eyes hadn't been so prominent when she told him about the rumored disappearances, Ryan wouldn't have bothered to try to research the claim. Sometimes, he wished he'd listened to the devil on his shoulder, and not the angel.

After all, he'd connected with Mrs. N and her elite friends to steal from them, bit by bit. Not turn into some do-gooder willing to risk his hide.

But here he was.

Even as his stomach dropped, he nodded. "Yeah. Soon, real soon."

"How do you know that they don't already know about it?"

He gestured to the laptop. "Because that website and all those videos are still there. If the Feds were on to them, it would have all disappeared. And that 'rumor' wouldn't still be floating around. My guess? If the Feds were on to whoever made that video, all these shit birds would've run for the hills by now. Maybe none of 'em are murderers aside from the one, but none of their hands are clean."

Lifelong thief or not, Ryan was confident there were fewer skeletons in his figurative closet than any one of the men or women with whom he kept company.

Unlike him, they had the power to bury their secrets.

"Hey." Though weary, Lil offered him a wide smile. "Do you want to talk to Erin and Evan? I'm sure they'd be okay with pausing *Pokémon* to come talk to their favorite uncle."

His smile was genuine this time. "Of course."

With a quiet rustle of fabric, Lil pushed herself off the edge of the bed and made her way out of frame. Her voice was muffled, but he could still hear her as she addressed Erin and Evan. "Hey, guys, Uncle Ryan is on video chat. Do you want to talk to him?"

"Yeah!" The two spoke almost simultaneously and with so much joy, Ryan felt a fist close around his heart. It was hard to keep the smile in place as all sorts of emotions burned through his sinuses, threatening to leak from his eyes.

This was his family. His only family.

And he needed to protect them. Needed to do what was right.

"Okay, I'm going to the bathroom. You guys go in there and say hello. I'll be there in a second."

A flicker of movement at the edge of the screen was followed shortly by a blur as eight-year-old Erin hopped on the bed. Evan, two years her junior, followed his sister's lead, waving at the camera as he settled in to sit.

Ryan donned the most convincing smile he could manage. Even though—to the best of Lil's knowledge—James had never laid a hand on Evan or Erin, the two kids had already been through more in their lives than most people Ryan's age. As diligent as Lil had been to hide her suffering at her husband's hands, kids caught on to more than adults realized.

Neither of them questioned the reason for their father's absence. Even without explicitly asking why, Ryan suspected he knew the answer. They'd both known they weren't safe with their father, and they trusted their mother.

"Hey, guys." Ryan returned his nephew's wave. "How are you? Today was your short day at school, wasn't it?"

Erin smiled as she nodded. With her dark hair and light blue eyes, she was a carbon copy of Lil. "Yeah, it was. Mom picked us up, and we went to the store with her. She even let us get candy. We might get to go to the zoo this weekend too."

Evan's blue eyes widened as he glanced at the camera. "Do you think you'll be here to go with us, Uncle Ryan? Mom said it's the second biggest zoo in the whole country."

His heart squeezed again. "I wish I could, but I'll be busy working." Technically, the statement wasn't false. He'd come to Virginia because of the opportunity to scam some wealthy people who had more money than sense. So far, the endeavor had proved lucrative, though he'd started to wonder how much he would have to pay to turn a profit out here.

As Erin looked to the doorway and then back, a flicker of sadness flitted across her face. "Do you know when you'll be coming back?"

Swallowing against the sudden lump in his throat, Ryan shook his head. "No, I'm not sure. I've got something I…" He had to pause for fear his voice would waver. "I still have something I have to do out here. There are some people I need to help."

"Mom's worried about you," Evan said. He glanced to his sister, and Erin nodded. "I told her you'd be okay, but she still cries a lot. I don't think she wants us to know about it."

Though Ryan could remain stone-faced in front of hardened criminals and grizzled law enforcement veterans, the struggle to keep the despondency off his face in front of his niece and nephew was arduous.

He swallowed in an effort to displace the lump that had turned into a stone. "I'll be okay. I'll be back before you know it, I promise."

He'd managed to speak with so much confidence, he almost convinced himself.

But no matter the conviction in his voice, it felt like each word was a lie.

THREE FULL DAYS passed before Ryan summoned up the fortitude to undertake the short trip to the Richmond FBI office.

After a little digging to refresh his memory on those federal agents involved in the Presley heists almost a year earlier, he'd been relieved to learn that Agent Winter Black—the same Agent Black who had helped him escape Heidi's clutches and shimmy into an FBI van to undo an elaborate collar bomb—still operated out of the bureau's Richmond field office.

Though he'd been too panicked to take note at the time, Ryan got the feeling that Agent Winter Black was one of the good guys. Not just because she operated on the right side of the law, but her demeanor on that distant day told him that her interest wasn't in serving herself and her own career.

She'd had a chip on her shoulder at the time, no doubt about it. But no matter her dark past, she struck him as a person who sought justice, not just an easy win.

Each step he'd taken to the front doors of the building had been painstaking. When his foot hit the ground, he wondered if he would be better off cutting his losses, taking his rich targets for all he could manage, and getting himself, his sister, and his niece and nephew to a country with lax extradition laws. Evan and Erin were young. They could still learn Spanish if they relocated to Panama.

Maybe, but he'd scoffed aloud at the notion, and Lillian had been reticent as well. Evan, Erin, and Lillian had been through enough. Ryan didn't need to heap any more onto what they already had to contend with on a day to day basis.

Like a sudden trip to Panama or the Ukraine, any thoughts he might have had to drop off the face of the planet for the alleged benefit of his remaining family were ridiculous. Despite his checkered past, Ryan knew he wouldn't be able to sleep at night if he abandoned his sister and her kids at such a pivotal point in their lives. Even from a prison cell, he'd be of more use to them than he would in Eastern Europe or South America.

That left him with one option.

Make a deal with the Federal Bureau of Investigation. He'd help them put away a potential serial killer—not to mention all the perverts and creeps who had commented on the photos and videos—and they would offer him leniency. And as a cherry on top, he'd make sure they knew about Kent Strickland and Tyler Haldane's manifesto. They probably already had a printed version locked up somewhere in the building, but it never hurt to be thorough. To use whatever you had.

The decision to work with the FBI was a gamble, but Ryan had never been one to cower when the odds shifted out of his favor.

The light creak of a door's hinges jerked him back to reality. He'd been about to drift off to sleep in the middle of an FBI interrogation room.

Scrubbing both hands over his face, he glanced at the two-way mirrored glass and then to the door.

As it swung inward, his pulse rushed in his ears. His hands were clammy, but his mouth was as dry as an Ancient Egyptian tomb.

This had to work.

They had to help him.

3

Almost a year had passed since Ryan O'Connelly slipped out of the FBI's grasp after the end of Heidi Presley's rampage. When Winter last saw Ryan, he'd been held prisoner by Heidi, shot, and beaten. Today, he didn't appear to be much better off.

As she and Noah Dalton entered the interview room, his blue eyes darted back and forth between them and the pane of two-way glass. Stubble darkened his cheeks, and strands of his dark hair had come loose from where they'd been neatly styled. His clothes, a white button-down shirt and dress pants, were clean and pressed, but the rest of him looked like he'd just escaped from the pits of hell.

Winter and Noah exchanged glances as they took their seats across the table from the prominent thief and conman.

Setting a little notepad atop the laminate table, Winter cleared her throat. "Well, good morning, Mr. O'Connelly. This is…unexpected. Agent Weyrick says you've got something for us about Tyler Haldane and Kent Strickland, is that right?"

As he threaded his fingers together, Ryan exhaled a long

breath. "Well. Yes and no." He paused to shift his wary gaze from her to Noah and back. "I do have information about Tyler Haldane and Kent Strickland, but that's not the main reason I'm here."

Whether because of time that had elapsed since he'd been in the States or a conscious decision of his own, Ryan's accent was less prominent. Winter knew based on a cursory background check that the man had never actually lived in Ireland, so his manner of speaking was unusual to begin with.

The accent was one part of Ryan's persona that had always piqued Winter's curiosity. Maybe this time around, she'd find the time to ask him why a man from Chicago would cultivate an Irish accent. After all, Aiden Parrish had grown up in the South Side of Chicago, and aside from the occasional sharply pronounced "a," he had no accent to speak of.

Noah's chair creaked lightly as he leaned back to offer Ryan a curious look. "You're not here to tell us more about a couple mass murderers?"

To Ryan's credit, despite his weariness, he didn't balk at Noah's skeptical tone. His eyes were tired, and his expression strained, but he held himself like a man with a purpose. "That's not the main reason I'm here. Strickland and Haldane are dead or in prison. They're not a danger to anyone anymore, so any information I've got on them is more to help your prosecutor than anything, yeah?"

With a thoughtful glance to Winter, Noah nodded. "True enough."

Narrowing her eyes, Winter propped her elbows atop the table and leaned forward. "You know we won't just let you walk out of here. Even if you do have something on Haldane and Strickland, you're a wanted fugitive, Mr. O'Connelly."

The shadows moved along his throat as he swallowed. "I

know. Believe me, Agents, I know. But I also think you know by now that I'm not anything like that psychopath Heidi Presley, yeah? I like money, not hurting people. And, honestly, who doesn't like money?"

Noah let out a quiet chuckle, playing "good cop" to the letter. "Can't argue that."

Waving a hand, Ryan gestured to the silver and black watch on Noah's wrist. "I figured you'd understand. How much did that thing set you back, anyway? Looks vintage, had to be at least fifty grand."

Winter could hardly stop herself from flashing Noah a wide-eyed stare. She forced a neutral countenance to her face and twirled a pen in her fingers. Fifty thousand dollars? For a watch? Who was this stranger she'd been sleeping with?

With a charming smile, Noah held up his wrist for Ryan to see. "Honestly? I've got no idea. My granddad collects watches. He gave me this one when I got back from my second tour in the Middle East. My gramma got it for him a long time ago. If I didn't have to wear a suit every day, I don't even think I'd wear it. It's more of a sentimental thing to me, but y'all don't seem to see it that way. Plus, it's a damn fine watch."

It better be. Winter kept the thought to herself and refocused on the task at hand. "You were saying, Mr. O'Connelly."

Folding his hands in front of himself, Ryan nodded. "Of course. Sorry. I'll just start at the beginning, then."

Clicking the end of her pen, Winter tilted her chin to bid him to continue.

"You'll have to forgive me if I don't want to go into too much detail about the first part, but please believe me when I say I'm only doing it to protect my sister. She was in a bad situation, and after you took out that crazy bitch Presley, I

helped her and my niece and nephew out of it." He paused to
flick an intent look back and forth between Winter and
Noah. "You're cops, so you know how abusive relationships
work, right?"

Winter did indeed. She'd written a paper about domestic
violence for one of her courses at SUNY in Albany. She
didn't have to ask why Ryan's sister hadn't gone to the police.
The woman was scared, that was why. Scared for herself,
scared for her children, scared for her future. Instead of
involving the authorities, she'd gone to someone she could
trust—her brother.

Winter watched him closely. She would have been
inclined to think Ryan was giving them both a line if it
weren't for the unmistakable pang of defeat in his eyes.

Ryan took the silence as his cue to continue. "I guess that
means you do. That's why I'm here. For her safety, that's all
I'll say about that."

Winter shot him a quizzical glance. "What do you mean?
You don't think we'd do anything to hurt her, do you?"

The corner of Ryan's mouth turned down in a look of
distaste. "No, I don't think you'd do anythin' on purpose,
Agents. But I've been through that whole song and dance
routine, and I know that when it comes to poor folks like me
and my sister, the wheels of justice don't carry us anywhere
good. Some lawyer in their ivory tower gets a wild hair up
their arse and decides to throw the book at me and her, you
know where my niece and nephew end up then?"

In the silence that ensued, he fixed Winter and Noah with
a hard look. As much as she wanted to protest, Winter knew
he was right. If Ryan's sister was sent to prison, the kids
would either wind up back with their abusive father or as
wards of the state.

Either way, their prospects would be grim.

Winter softened her tone. "That's fine. Just tell us what

you found. Agent Weyrick said that you had information about some young women who've gone missing."

The cloud of petulance lifted, and Ryan's expression turned bleak. "That's right. I came to Virginia because I met some people online. Some people who had more money than sense, you know the type, right?"

With an amused snort, Winter nodded.

"I'll spare you the details there. I figured they were just your run of the mill arseholes. You know that type too, I'm sure. The bad parents, unfaithful spouses, crooked businessmen, that type. And don't get me wrong, plenty of them are, but..."

Noah lifted an eyebrow. "But?"

Ryan pursed his lips. "I'm here because I want to do the right thing, Agents. I had a chance to do the right thing when Heidi was on her bloody rampage, but I didn't have the guts. On the one side, I had her crazy ass, and on the other side, I had a prison cell. Today, I'm here to do the right thing, but I need your help too."

Based on her past experience with Ryan, Winter knew the man wasn't cruel or maniacal like his former blackmailer, Heidi Presley. Ryan didn't even steal from people who couldn't afford it. He stole valuable, sometimes priceless items from those who hardly noticed they were gone. At the beginning of the Presley heists, he'd even donated the two-hundred thousand dollars from a bank robbery to a local church. In some respects, Ryan O'Connelly was akin to a modern-day Robin Hood.

Before Winter could reply, Noah broke the silence. "We'll do the best we can. We can't make you a deal right now. That's something the SAC and the U.S. Attorney have to hammer out, but they tend to listen to our recommendations before they make a final decision."

Clenching his jaw, Ryan nodded. "I guess that's the best I'll get right now, isn't it?"

Winter exchanged a knowing look with Noah. She'd seen the U.S. Attorney cut deals in the past. In fact, word in Baltimore had it that Tony Johansson—the crooked cop who'd worked with the Russian mob for over a decade—was in the process of ironing out an agreement to testify for the prosecution in exchange for leniency. Not only would the man testify, but he'd become a valuable source of information into other dirty cops in Baltimore and Washington, D.C.

Winter made her best effort at a reassuring smile. "We'll do our best."

When Ryan returned the expression, he looked even more tired than he had before. "That's all I can ask, isn't it? I'll get down to it, then. I've been around these arseholes for a few weeks now, and aside from my contact, there ain't a one of 'em who's squeaky clean. If you want to paint me in a good light to your prosecutor or district attorney, just put me up beside some of this lot."

Though the sound was muted, Winter chuckled at the candid observation. "So noted, Mr. O'Connelly."

With a dismissive wave that reminded Winter of her good friend, Autumn, Ryan leaned back in his chair. "Anyway. One of the women is a widow, and her husband left her with a sort of membership in this weird little club they've established. They don't have a name for themselves or anything like that, and it's all very hush-hush. They'll get together to come up with new business ventures and strategies, to talk about politics, their yacht club memberships, that sort of thing."

Winter fought against rolling her eyes. There was a reason she wasn't in the White Collar Crimes Division. If anyone ever came to her to cry about how they'd been scammed out of their third yacht, she'd be just as likely to shove them out the door as she would to file a formal investigation.

For the first time that morning, Ryan's expression seemed to brighten. "I saw that look, Agent Black. I think we're on the same page here."

She snorted out a laugh. "That obvious?"

He shrugged. "Not all wealthy people are bad. I've met plenty of kind ones throughout my...career. But these people, with the exception of the woman I've befriended, they're not kind. The bad ones, they tend to cluster around one another, you know what I mean?"

"Misery loves company," Noah muttered.

Ryan's look of amusement was short-lived. "It does. But that's where the missing girls come in. About a week ago, my contact told me she'd heard rumors circulating that one of these people had been moonlighting by kidnapping prostitutes and filming their captivity. She didn't know many of the specifics, but her guess was that they charged people to watch the videos."

Scribbling down a few notes, Winter nodded for him to continue.

With a sigh, Ryan rubbed his scruffy cheek. "I thought that'd be an easy way to get some creeps to give away their money, and maybe one of these guys was doing it to make a few extra bucks. Not by actually kidnapping women, but by getting someone to act like they'd been kidnapped. It seemed like a good scam, so I figured I'd check it out. I'm sure you're familiar with the dark web, Agents, but have you heard of the Marianas web?"

Neither Winter nor Noah confirmed their knowledge or lack of it, which almost made Ryan smile. For a moment, he'd almost forgotten they were both FBI agents, trained to neither confirm or deny.

Ryan went on. "It's the deepest part of the dark web that

can be accessed by the technology we have now. Soon, when quantum computers become a reality, the trench from which it was named will grow deeper and deeper, but at this point in time, this web is as low as you can go, pun intended."

Ryan looked between the two and continued when they nodded their understanding.

"Between those two places, there's all kinds of unbelievable stuff out there. I'll cut a long story short and just tell you that I found what she was talking about. There were the videos, and then there were pictures. He'd take those while he was stalking the women."

Winter tapped the end of her pen on the notepad. "How do you know they were in Virginia?"

Ryan folded his hands, hating how his fingers trembled. "People on those sites, they tend to be open to paying higher premiums to watch videos of people from certain countries. A lot of snuff films are made in Indonesia, but people are willing to pay a lot more to watch an American instead."

"Wait." Winter raised a finger. "You're talking about a snuff film? I thought you said these were videos of kidnapped women?"

Ryan's eyes met hers. "They were. That's how he started."

The look on Noah's face landed somewhere between ominous and befuddled. "How do you know it's real, and it's not like what you were saying? An actor, someone scamming all the creeps out there."

Ryan was only a year or two older than Noah, but in that moment, he looked like he'd aged two decades older. "Get me a laptop, and I'll show you how I know it's real."

An involuntary shudder worked its way down Winter's back.

She didn't even need to see the video. Ryan's demeanor was all the authentication Winter required.

4

Noah Dalton had seen death before. He'd been on the scene of the gruesome murders committed by the madman referred to as The Preacher. He'd shot and killed that very madman, and months before that confrontation, he'd killed a twisted pharmaceutical researcher named Scott Kennedy. During his two tours in the Middle East, he'd seen his share of combat. He'd seen people die.

Not like this.

Not a helpless young woman who'd been all but decapitated by a psychopath with a butcher knife. He'd never watched the life so senselessly drain from another person's eyes as blood soaked the front of their shirt.

At first, the sight had made him nauseous. Then, it made him angry.

Better than most, Noah knew the dark side of human nature. Just because he knew what human beings were capable of doing to one another didn't make his ire any less palpable.

They sent the website with the video of the murder—along with four other videos of young women who appeared to have been held captive in the same space—to Cyber Crimes. It didn't take long for the tech team to confirm what Winter, Noah, and Ryan already knew. The video hadn't been altered.

By the time Max Osbourne let himself into the interview room, the three of them had already finished their lunches. Winter had been kind enough to go out to buy them Chinese food while Noah stayed with Ryan O'Connelly to await the news from Cyber Crimes.

Noah glanced over as Max eased the door closed behind himself. The SAC paused to sweep his gaze over the little gathering, a patented wordless method Max used to let them know their briefing had officially started. Apparently, the look had more than one use.

"Agents, I would've been here sooner, but I had back to back meetings this morning. Mr. O'Connelly, I didn't expect to see you so soon. You've got a reputation for staying away from buildings like this."

Ryan shrugged, but Noah didn't miss the glint of uncertainty in his eyes. "I'm hoping that's something we can finally settle."

With a quick nod, Max took a seat at the end of the table. "Let's hear it, then."

Though Ryan omitted the part of his story that involved his sister, he gave Max the same rundown that he'd given Winter and Noah. For the duration of the explanation, the SAC's face was unreadable. Despite the seemingly blank look on Max's face, Noah had been in the Richmond office long enough to know that the man had soaked up each word like a sponge.

As Ryan wrapped up, Noah shifted in the uncomfortable metal chair. They provided suspects with the cheaply made chairs to keep them from getting too comfortable, but he still couldn't figure out why the agents had to suffer too.

Lacing his fingers together, Max leaned back in his seat. "So," Max's gray eyes settled on Ryan, "what are you asking us for, specifically?"

"Specifically?" Ryan echoed.

The SAC nodded. "The U.S. Attorney likes specific, son."

Ryan swallowed. "I don't want to go to prison. Honestly, that's as specific as I care to get. I don't want to go to prison, and I want to make sure my sister and her kids won't get caught in the middle of any of this."

Though Ryan's concern that his younger sister could be charged with aiding and abetting or harboring a fugitive seemed farfetched at first, Noah had to remind himself that the man was a lifelong criminal. He and his ilk were nothing if not paranoid, and the glint in Ryan's eyes left no doubt that the man was protective of his sister.

The worry might have seemed farfetched, but Noah knew better than most that the fear was based in reality. If the U.S. Attorney needed to leverage Ryan for whatever reason, they wouldn't hesitate to throw the so-called book at anyone involved in Ryan's efforts to elude law enforcement.

SAC Osbourne shook his head. "They won't be. As long as you aren't trying to pull a fast one on us, they'll be fine. You'll have to forgive me here, Mr. O'Connelly, but you don't exactly have a history of cooperation with the bureau. I'm not saying that I personally doubt why you're here. If there were any doubt about your sincerity, I'm confident Agent Black or Agent Dalton would've told me by now."

Some more of the color drained from Ryan's face, but he nodded. "I understand."

With an upraised finger, Max rested his arm against the table and scooted forward. "That being said, there's only so much I can do right now. I can talk to the U.S. Attorney on your behalf and give them my opinion, and so can Agents Black and Dalton here, but the decision is theirs to make. I can tell you one thing, though. They'll want whatever information you're giving us here to end with an arrest and a trial."

Though it was fleeting, Ryan's expression turned pensive. "A trial?"

"That's right. Chances are, depending on what evidence they use, you'll have to testify. Are you willing to do that, Mr. O'Connelly?"

"Of course." Ryan's response came without hesitation. "I want these sick bastards put away just as bad as you all do. But, considering my history with the law, I'd have to be some special kind of idiot to do that for free."

Noah stifled a chuckle. He'd had a chance to mull over Ryan's situation, and he couldn't say he would approach it much differently. At the end of the day, Ryan wasn't a violent offender. He wasn't a gangster or a drug trafficker, and he wasn't in the business of exploiting those less fortunate than himself.

He was a thief who'd made off with millions of dollars' worth of valuables in the course of his career, but he had a reputation for being as unobtrusive in his heists as was humanly possible. No one saw him, no one caught him, and most importantly, no one fought him. As far as Noah was concerned, he was the ideal candidate for a bargain with the U.S. Attorney.

Not only did he have valuable information about whoever had made the four kidnapping videos and the single murder video, but he'd honed an entire list of criminal contacts over the course of his life. Noah had kept the sentiment to himself so far, but he wouldn't be surprised if part of Ryan's agreement with the U.S. Attorney would involve his cooperation with a host of other investigations.

However, Noah wasn't naïve. If the U.S. Attorney saw the capture and conviction of Ryan O'Connelly as a feather in their professional cap—as a guaranteed conviction that could give them a ticket to a promotion or a raise—they'd take the sure thing over the gamble that they may or may not find the lunatic responsible for the twisted videos.

That was politics, which was exactly why Noah had no desire to advance to any role beyond field agent or Supervisory Special Agent. He hadn't been raised to play those games. He'd been raised to do the right thing, even if it meant the more difficult path.

"We'll find him."

In tandem, Noah, Max, and Ryan all looked over to Winter.

Between the determined glint in her eyes and the matter-of-fact tone in which she'd spoken, Noah was hard-pressed to keep the grin off his face as he turned to Max. "We're going to need O'Connelly for this investigation, sir."

The SAC scratched his chin. "Yeah, I think you will. Mr. O'Connelly, I know we don't know one another, but I'm familiar with your reputation. Lucky for you, you're a non-violent offender, and before you hooked your wagon to Heidi Presley, there's no concrete evidence that ties you to any prior crimes. No charges have been filed against you directly for those, or if they were, they've since been dropped or passed the statute of limitations. But getting them to look past the Presley case won't be easy."

Any amusement was sucked from the air around them at the bleak statement. Noah gave SAC Osbourne a sober nod in response.

"You're familiar with the felony murder rule, aren't you, Mr. O'Connelly?" Max's gaze didn't waver from where he'd fixed it on Ryan.

"I am," Ryan replied.

"Then you know that, under the felony murder rule, the U.S. Attorney can charge you with all those murders even if you didn't actually commit them. You were there, and you were present for the acts that led up to the murders. In the eyes of the law, that makes you just as culpable as Heidi Presley."

At the sudden discomfort on Ryan's face, the man might as well have been sitting on a pile of rusty barbed wire. Then again, Noah was sitting on the same type of chair, and a pile of barbed wire wasn't much of a downgrade.

Max rested his elbows on the laminate table. "I don't say that because I think that's what they're going to do. Honestly, with a defense lawyer that's worth even half a shit, they'd be hard-pressed to get any of those convictions to stick after what Presley put you through in the end. I just want you to know that I plan to go through this with the U.S. Attorney, but like I said, it won't be easy."

Noah barely suppressed a sigh. More politics. Great.

Ryan nodded. "I understand."

"In the meantime," Max paused to gesture first to himself and then to Winter and Noah, "here's what we can do for you. I think it goes without saying that we need to make sure you don't split in the middle of this thing. Instead of tossing you in a holding cell, I'll make you a deal. You're going to have to sign it before you can walk out of here, provided you're interested."

A portion of the shadow left Ryan's eyes. "I am."

"Agents Black and Dalton think you'll be able to help them with this thing, and I'm in agreement. Now, Mr. O'Connelly, you're going to wear an ankle monitor while you do your part, and we're going to have one of our agents keep an eye on you. This isn't the old school ankle monitor you're thinking of, either. This one records your pulse, your blood pressure, hell, even the conductivity of your skin. It can literally tell whether or not you're planning to escape."

"Jaysus," Ryan muttered under his breath.

For the second time, Noah had to fight back laughter.

A slight smirk tugged at the corner of Max's mouth as he crossed his arms. "You're dealing with the FBI now, son. It's not quite as easy to get away from us as it is to get away from the police in Erie, Pennsylvania. I'll work with the U.S. Attorney to get something ironed out that you can live with, but Mr. O'Connelly…"

The SAC's eyes glittered icily as he pinned Ryan with a foreboding look. Noah had been fortunate enough so far not to have been on the receiving end of that glare, and right now, he hoped his streak would continue indefinitely.

"…if you try to sneak away," Max's voice was deathly calm, "or if you make me or my agents look like idiots for trusting you on this, I will personally hunt you down. And when I find you, and I will find you, I will make sure you stand trial for every last innocent person Heidi Presley killed, including a federal agent. Mr. O'Connelly, if you try to fuck me over, I will hang you from the highest rafter I can find. Do you understand me?"

When Ryan swallowed this time, Noah heard the gulp.

Before an uncomfortable silence could settle over the room, the man nodded. "I understand."

Max's stony countenance remained as he returned the nod. "Good. Because right now, there's a psychopath out there kidnapping and murdering young women in our city and filming it so they can sell it on the web."

5

As he raised a hand to stifle a yawn, Bobby Weyrick wondered why he didn't just move into the FBI office. There had to be a spare room where he could put a mattress and television. A small closet for all his stuff. Or maybe it was finally time for him to leave the night shift to work during the hours when normal human beings operated.

He'd only been content with working nights for so long because his soon to be ex-wife had also worked the same shift. But Kara had cheated on him for years, and he'd known about the infidelity for almost the entire time. So, why, exactly, had he stayed on this bloody shift?

Covering his mouth as he yawned again, he couldn't come up with an answer.

To him, the five o'clock evening briefing was equivalent to three in the morning for a person with a normal sleep schedule. There were only a couple other agents who worked the night shift in Violent Crimes, and they all joked about what it would be like to schedule a mandatory meeting at three in the morning. Of the night crew, he was the only agent who had been summoned to the briefing that evening.

After he set his paper cup of coffee on the table, he slumped down to sit behind Winter Black and Noah Dalton. At his light groan, Winter glanced over her shoulder and arched a dark eyebrow.

As he took a tentative sip of the potent coffee, he shook his head at her unasked question. "I just woke up."

A touch of amusement rose to her face as she nodded her understanding.

He snapped his gaze over to a flicker of movement as the final two attendees made their way to the cluster of tables that faced the podium and whiteboard at the front of the room. The fluorescent light caught the shine of Sun's glossy black hair. Not a single strand of her angled bob was out of place, and her pastel blue dress shirt and gray slacks were as neatly pressed as ever.

Though Sun's eyes flitted over to him, her expression changed little. Rather than acknowledge his presence with a wave or even a nod, she took a seat at the side of her companion, Miguel Vasquez. Miguel, at least, offered a quick wave.

In the days since Bobby had returned from the Baltimore assignment he'd worked with Winter, Sun had regarded him with the same suspicion one would most likely give a leper. He'd gleaned that she wasn't keen on Winter, but he still wasn't sure how the feeling of distaste differed from her attitude toward the general populace.

Was she jealous?

At the thought, he wrinkled his nose. That was ridiculous. He liked Winter as a person. She was sharp, and her sense of humor was remarkably similar to his, but there were zero romantic aspirations between the two of them.

Sure, he could admit that she was an attractive woman. He could also admit that Noah Dalton was a good-looking man, but he didn't want to sleep with the big Texan, either.

Jealousy had never been an attribute to which Bobby devoted much attention, and his understanding of what could provoke such a sentiment was sorely lacking. He pushed aside the internal debate as Max Osbourne strode over to stand behind the wooden podium.

"Evening, ladies and gentlemen." The SAC swept his gaze over the gathering. "Most of you know why we're here already, so let's just get right to it. We're here because of Ryan O'Connelly."

Sun's dark eyes swept across the room. "Where is he?"

Max leveled a finger in her direction. "If you'll allow me to finish, Agent Ming, you'd very quickly learn that he's in the building, at least for now. We aren't booking him. Not officially, anyway. He's an integral part of this investigation. He's got a line of communication straight to our pool of suspects, and he's the one who found where one of them has been posting kidnapping videos and homemade snuff films online."

As she set her jaw, Sun crossed her legs. So, maybe Bobby wasn't the only object of her irritation. Maybe she was mad about their case.

"Agent Black and Agent Dalton are heading up this investigation. Mr. O'Connelly will be moved to a secure location once we're done with this briefing." Max's gray eyes met Bobby's. "Agent Weyrick, you're responsible for keeping an eye on O'Connelly."

The flash of indignation on Sun's face was more noticeable. As she opened her mouth to protest, Max cut her off.

"Agent Ming, I can see you're chomping at the bit. Agent Weyrick will be responsible for O'Connelly at night, and you'll take the day shift. O'Connelly has expressed interest in making himself useful, and I expect the two of you will take advantage of the close contact to glean any information you can. This isn't a babysitting assignment."

From the short interaction he'd had with the renowned thief the day before, Bobby figured he and O'Connelly would get along fine. With a nod, he took another sip of the black coffee in his hand.

Max returned the nod before he gestured to the brunette woman seated at the table in front of Sun and Miguel. "Now that we've got that settled, I'll turn this over to Agent Welford from Cyber Crimes."

Agent Welford offered a polite smile as she rose to stand. She'd fashioned her dark brown hair into a neat ponytail, and her flats tapped lightly against the tiled floor. Max moved to the side as she took her spot at the front of the room.

If Bobby met Special Agent Ava Welford on the street, he wouldn't have guessed she was an agent with the FBI. Her honey-brown eyes were warm and kind, and there were just enough laugh lines on her fair face to make her seem approachable. She looked like someone's aunt, not a federal agent. Then again, the two things weren't mutually exclusive.

Before his mind wandered down the inane path, he took another long pull from the dark coffee. He felt like he'd slept for five hours in the last six days. If it hadn't been for the trusty combination of energy provided by caffeine and metal music, he'd have curled up in a ball on the floor like a cat.

"Okay," Agent Welford's voice cut through the haze that had threatened to overtake Bobby's thoughts, "we all know by now that there have been a total of five videos posted to the sub-forum of a website that Mr. O'Connelly found on the dark web. In the first four videos, the camera doesn't move. All that's captured in the frames is the women pacing and searching the room. Then, the feed just goes dead."

The mention of a serial kidnapper turned murderer was enough to push the cobwebs from Bobby's head.

Agent Welford cleared her throat. "Until the fifth video,

that was the MO. But at the end of the fifth one, there was a new video after the feed of the captivity ended. In that shot, an unknown masked man produces a butcher knife and slits the young woman's throat."

"We know the videos are real, right?" Sun asked.

Ava Welford nodded. "Yes. And as best as we can tell, there weren't any special effects used. To the best of our knowledge, the video of the young woman being killed is authentic."

"What are the odds it's not real?" This time, the query came from Aiden Parrish, the Supervisory Special Agent of the Behavioral Analysis Unit.

In response, Agent Welford shook her head. "The odds are slim, SSA Parrish. To create something that realistic, the actor and the filmmaker would need access to a state-of-the-art special effects studio and an artist capable of pulling off that type of realism. I'm not sure how many high-budget movies you all have seen recently, but considering half the time Hollywood can't even get it right, I think it stands to reason that a random person in a basement won't have what it takes."

Bobby half-expected Aiden Parrish to sneer. Instead, his mouth twitched with a slight smile as he nodded. "Thank you, Agent Welford."

"What about the IP addresses of the person who posted the videos?" Sun's tone was as pointed as her expression.

The attitude change might have been Bobby's imagination—after all, Sun had been irritable since she walked into the room—but he thought there was a twinge of hostility whenever she spoke after Aiden Parrish. Though Bobby had no idea of the reason for the antagonism, it became clearer and clearer with each of Sun and Aiden's interactions that there was bad blood.

Agent Welford spread her hands as she glanced over to

Sun. "The IP address was generated by a proxy server to mask the real log-in. We looked through the IP addresses of the commenters on the video, and they all used proxy servers too. It's not all that uncommon. More often than not, when we're dealing with people tech-savvy enough to navigate the dark web, they're using a proxy. With something on this scale, IP addresses are usually a dead end."

Though the movement was grudging, Sun nodded.

"We're still looking into the posts, and we'll continue to track down what we can while you work through the investigation on your end," Agent Welford said.

Max stepped up to the podium as Agent Welford returned to her seat. "First order of business is to identify the victims. If any of you learn anything new that might relate to this investigation, you're expected to relay the information to Agent Black and Agent Dalton. Otherwise, you're all dismissed."

When Bobby lifted his coffee for another drink, he was surprised at how light the cup had become. *If I have to sift through missing persons reports all night, I'm going to need an entire pot.*

He almost groaned aloud at the thought.

As Sun strode past without so much as a sideways glance in his direction, he grated his teeth. He wanted to ask her what was on her mind, but right after a briefing wasn't the time, and the FBI field office wasn't the place.

Ryan O'Connelly had better be good company, because this was going to be a long night.

6

W hen Winter stepped into the conference room the next morning to meet with Bobby Weyrick, the weariness on his face was so pronounced that it made her tired. Though Winter had received a message from one of their office's leading forensics experts to tell her there was an update on the evidence they'd collected from her old family home in Harrisonburg, she was glad she'd decided to meet with Bobby first. If she'd waited, she would have had to wake him up.

With a light click, she closed the glass and metal door behind herself. "When's the last time you slept?"

As he yawned, Bobby shrugged in response. "I'm not sure anymore. Honestly, I think I got more sleep when I was deployed in Afghanistan."

Winter sat down at the circular table across from him. "Before you know it, we'll be back to paperwork and court hearings."

He dropped his face into one hand. "Yeah, when people stop murdering one another. I'm not holding my breath."

At the sarcastic remark, she couldn't help a quiet chuckle.

"Are you and Autumn related? Because you sounded just like her with that comment."

He wrinkled his nose. "Autumn Trent? The redhead? God, I hope not."

Winter froze midway through pushing open the screen of her laptop. As she narrowed her eyes, she closed the computer and laid both hands atop the matte surface. "What does that mean?"

With a light sigh, he straightened himself. "It means that I need to go to bed because now I'm saying things that don't make any sense. You don't really need me to explain that, do you? It just...it came out wrong."

She crossed her arms over her chest. "I think you'd better. You're talking about my friend, you know that, right?"

As he nodded, he rubbed his eyes with one hand. "I sure do," he muttered. "I didn't mean anything bad by it, okay? It's just, she's..." Holding out both hands, he gave her a hapless look.

"She's what?" Winter's voice was so flat it bordered on outright irritable.

"She's an attractive woman, and if we were related, that'd be..." he made a face like he'd just bitten into a lemon, "that'd make me feel gross."

Even as the laughter bubbled up in her throat, Winter couldn't curb the outburst. As she lapsed into a fit of laughter at Bobby's awkward explanation, the tension she'd carried since the end of the investigation of Tony Johansson—a corrupt Baltimore City narcotics detective—lifted from her shoulders.

She held up a hand to stave off any potential remarks, covering her face with the other as yet another wave of laughter threatened to roll over her. She felt punch-drunk, which might mean she could use some extra sleep too.

"I'm sorry," she finally managed. As she paused to sniffle,

she glanced over to take stock of the mix of confusion and amusement on Bobby's face. "Sorry. It's…it's been a long couple of weeks, and I guess sometimes you need a little fifth grade humor to help cut through the stress."

He chuckled. "Yeah, I understand that. On the plus side, I'm definitely more awake now." As he flipped open a beige folder, he spun the file around to face Winter.

Like a switch had been flipped, the good humor in the room evaporated.

Winter studied the glossy printout of a zoomed-in still frame of one of the five videos. Before she turned over the page, she glanced at Bobby.

"I found two of them." He gestured to the folder. "I printed these stills off before I left with O'Connelly last night. Took down the time that each of the videos was posted, and then I went through missing persons reports from around the same time. This young woman here, that's the girl who was killed."

With a grim look and a nod, Winter returned her focus to the printed information behind the blonde's picture. "Dakota Ronsfeldt. Nineteen, lived in…" Giving her head a little shake, she looked back to Bobby, giving him an *is this right* stare.

"Lived in Maine," he finished for her. "That's why it took me so long to find her. Her older brother and sister reported her missing, but they just made the report a couple days ago. Dakota was a recovering addict, and when she relapsed, her whole family cut her off. My guess is that's why she came to Virginia. She got popped here in Richmond for solicitation about a month ago."

Winter turned to the next page—the missing persons report. "How long had she been here?"

"I got ahold of her brother last night." Bobby shrugged his shoulders as if trying to work out a knot. "He said she left

Maine something like six weeks ago. She'd call them on a regular basis, usually to ask for money. When she didn't call them for a week straight, they tried to get ahold of her. Then, when they couldn't, they filed the report."

Behind the missing persons report was a printout of Dakota's senior picture. Fall leaves of gold and red decorated the ground at her back, and her smile was wide and hopeful. What had happened between then and the time she was arrested for prostitution in Richmond, Winter suspected she'd never know.

Compressed into a few sheets of paper and an eight-by-ten photograph was the entire tragedy of the end of a young woman's life.

Any doubts she might have had that the video was a fake could be officially laid to rest.

Swallowing back the horror that must now be faced, Winter moved the first bundle of papers aside to peer down at the next eight-by-ten. This young woman was also blonde, though she had been only seventeen at the time she was reported missing.

Bobby cleared his throat. "That's Anastasia Mitchell. She was reported missing by her mother after she'd been gone from home for more than two weeks. That was a couple months ago, right around the time her video was posted. I got ahold of her mother this morning, and it sounds like they were a really strict household. Jehovah's Witnesses, I think."

Lips pursed, Winter returned Dakota's file and closed the folder. "It took them two weeks to report their seventeen-year-old daughter missing? Why?"

Spreading his hands, Bobby leaned back. "I don't know. From what the mom said, Anastasia ran off to be with a boy. The mother claimed that the boy had turned her daughter into a prostitute, and if it wasn't for Dakota's solicitation charge, I'd have thought she was exaggerating."

Winter tapped a finger on the closed folder. "During the Augusto Lopez investigation, some of the killers Augusto targeted picked on working girls too."

"So did Ted Bundy, The Green River Killer, Jeffrey Dahmer, BTK."

Winter nodded. "Yeah, it's a signature move among creeps who like to kill women."

Bobby lifted a shoulder. "I hate to say it, but I think we've got ourselves another serial killer."

Another serial killer.

Looking at the girl's picture again, Winter wondered if they'd ever have the manpower to devote to a fresh look at her brother's case.

Not if these psychopaths keep popping up, she thought bitterly.

The sooner they took this bastard off the streets, the sooner she could focus her efforts on finding Justin.

RYAN WAS glad the bureau had sprung for a hotel suite with a separate bedroom. He'd been advised against closing its door completely, but he was satisfied with the thin slat of light when he left it ajar. As long as Agent Sun Ming wasn't staring at him while he shoved his face under a pillow and squeezed his eyes shut, he didn't care.

He couldn't blame the agents for their wariness. He'd earned the suspicion and mistrust of the entire Federal Bureau of Investigation.

At least they won't drug me and strap a bomb around my head.

Though he still felt like a captive, the accommodations on the fifteenth story of the mid-grade hotel was much better than his time under Heidi's thumb.

He assumed the FBI had chosen the fifteenth floor in

order to make an escape more difficult for Ryan, but between the eagle-eyed agent in the next room and the sci-fi ankle monitor he'd been fitted with the day before, he doubted he could have broken free from their oversight even if he tried.

As he'd been pointedly told by the Richmond SAC, the Federal Bureau of Investigation was far more acquainted with flight risks than the Erie police had been.

Even if he made it past his vigilant babysitter and managed to ditch the high-tech ankle monitor, what then?

He didn't doubt Max Osbourne's conviction when he'd assured Ryan he would find him if he ran, nor did he doubt the man's capabilities.

If Ryan made it out of the hotel, even out of the city, what did he do then? How did he keep his sister safe from her abusive ex-husband if he was constantly forced to look over his shoulder for the rest of his life?

Before he'd left the field office the day before, Agents Black and Dalton had thanked him for his help and vowed they would find the person responsible for the macabre videos.

If Ryan's fate was in the hands of the two agents and their SAC, he would feel a bit better. But his future was in the hands of a lawyer.

Ryan had always hated lawyers.

With a muffled groan, he tightened his grip on the pillow that covered his head. He'd been so tired when he met with Agent Black and Agent Dalton, but even though he'd barely managed a couple hours of sleep since then, he couldn't will his eyes to stay closed. No matter how hard he tried to blank his thoughts, they kept spiraling.

He'd feel better if he could at least talk to Lillian, if he could at least confirm that she was okay, but he wouldn't risk an outreach to the person he'd tried so hard to protect. Even if the FBI had Ryan dead to rights, they didn't have Lil.

The bureau wanted him around for the course of the investigation, but after an entire night in the company of an agent, Ryan still didn't understand what they expected from him. He'd given them all the information he found—wasn't that enough?

Sure, he had gained access to the portions of the dark web where the videos had been found in the first place, but he had given the bureau's tech department the information to do the same.

Clenching and unclenching both hands, he finally lifted the pillow, rolled to his back, and took in a deep breath.

You made your choice before you even came here, he told himself.

Coming clean to the FBI was the only way to restore some semblance of normalcy to Lil, Evan, and Erin's lives. It was the only way he could be sure the Feds wouldn't paint a target on his sister's back.

If he ran, Lillian would be their first stop.

Ryan flung an arm over his eyes to block out the sight of the room.

If he had a choice before, he didn't now.

7

After Winter made copies of all Bobby Weyrick's notes and files he'd gathered the night before, she dropped the folder off at Noah's desk. She'd hoped he would be there, but he must have been tasked with a meeting or an errand.

As she made her way to the elevator that would take her to the cluster of offices that belonged to the forensic lab's senior members, she felt like she was on her way to her first day of school. Though Stella Norcott had told her she'd finished her evaluation of some of the items from the house, she hadn't elaborated. If any pertinent information had been found, Winter was sure she would have called or written a more detailed note.

A little over a week ago, Autumn had accompanied Winter to her childhood home in Harrisonburg, Virginia.

Visiting the house was a follow-up to the cryptic email Winter had received from Justin: *Hey, sis. Heard you've been looking for me.*

The FBI Cyber Crimes Division had determined that the email originated from Harrisonburg. Right away, Winter had been certain not just that the sender was her little brother, but that he'd set foot in the house that had been abandoned since their parents were killed.

Her hunch had been right.

On the drywall of the area that had once been their family's living room, he had written: *Hey, sis, you just missed me.*

When Winter and Autumn had followed a foul stench upstairs, it led them to the same bedroom where Winter had found her parents' bodies all those years ago. Written in the same substance as the message downstairs was another cryptic message: *See you soon.*

What that meant, Winter was still no closer to knowing. The short message had been rendered even more ominous by the pile of desecrated rat corpses in the corner of the room.

With a long exhale of breath, she shook herself from the recollection and jabbed the button for the third floor.

To hope that a few dead rats and the dust in an abandoned house would unequivocally point them in Justin's direction was naïve, to say the least. Any time her thoughts drifted toward the realm of wishful thinking, she abruptly reined them back into reality.

Over the past few days, she'd started to wonder if her brother even wanted to be found. Did he think he was in danger? Did he think that because Douglas Kilroy had stolen him away from his family, he was somehow responsible for the man's crimes?

Clenching her jaw, Winter pushed aside the ridiculous questions.

He was nineteen now, not six. She was searching for a young adult, not a little boy. He may have even attended college. Either way, he was a much more complex person than he'd been in the first grade.

As the cheery ding sounded out and the silver doors slid open, she took in a steadying breath and stepped into the hall. Stella had a busy day, but she'd told Winter she was welcome to stop by the office during her lunch hour.

Stella Norcott's door was the last in a row of three, and light from the sunny office spilled out into the dim hall. As Winter stepped into the doorway, Stella's jade green eyes snapped up from the container of food on her desk.

With a smile, she rested her fork on the edge of the Tupperware. "Hey, Winter. How's it going?"

Winter returned the expression to the best of her ability, but she was sure she'd failed miserably.

"I'm all right. How are you?" The question felt perfunctory and robotic.

Shrugging, Stella set her food aside. "I'm all right too. Yeah, that about sums it up. Tired. Busy. Stressed. You know, the usual."

As she dropped down to sit in front of the polished desk, Winter maintained her wooden smile.

Fortunately, Stella's attention wasn't fixed on Winter's strained expression. With one hand, she turned the widescreen monitor to face Winter as she tapped a couple keys with the other. "The lab is chaos right now, so that's why we aren't in there. You know those performers who spin plates on sticks, right?"

Brushing a stray strand of hair away from her eyes, Winter nodded.

"That's what I feel like every time I go back there. We had a couple people quit out of the blue, and then my ballistics guy, Ted, is on paternity leave." As she dropped a hand to the top of the desk, she sighed. "I'm sorry. You aren't here to listen to me complain about personnel issues. You're here to talk about a case."

For a moment, Winter's smile didn't feel so strained.

Sometimes, knowing there were others nearby who ran around their day to day lives with the same frenetic pace as a person on fire was enough to keep Winter from spiraling down into the realm of anxiety. Stella Norcott had always struck Winter as a woman who had her life together, but even the best and most organized men and women fell victim to the chaos every now and then.

"Here we go."

When Winter glanced back to the forensics specialist, her eyes were on the monitor. As Winter followed her gaze, she had to fight to keep from wrinkling her nose at the gory sight. Somehow, seeing the dissected rodent displayed in high definition on a screen was more jarring than seeing a dead rat in real life.

"Oh, sorry. I guess I should have warned you before I pulled this up." Stella's eyes flicked over to her lunch and then to Winter before she shrugged. "I'm used to it. Animals and gore like this aren't usually my specialty, but I see enough of it that I can watch a surgery while I eat spaghetti."

Winter hoped her chuckle sounded less like a nervous cackle than it did to her own ears. "It's okay. Were you able to find anything from the rats?"

Stella pursed her lips as she tapped the keyboard again. In the next image, the item of the camera's focus was smudged with coagulated rat blood, but it wasn't organic.

Squinting at the monitor, Winter scooted forward. "Is that...what is that? Is that a Black Cat? A firecracker?"

Stella nodded. "It is. We've got no idea why they were there, but we found one in the belly of each rat. Do you know what they might mean? Is it something that might have been significant to Justin somehow?"

Just as Winter was about to shake her head, she was struck with a sudden memory. "Oh my god."

"What?" She could feel Stella's curious gaze on the side of her face.

Winter couldn't pry her attention away from the monitor.

"That summer, the summer before my...my mom and dad were killed, that Fourth of July. Mom and Dad let Justin light some fireworks, just the small stuff, sparklers and a couple bottle rockets. I remember, earlier that day, he'd done something to irritate me, so I put his favorite stuffed animal on the top of the bookshelf down in the living room."

When she paused to swallow, Stella remained quiet.

"It was a lion, a stuffed lion named Rory. My parents were busy doing yard work, so it was hours before one of them had a chance to come in and get Rory down for him. We ate dinner, and I just figured everything went back to normal. He'd annoyed me, and I got back at him, so we were square. But then, when we were out lighting off fireworks." Winter glanced over to Stella and pointed to the screen. "He threw a Black Cat at me."

Stella gave her a commiserating look but didn't appear shocked or even a bit surprised. "My mom's brother stabbed her in the back with a screwdriver once when they were eight or nine."

"Oh my god," Winter managed.

Patting the air with both hands, Stella shook her head. "Sorry, I'm not trying to steal your thunder. It just seemed relevant. Siblings can be jerks to one another."

With a quiet chuckle, Winter nodded. "Yeah, they can. My mom and dad chewed him out for it and told him how dangerous it was to play with fireworks like that, and he apologized for it later that night. It was just one of those things. He didn't know any better. He threw it at my feet to try to scare me, and it worked."

"No doubt."

Winter could feel the creeping horror walking up her spine as she met Stella's gaze. "Why would he do that?" But she already knew.

Stella's cool composure didn't waver as she casted a

thoughtful glance to the monitor. "Maybe he just wanted to make certain that you had no doubt that it was him."

"Maybe." The word was barely above a whisper.

There was no way she could have mistaken the author of those two messages for someone else.

"Other than that, we ran through the fingerprints we collected from the house. The prints and these guys." Stella pointed to the headless rat on the monitor. "Those were the most time-consuming parts of our investigation. The only prints in the house were from the realtor, Dr. Trent, yourself, and a couple other agents."

"How did he get in? The lock to the door was still intact when we got there, and it didn't look like anyone had walked through the living room for quite a while."

Stella closed the gory image and straightened her computer screen. "We found a footprint outside one of the windows. We're still looking at it, trying to see if we can figure out a size, style, that sort of thing. Right now, we think that's how he got in."

"That makes sense," Winter murmured.

None of this made sense, but she wasn't about to put Stella down when she'd clearly gone above and beyond her normal duties to get the analyses to Winter so soon.

As if she could sense Winter's underlying nervousness, Stella's expression sobered. "I'm sorry we don't have more for you right now. The writings on the walls were definitely done with rat blood, but otherwise, we didn't find any indication that there were even rats in the house. They had to have been killed somewhere else."

Just when Winter thought the situation couldn't make less sense, Stella threw her a curveball. Was it more or less disconcerting that Justin had mutilated the rats before he arrived at the house where their parents had been killed?

At the thought, her stomach roiled.

"When do you think you'll make it through everything that's left?" The question had been spoken in Winter's voice, but she felt like someone else had said the words.

"Aside from the paperwork, we should have it all wrapped up by tomorrow. The paperwork usually lags behind by a couple days, or lately, by a week."

"Tomorrow, okay." Winter clenched one hand and focused on the sting as her nails dug into her palm.

Like everything else so far in the search for Justin, the most recent discovery only left her with more questions than answers.

Chief among them was what had happened to the little boy who'd been taken from her so many years ago.

Where was he, and who had taken his place?

8

Though working out a psychological profile of a serial killer was more specifically within Aiden Parrish's realm of comfort than interrogating a Russian mafia foot soldier, part of him preferred to deal with the mob. More often than not, the mob made sense. They were motivated by one thing and one thing only—money.

To be sure, they committed plenty of atrocious acts in their pursuit of money and power, but their motive was always the same.

When Aiden was faced with a puzzle like the one that had been delivered to the FBI by Ryan O'Connelly, he wondered if he had finally come across a mystery he couldn't solve.

He would never admit the uncertainty to anyone else, but after almost a decade and a half in the BAU, he figured the initial pang of doubt was part of the process. This time, his immediate response to the fleeting uncertainty had been to reach out to a certain forensic psychologist.

With a groan, he leaned back in the office chair and rubbed the bridge of his nose.

When he'd started at the bureau, he'd always thought he

would make it through his career without the mistake of mixing his professional and personal lives. Then he'd met Sun Ming. Of course, that was only after the one-time affair he'd had with Cassidy Ramirez during the start of The Preacher case nearly fourteen years ago. And the feelings that had grown for the girl who had been orphaned by that particular psychopath.

He mentally cursed himself. Maybe he wasn't as adept at separating professional and personal business as he liked to think.

The realization elicited another groan, and he was suddenly glad that Winter and Noah were late to the last-minute meeting.

Somewhere in the back of his mind, he knew Autumn Trent was different.

They'd only known one another for a few months, but he was sure she already knew more about him than most of his friends and acquaintances. She knew about his secret affinity for Code Red Mountain Dew, about every computer game he'd ever played, every concert he'd ever been to, every college exam he'd ever bombed.

And yet, he couldn't bring himself to act on the inexorable pull he felt when he saw her. Especially now that she'd started to dress like a runway model instead of a roadie for Nirvana. Not that she'd looked bad before. If anyone could make ripped jeans and flannel look good, it was Autumn. But now, she wore those heels...

As much as he wanted to avoid mixing the personal and professional, he couldn't help but wonder why he was so hesitant to act on the undeniable attraction. Maybe the conundrum itself was the problem. Not only was Autumn a professional colleague, but she was one of Winter Black's best friends. Unless he was sure the outcome would be positive for everyone involved, it was best to stay far away from such an impulse.

When the creak of the door cut through the stillness of the little conference room, he jerked his attention back to the present.

He arched an eyebrow at Winter as she closed the door behind herself. "Where's Dalton?"

"He sent me a text a few minutes ago. He was with Miguel Vasquez checking up on one of the victim's families." She dropped down to sit across from him.

"You didn't go with him?"

She shook her head. "No. I was stuck on a phone call trying to get ahold of the other victim's parents. A phone call that went nowhere, so, whatever." Crossing both arms over her chest, she turned those vivid blue eyes back to him.

He chuckled quietly. "Whatever, indeed. I suppose we might as well get started then."

With a half-smile, she nodded. "Yeah, we might as well. I'm assuming you already know everything we've found so far, so I was hoping I'd be able to pick your brain about it."

Straightening, Aiden propped his elbows on the table and returned her nod. "Of course. I looked through those videos and all the posts under them in that forum. Most of them seem like run of the mill predators, but our voyeuristic OP, or original poster as they say, is cut from a slightly different cloth."

"Different how?" She scooted forward, her eyes fixed on his.

"Well, for starters, all signs point to the fact that he's a sociopath. He knows right from wrong, and that's why he wore the mask, the sunglasses, all of it. It's why he hid his location with a proxy server and removed any distinguishing marks from the room where he held those girls. But..." He raised a finger.

Winter gave him a *don't play with me* stare. "But?"

"But, he's not exactly an unfeeling, methodical murderer either. There's some repressed rage buried underneath the calculating veneer. When he cut that girl's throat, he almost decapitated her. His expression wasn't visible, but the way he held himself wasn't cool and collected. His movements were uneven and erratic. He turned the camera off, but I don't doubt that he stabbed her a few more times before he got rid of the body."

"Okay," Winter said. "He's pissed about something, so he abducts and murders women to try to turn a profit on 'pervs are us dot com' all while he tries to satiate his rage?"

Aiden tapped his knuckles on the table. "Close, but I think there's more driving his behavior than just plain anger. It could stem from attachment problems with his mother during his development. Then, when one of his advances was rejected during his teen years, he snapped. And just to be clear, it wasn't the girl's fault for rejecting him." He flashed Winter a matter-of-fact look. "He was a psychopath before she turned him down. She didn't drag it out of him. People like this, they're wired differently."

The corner of Winter's mouth twitched in the start of a smile. "You've been hanging around Autumn, haven't you?"

He tried to look confused. "What?"

With a light laugh, she rolled her eyes. "Yeah, okay. So, we've got a guy who's angry at women due to attachment issues with his mother and then probably rejection when he was older. What are you thinking in terms of demographics?"

"If the videos he posted are any indication, he's still evolving, still changing parts of his routine. He went from recording the girls while they were being held captive to murdering one of them up close on camera. Something might have happened in between the last captive video and the homemade snuff film. It could be that he was stressed about something unrelated, or that he got turned down by another girl."

Winter scoffed.

"I agree. But the fact that he's prone to these outbursts, to changing his MO so drastically out of anger, means he probably hasn't been doing this for long."

Nodding her understanding, she shifted her eyes away from him as they lapsed into silence.

"What about Justin?"

The question leapt out and struck him with the force he'd expect from a boxing heavyweight champ.

The effort to say something other than a dumbfounded "what" felt Herculean. Aiden wasn't knocked off-balance by a question often, but when it happened, it made him nervous.

He hated to be nervous. Anxiety was an aspect of his mind he liked to think he'd conquered a long time ago, and a reminder that the unease still lurked beneath his polished, purposeful exterior brought a bitter taste to his mouth.

"What about Justin?" he echoed when nothing more substantial came to mind.

The motion slow and measured, Winter nodded. "I know you, Aiden. I know you've probably had a profile or a theory put together about him for months. Ever since Kilroy told us he was still alive. Even if you didn't write it down or make it official, I know you've at least got an opinion."

He linked his hands behind his head and let the room lapse into silence.

She was right. He did have an opinion about what had happened to Justin Black, but he knew she wouldn't want to hear it.

However, if he refused to answer the question, or if he offered some half-assed explanation, she would know. Winter might not have had the same bizarre knack to see straight through someone like Autumn did, but she'd known him for nearly fourteen years. She knew better than to think he hadn't formed an opinion about Justin.

He'd done more than form an opinion.

He'd pulled in the expertise of Autumn Trent, and he'd done so officially. There were records at both the bureau and with Shadley and Latham—the prestigious firm that specialized in criminal and forensic psychology—that confirmed Autumn's involvement in Justin Black's kidnapping investigation.

For the time being, he would make a point to leave Autumn out of the clash that was on the horizon. Well, it had been on the horizon, but now it was knocking on the front door.

Even when Winter was a teenager, Aiden had never coddled her. She was a smart, strong young woman, and she didn't need to be shielded from the harsh realities of the world. After all, she'd been dead set on working for the FBI since she was in junior high. If she wanted to work for the FBI, she needed to know the truth.

The truth about the world, and now, the truth about her brother.

When the blinds clattered against the glass door as it swung open, he barely kept himself from heaving a sigh of relief.

As soon as Noah Dalton stepped into the room, the man froze in place. His green eyes darted from Aiden to Winter and back before he released his hold on the handle to let the door swing closed.

"Did I interrupt something?" Noah didn't move from his spot just in front of the doorway, unabashed skepticism written on his face.

Winter's intense stare on Aiden didn't relent. "No. Aiden was just about to tell me his thoughts on Justin's kidnapping."

Noah opened and closed his mouth a couple times before he clenched his jaw and nodded. "Okay. Do I need to be here for this, or…?"

As he reached for the door handle, Aiden held up a hand. "You're fine, Dalton." The first rush of irritability rose up to greet him, and he embraced it like an old friend. "This will just take a second."

Winter's nostrils flared. "Go ahead then. Enlighten us."

"Winter," he swallowed another sigh before continuing, "your brother left the mutilated corpses of four rats in a corner of the same bedroom where your parents were murdered. He wrote you two ominous messages in blood. What would you say if you saw that in a case file? If you saw that a serial killer had abducted this person when they were six years old, and that they were now taunting their older sister by leaving messages at an old murder scene?"

She opened her mouth as if she intended to respond, but he cut her off.

"That was rhetorical. I didn't want to tell you this yet because I wanted to know for certain that it was true, but anymore, I don't think there's much room for doubt. Something isn't right with your brother, Winter. During the last thirteen years, he's likely been with Douglas Kilroy, and it changed him. When you find him, it'll be when he wants you to find him, and I guarantee he won't be a damn thing like the kid you remember."

Resting both palms flat on the table, she pushed herself out of her seat. "You mean to tell me you think that my brother is just like this psychopath who's out there hunting down girls and filming their murder? Is that what you're telling me?"

He grated his teeth together. "Take it at face value."

Even as he rose to stand, he was struck by a sudden thought. A peculiar thought.

Aiden hated to be wrong. He hated when he discovered a hole in a theory he'd spent hours or days perfecting.

But for what might have been the first time in his professional career, he hoped he was wrong.

Hope in one hand, shit in the other.

9

Tomorrow would mark two weeks since Nathaniel found the envelope his son had left in his upstairs home office. The flash drive that held a four-hour-long video of a young woman in captivity. The video of that same woman's brutal murder.

For two weeks, Nathaniel had scarcely been able to get the imagery out of his head.

He was sure the blood and gore were fake, and he'd even tried to lighten his thoughts by considering how he could get the young woman a position in an upcoming horror film.

No matter the number of times he tried to mentally nominate her for an Oscar, his memory always returned to her eyes.

With a weary sigh, he closed and locked the door behind himself as he stepped out of the garage and into the mud room. It was just as immaculate as it had been on the day he had come home to find that flash drive.

At least today, he could hear the faint drone of the television where Maddie had taken up residence in the great room.

Like he did every day, he stepped out of his dress shoes and hung his light jacket on a hook above the wooden bench. Loosening the black tie around his neck, he headed to the kitchen. Sure enough, he caught the faint whiff of cooked onions.

He'd hired staff to clean the spacious house, and he paid them extra to prepare meals in his absence. But recently, with her discovery of a popular mobile app that displayed countless recipes, Maddie had taken the task of cooking upon herself. Plus, if she made the food, she could double the amount of onions in each dish.

As he approached the stainless-steel refrigerator to retrieve a beer, his eyes were drawn to a black and silver knife block beside the range. He bought the knives years ago, and they'd set him back a few hundred dollars. But right now, he wasn't interested in the price or the craftsmanship.

Right now, the knives were familiar for a different reason.

Just as clearly as if the image was projected in front of him, he saw the man's gloved hand clamped around the matte black handle of a butcher knife. The same matte black finish. The same polished steel blade.

When he spotted the butcher knife, he wanted to be relieved.

As he neared the counter, his focus was fixed on the handle. Each move more painstaking than the last, he pulled the knife free from its spot at the edge of the block.

Was his mind playing tricks on him, or was there a rust-colored line where the steel of the blade was fastened to the handhold? With a fingernail, he gingerly scraped at the discoloration. As the substance flaked away, a pit of anxiety coalesced in the bottom of his stomach.

It's rust, he told himself. *These things have been here for years. Someone forgot to dry it before they put it back, and it started to rust. That's all it is.*

"Dad?"

The quiet voice jerked him from the contemplation with the same force he would have expected if he'd been physically struck. As he leapt backward in the direction of the refrigerator, he almost lost his grip on the knife.

Maddie's green eyes widened at the sudden movement, and she raised both hands. "Whoa, I didn't mean to scare you. Is something wrong? You were just staring at that knife."

With a sharp breath, he glanced to the knife one more time before returning it to the block. "I'm fine. Yeah, sorry. I was just, it looked like there was rust on the handle." He blew out a weary sigh and raked a hand through his hair. "Guess I was more focused on it than I thought. How was school?"

She shrugged as she stepped around him to pry open the fridge. "It was all right, I guess. It was school. Boring, but necessary."

He managed a quiet chuckle. "Definitely boring, and definitely necessary. Trust me, kiddo, college will be more your speed. You'll have to take some gen eds, but you'll actually be able to study the subjects that interest you."

"As long as there aren't any more of these stupid social cliques, I don't really care what I study," she muttered as she cracked open a can of sparkling water.

Even as he offered her a reassuring smile, he reached down to where his phone buzzed in the pocket of his slacks. "Damn it. It's seven at night."

"Work?" It was said with such an expression of wide-eyed sarcasm that Nathaniel smiled. A real one this time.

Swiping the green answer key, Nathaniel cleared his throat. "Judge Arkwell speaking."

❄

AFTER THE POINTED, borderline hostile observation Aiden Parrish made about Winter's younger brother, Noah had honestly been unsure how to approach his friend.

His friend, and now his lover, though he doubted sex was in Winter's plans for the night.

As much as he wanted to reassure her that Parrish was mistaken, he wasn't convinced that the man was all that far off base. In fact, the more he thought about it, the more Noah agreed with the behavioral analyst.

Apparently, he and Winter had switched roles in their interaction with the Supervisory Special Agent.

Rather than broach the treacherous subject on the drive back to their apartment complex, he'd made an effort to steer their dialogue toward television shows. But the conversation hadn't taken long to peter out.

Though the drive was quiet, he didn't get the sense that she'd vanished into her own little world. She might not have been talkative, but she was still there.

Of course she was upset. How would he feel if someone he trusted, someone whose opinion he'd valued for more than a decade, had told him that the one remaining member of his immediate family was a sociopath?

Would he be devastated? Angry? Both? He couldn't say for sure.

"What did you think about it?" Her unexpected question cut through the silence like a knife.

He opened and closed his mouth a few times before he found his voice. "About what Parrish said?"

Her blue eyes flicked to him, the strain of the conversation reflecting in their depths. "Yeah. Do you think he's right?"

He should have been prepared for the question, but he felt like a novice swimmer struggling against a riptide.

Noah didn't think Aiden Parrish was right. He knew

Aiden Parrish was right. No one in a reasonable state of mind decapitated and gutted a bunch of rats just to paint a cryptic message on the wall. On the wall of the house where their parents had been brutally murdered.

Something was wrong with Justin. There was no doubt in Noah's mind about that.

But after the blow she'd just been dealt by the man who had effectively mentored her, he didn't want to add to her turmoil.

With a sigh, he reached over and squeezed her hand. He was fully prepared to face her ire for his response, but right now it was the best answer he could give.

"I don't know, sweetheart," he said, his voice hushed. "None of us do, not for sure. I just...I think maybe we ought to cross that bridge when we get to it, you know? It's not like we've got a lack of stuff to worry about right now."

To his relief, she seemed to relax into her seat, her fingers curling around his. "You're not wrong about that."

As they lapsed back into silence, he felt the tentative creep of relief.

"I'm sorry," she blurted. "I shouldn't have asked you that. That put you in a weird spot."

Flicking on the blinker, he glanced to her as he shook his head. "It's okay. I'm not really qualified to give an opinion about it, you know? At least, it doesn't seem like I am. That's Autumn and Aiden's territory. And, I don't know, it probably sounds a little weird right now, but I think the only reason Parrish said any of that is because he's looking out for you."

When he was greeted with more silence, he wondered if he'd gone too far.

Definitely no sex tonight.

Rather than drop the subject, he doubled down. "I'm not saying he couldn't have gone about it better. He definitely could have. But I don't know. The guy's an asshole, but he's not that kind of asshole. Not the kind who'd lie just to be a dick about something. If that's what he's saying, then that's what he really thinks."

With a weary sigh, she nodded. "I guess."

Once he pulled into a spot, he let go of her hand to shift the pickup into park. When he turned his full attention back to her, there was a glimmer of despondency in her blue eyes as she twirled the ends of her hair around an index finger.

With one hand, he reached out to touch her shoulder. Her gaze flicked away from the windshield, and as her eyes met his, her lips curved up in a slight smile. Though he wanted to offer words of wisdom to drive the sadness from her face, he doubted he could come up with an observation powerful enough to offset Parrish's assessment.

Instead, he leaned forward as he clasped her shoulder. When she closed the remaining distance and pressed her lips against his, the rush of anticipation was almost immediate. Her hand was warm on the side of his face as they separated, and he tilted his head to the side to offer a fleeting kiss to her palm.

He kept his eyes on hers as he squeezed her shoulder. "Whatever happens, however any of this turns out, you know I've got your back, okay?"

The strain in her expression lessened. "Thank you, Noah."

When he smiled at her this time, the look didn't feel so forced. "Come on. Let's go figure out what we feel like eating and find something to watch."

Her face brightened. "That sounds like a plan."

Good plan or not, he didn't even get a chance to turn on the television. He was hungry, but food was the last thing on his mind as she sidled up next to him and slid both hands beneath his shirt and up his chest.

He would find food later.

10

I f Winter hadn't awoken in such a good mood, she would have been spitting four-letter words with every other step as she made her way down the hall after her morning visit with Stella Norcott.

She wasn't angry with Stella, of course. The senior forensics analyst and her team had done their job, and they had done it well. But despite their best efforts, the evidence they'd gathered didn't point to any definitive direction Justin might have taken. Though they now had a cast of the footprint from outside the kitchen window, they hadn't been able to identify the shoe based on the imprint.

All they could be sure of was the fact that Justin had been at that house. Even then, Winter figured there was always the possibility, however remote, that someone could be playing a cruel prank on her.

The idea was just one step short of flat-out stupid, but she'd learned to embrace the unexpected since starting her FBI career.

For now, she would turn the lingering irritability into

fuel for the murder and kidnapping cases that had landed in her team's lap.

Between Winter, Bobby, and Noah's efforts, they'd managed to identify all but one of the victims. All the women were under twenty, and as best as they could tell, all four of them were prostitutes. Apparently, their killer had torn a page straight out of Ted Bundy's *How to Become A Serial Killer for Dummies* manual.

Ted Bundy wasn't the only serial killer who had preyed on prostitutes. Picking on the vulnerable members of society was a common practice for serial killers. Men like Ted Bundy chose working girls not only because they were easy targets, but because their status on the fringes of society meant a lower likelihood of detection.

If Bundy was still alive, Winter would be inclined to take a personal day just to go kick him in the balls. But for the time being, her make-believe trip would have to wait.

They'd identified four of the five women, and now, the legwork of the investigation had started. For the first part of the day, she and Noah flipped through Bobby's notes to make a list of names, phone numbers, and addresses.

Based on the missing persons reports, they established an approximate timeframe for each young woman's disappearance. With any luck, they could find a handful of friends or other working girls who could point out any abnormalities in the days leading up to the kidnappings.

First things first, however, she and Noah needed to find out if any unidentified bodies at the morgue—or at least any bodies that had passed through the morgue—matched their victims. A body would be a valuable source of forensic evidence, but she had a sneaking suspicion they wouldn't be so lucky.

Though it was a little after one by the time she and Noah left the FBI building to go pay their visit to the medical examiner, they still swung by a coffee shop to bring Dan a peace offering.

Winter set the paper bag of pastries in her lap as she fastened her seat belt. "You do know that Dan gets paid, right? He probably makes more than either of us. He probably makes as much as Aiden. He's an adult, and he's more than capable of buying his own coffee and donuts."

Noah looked appalled. "They're not donuts, darlin'. They're croissants. Chocolate croissants."

She rolled her eyes in feigned exasperation. "Oh, okay. I'm sorry. Dan can buy his own chocolate croissants. Can't he? Or was he banned from the coffee shops around Richmond?"

Chuckling, Noah turned the key over in the ignition. "You'll have to ask him that. We haven't seen him in a while, okay? Bringing him some treats seems like the polite thing to do."

The paper crinkled as she reached into the bag. "You're lucky I like Dan, but I'm still going to eat one of these. That man doesn't need three."

For the remainder of the drive, Winter ate her pilfered pastry in silence as Noah flipped through radio stations. When they pulled into the worn parking lot of the unassuming building, Winter had licked the chocolate off her fingers and dusted any evidence of crumbs from her shirt.

As they strode through the entryway and down a hall to Dan's office, Winter was drawn to a short pine tree in the corner of the room. She'd seen it before but had never commented on its presence. She commented now. "Isn't it September?" she asked as she set the bag of breakfast treats on the medical examiner's desk.

Like always, Dan looked ready to head to work at a large bank or a stockbroker's office. His ebony hair was neatly styled, and though he wore a white lab coat over his dress shirt, there was a suit jacket draped on the back of his chair.

The corners of Dan's eyes creased as he grinned. "Did you see the ornaments? The tree might not be seasonal, but the ornaments are. I've always liked holiday décor. There's something about it that makes a place feel homey, but having to go through three distinctly different sets of decorations just seems like too much. I streamlined it all into a tree. See?" He pointed, and Winter followed the motion.

Winter squinted. "Are those?"

Still grinning, Dan nodded. "Ghosts and black cats, yes. I got the idea from an ex-girlfriend."

As Noah glanced to Winter, he scratched his cheek. "A Halloween Christmas tree. Why does that sound so familiar?"

Winter didn't have to think for long. "Autumn. She was shopping online for ghost ornaments when I went to visit her the other day. She said her cat knocked some of the old ones off the tree last year and she couldn't find them."

Noah's green eyes brightened with sudden recognition, and he snapped his fingers. "That's right."

As he pulled open the bag of pastries, Dan lifted an eyebrow, gesturing for them to take a seat. "Autumn Trent?"

"Yeah, that's...wait." Winter gave Dan a curious look. "How do you know Autumn?"

Though Dan offered a nonchalant shrug in response, a hint of his good humor slipped away. "I used to teach at VCU Law School. She was a student of mine years back."

Winter wasn't convinced of his casual dismissal, but she let the subject rest. They weren't here to delve into the six degrees of separation that connected them to every other stranger on the planet. Instead, she held up a manila envelope before she slid it across the polished desk. "This is for you."

Reluctantly, Dan set aside his newly acquired croissant to open the folder. As he produced the printout of a blonde woman's Department of Motor Vehicle registration, his dark eyes flitted back up to Winter and Noah.

"Dakota Ronsfeldt," he said.

Winter nodded. "There's information on three other women in the folder too. They've all been reported missing, and her..." she gestured to Dakota's picture, "there's a video of her murder on a dark web forum where creeps and perverts tend to congregate. Our informant pointed it out to us."

With a nod of understanding, Dan pulled out the rest of the contents of the envelope. "Like a snuff film, then?"

As Winter glanced to Noah, they both shrugged.

"Something like that, yeah. Though it seemed less like a snuff film and more like a livestream," Noah said. "We're here today because we wanted to see if there were any Jane Does that have been through here that match our missing girls. There was footage of Dakota being killed, but the other three were just videos, probably livestreams, of the girls while they were held captive."

The room lapsed into silence as Dan shuffled through the printouts and photographs. After he looked over the final victim's picture, he straightened the stack of papers and shook his head. "No, none of them look familiar. I'll double-check through our records and ask the rest of the office staff, but I don't think I've seen any of them in here before."

Blowing out a quiet breath, Winter shifted in her seat. "Okay. Keep that envelope and let us know ASAP if you see any Jane Does that might match one of the missing girls."

Dan nodded. "Of course. I'll make sure all the staff knows what to look out for too. Is there anything else I can help with?"

She swallowed another sigh as she pushed to her feet.

"No, that's it for now. We'll let you know if anything changes."

Dan offered a quick wave before she and Noah turned to let themselves out of the office.

Earlier that morning, when Aiden Parrish had presented his profile of the killer, he speculated that they wouldn't find the bodies of any of the five victims.

The perpetrator had taken steps to ensure he wasn't traced via the online posts he made, so there was no doubt he'd do the same for physical evidence.

And even though Dan still had to sort through the office's records to confirm, all signs indicated that Aiden was right.

Winter gritted her teeth.

Aiden was always right.

11

I n the three days since I'd left the flash drive in my father's home office, I hadn't so much as caught a glimpse of the man. That wasn't to say I was purposefully avoiding him. Judge Nathaniel Arkwell was a busy man, and I'd never ranked all that high on his list of priorities.

I'd left the video to frighten him. But what he didn't know then, and what he still didn't know now, was that I'd planted a nanny cam in a potted plant near the window of his office.

Though I was still disappointed I hadn't gotten to see his reaction live, I'd watched the footage three different times over the past few days.

As I stretched my arms above my head, I pulled myself out of the memory and glanced around the living area. The staff kept the place so immaculate that it rarely looked like anyone lived here.

A gray and blue patterned blanket was draped diagonally along the end of the overstuffed sectional couch, and a handful of matching pillows had been arranged neatly just behind it.

With the rustic driftwood coffee table and the glass bowl

of decorative beige and blue wicker balls, the entire room looked like a scene ripped out of an issue of *Better Homes and Gardens*. Even without the staff, I suspected the house would be just as clean.

My mom always used to say that my father had been a disorganized slob when she met him. Over their years together—before they had me, anyway—she'd converted him into a clean freak. It wasn't surprising that Maddie and I picked up on the same penchant for cleanliness.

Scooping the remote for the expansive television from atop the coffee table, I dropped down to rest my back in the corner of the couch. Just as the screen flickered to life, I caught a glimpse of movement in my periphery.

At seven in the evening, the staff had gone home, and Maddie had already left for a friend's house when I got back from my afternoon class.

"Nathaniel."

My greeting was as crisp and professional as if I was addressing one of my instructors. As far as I was concerned, I only had one parent, and she had been dead for over a decade.

With a weary sigh, Nathaniel loosened the black tie around his neck. Though his face was perpetually clean-shaven, flecks of silver were visible amidst the five o'clock shadow on his cheeks. As his light brown eyes met mine, the shadows on his face made him look every bit his forty-four years of age.

The corner of my mouth twitched, and I didn't try to disguise the smile.

The decision to leave the flash drive for him to find had been made at the last minute, but when I saw that defeated look, I was glad I had.

Though I half-expected him to turn around to make his

way back upstairs, he stood his ground. "I need to talk to you, Cameron."

Shrugging, I turned my attention back to the television. "Then go ahead and talk."

I could almost hear his teeth grind together at the flippant remark.

"You want to explain that flash drive you left in my office?"

I shrugged again, but I didn't turn to face him. "Thought you might find it interesting."

He scoffed. "Interesting? Yeah, that's one way to put it. What is wrong with you? Where did you get that?"

I almost laughed. As much as I wanted to come right out and tell him that I'd made it myself, the moment didn't feel quite right.

Nathaniel's time was coming. It wouldn't be long before he discovered firsthand what I'd learned to do over the years.

For the third time, I shrugged noncommittally. "Got it on the internet."

"Really?" His incredulous tone was tinged with indignation. He looked mad. Pissed, really. For a moment, it even looked like the good judge might be able to kill me.

Unbidden, I remembered there was a handgun—a forty-five, if memory served—stashed in a false bottom drawer of the end table by my feet.

Nathaniel was a public official, after all.

Such a position came with its fair share of security risks, and my father had always been a gun aficionado. If someone with an ax to grind with Virginia State Supreme Court Judge Arkwell barreled through the front door and into the great room, the great man would be able to defend himself.

I finally pried my attention away from the flickering screen as I pushed myself to sit upright. If I wanted, I could scoot to the end of the chaise, pull open the drawer, and retrieve the handgun before Nathaniel could even close the distance between us.

Sure, he was a veteran, but he'd been out of the Navy for more than twenty years. Two decades was plenty of time for rust to slow down his reflexes.

Rather than leap for the weapon, I feigned an exasperated sigh. Killing the asshole would take away much of my fun.

"It sounds like you don't believe me. Then again, that wouldn't be new, would it? You'll believe everything Maddie tells you, though, right? You know where she is right now, don't you? Did she tell you she's at her friend Katie's house? Because that's not where she actually is."

When the familiar spark of ire flickered to life in my father's eyes, I had to make a concerted effort to keep my expression neutral.

Maddie had always been the golden child, but Nathaniel didn't know that his perfect little princess had matured into another degenerate high school tramp just like all her friends.

Before I could go on, Nathaniel cut me off. "Actually, Cameron, I do know where she is." Though calm, there was an unmistakable anger that simmered beneath the words. "I know where she is because she told me. She didn't tell me she was at Katie's, she told me the truth. Because that's what she does. She tells me things. She's with her boyfriend. Well, she's not sure if they're officially dating yet, but yeah, I know who she's with. Besides, Maddie isn't the one who left a video on my desk of a girl getting her throat slit, is she?"

My heart knocked against my chest as the chill of apprehension and excitement rushed through my body. "You know she's been having sex with him, right?"

Nathaniel rolled his eyes. "Yeah, last I knew, that's what seventeen-year-olds do with their boyfriend or girlfriend.

Are you trying to tell me you're saving yourself for marriage? Because that's bull."

I reflexively glanced to the end table, but I tore my gaze away and fixed Nathaniel with a petulant glare. I didn't need him to know that I had figured out his secret firearm stash in the living room. There were undoubtedly other hidden caches around the house, but I hadn't found those yet.

If Nathaniel had learned that I was screwing around with a girl during my senior year of high school, I would have never heard the end of his lectures. But now that it was Maddie, of course it was fine.

As the warmth of rage settled in beside the adrenaline, I shoved myself to stand. If I stayed here for the rest of this conversation, there was a distinct possibility I would venture down a path from which there would be no way back.

That forty-five had started to sing a siren's song, and I was its only audience.

Not that I cared if Nathaniel lived or died. I didn't. But he was useful. He'd proven that when he decided to keep the contents of that flash drive to himself.

I'd handed him a video of me slitting a whore's throat, and he hadn't even mentioned it to the authorities. The hallowed judge had kept the video of a prostitute's murder to himself.

Without bothering to turn off the television, I spun on my heel and stalked to the other end of the room.

"Where are you going?"

I glanced over my shoulder, but Nathaniel hadn't moved. "I'm going out," I replied. "Maybe I'll go fuck around with my girlfriend."

"Where did you get that video?" His voice cut through the air like a boomerang.

"I told you." I painted an uncaring expression on my face as I turned to him. "I found it on the internet."

Before he could let loose another volley of questions, I strode through the arched doorway to the kitchen. As I passed the stainless-steel appliances and granite countertops, I caught a glimpse of the block of knives.

The wooden block was new, and the old matte black knives were nowhere to be found.

My dick began to fill with blood at the realization.

When my pulse rushed through my ears this time, it was driven by a sensation just shy of outright giddiness.

I didn't have to tell Nathaniel. He already knew.

He knew, and he'd gotten rid of the evidence.

Just like I knew he would.

THE FBI HAD BEEN KIND ENOUGH to provide Ryan with a laptop he could use to aid them in their investigation. But if Ryan was honest, his stomach turned every time he pulled up the forum where he'd found the video of Dakota Ronsfeldt's murder.

The entire scenario was too familiar, and the irony hadn't been lost on him.

Heidi Presley had gone to some lengths to ensure she had a front row view of Ryan's demise during the final portion of her sadistic plan. Apparently, she wasn't the only sociopath out there who liked to immortalize their handiwork. At least the video of Ryan's ordeal hadn't been uploaded to the internet.

As the door of the hotel room creaked inward, Ryan snapped himself out of the daze and shifted in his seat.

The suite was outfitted with a bedroom, a small living area, and even a kitchenette. Though leftover pizza from the night before was still stashed in the miniature refrigerator beside the entertainment stand, Special Agent Bobby Weyrick arrived bearing a late dinner.

Ryan had been prepared to make do with ramen noodles and instant oatmeal, but for the last two nights, Agent Weyrick had provided real food.

"You really don't need to bring me food." Even as he made the half-hearted protest, Ryan rose to accept the plastic bag of Chinese takeout.

Agent Weyrick shrugged as he dropped down to sit at the other end of the couch. "No, but I was hungry, and my mama didn't raise me to be a jackass. I'm not going to sit here and shovel crab rangoon and lo mein in my mouth while you sit a few feet away from me with nothing."

Despite the grave situation, Ryan chuckled at the Southerner's unfaltering hospitality. "Well, I appreciate it. Thank you."

With a slight smile, the agent nodded. "No problem, man. I get to write it off as a business expense, anyway. Means I get a free meal out of it too."

Ryan returned the quick smile as he moved his laptop to the floor.

They spread out the veritable feast in silence, the quiet din of the television the only sound. The hotel might not have been the luxurious real estate to which Ryan had become accustomed in his years of illicit work, but he would give credit where it was due. He had yet to hear any of the neighboring guests.

"You were born in Chicago, right?" Agent Weyrick asked.

Nodding, Ryan turned his gaze away from the generous portion of fried rice to meet Agent Weyrick's curious glance. "I was, yes. Born and raised."

The agent looked thoughtful as he took a bite of an eggroll. "How'd you wind up with an Irish accent then?"

Ryan dumped some of the fried rice on a paper plate. "My

uncle raised me and my sister, and he didn't move to the States until he was twenty-something. He lived in Belfast all his life before then, so I just picked up on how he talked. My sister's a little younger than I am, so she never really caught onto it as much as I did. There's a little of it there when she talks, but nothing really that noticeable."

Bobby took another bite as he nodded his understanding. "That makes sense."

"The neighborhood we lived in was home to a bunch of other Irish immigrants and their families, so all the kids we played with had accents. I think that probably had more to do with it than anything."

Another slight smile made its way to Bobby's face. "Fair enough."

Ryan's pulse picked up as a question began to form on his lips. So far, he hadn't mentioned the deal he'd intended to cut with the Federal Bureau of Investigation. The silence wasn't a wise move on his part, but if he was honest with himself, he still wasn't sure he was ready to hear their answer.

The phrase "ignorance is bliss" had never sat well with Ryan O'Connelly. Even if the truth was dire, he'd rather know than be left in the darkness of not knowing.

But this was different. There were too many unfamiliar variables—the poor woman he'd watched die on camera, his sister, her children, and their precarious living situation—for Ryan to operate under his normal high-stakes mantra.

Normally, if he was involved in a sticky situation like his current standing with the FBI, he had the option to bail out altogether. The ankle monitor that the Richmond SAC had given him was as technologically advanced as monitoring devices came, but it wasn't infallible. Ryan still hadn't figured out a way around it, but he knew there was a way.

But this was different.

Lil, Erin, and Evan were counting on him. If he failed to

follow through with his end of the bargain with the FBI, Lil would become a person of interest in the capture of a fugitive. That fugitive, of course, would be Ryan.

Even if the prosecutor decided not to press charges against Lil for hindering an investigation, obstructing justice, harboring a fugitive, or any other crimes they could think to toss out, they would still seek her out to ask questions.

And if they found her, then it was only a matter of time until James found her. Ryan wouldn't put it past the son of a bitch to press charges for her leaving the state without notifying the court.

Even though Ryan was bound to his fate, he still wanted to know what that fate was. Because ignorance was not bliss, and at the least, he wanted to know what his future held.

He glanced to Bobby Weyrick, and then back to his fried rice. "Can I ask you something, Agent?"

From the corner of his eye, Ryan saw Bobby nod. "Sure. What's up?"

"I know this is in the U.S. Attorney's hands, but have you heard any update from them? It's only been a couple days, but I was hoping maybe you'd heard something." He bit off the rest of the query.

He didn't want to ramble. Rambling made a person sound desperate.

But he was desperate, wasn't he?

With a quiet exhale, Bobby set his egg roll down on a paper plate and wiped his fingers with a napkin. "I haven't heard anything, no. I'd tell you if I had. SAC Osbourne hasn't had a chance to sit down with the U.S. Attorney to hash it out yet. I don't know if you've heard of Augusto Lopez, but the U.S. Attorney is trying that case right now. If I had to guess, I'd say that's why he hasn't had time yet. It's an open and shut case, but the publicity on it is a nightmare."

Nodding, Ryan scooped up another bite of fried rice.

"Yeah, I've heard of him. He was the guy who went around killing rapists and murderers, wasn't he? Ex-Army Ranger, or something like that? The media called him The Norfolk Executioner. He's not all that popular on the forums where I found these videos."

Bobby snorted. "Considering Lopez would leap at the opportunity to kill just about anyone on that website, and especially considering the fact that there's probably nothing any of them could do to stop him, no. I don't imagine they're real keen on him."

Ryan managed a chuckle. "Exactly."

Though Ryan knew better than to vocalize the sentiment, he wished Augusto Lopez was a free man. Maybe if Lopez hadn't been caught, he'd have beaten Ryan to the punch and wiped out the voyeuristic creep who had taken to abducting and filming helpless young women.

Maybe Ryan would get lucky, and Augusto Lopez would be his cell mate if the Feds decided to send him to prison.

The bleak thought wiped out what little of his appetite had remained, but he shoveled the fried rice into his mouth nonetheless.

This wasn't about him.

Until he was guaranteed Lil's safety and comfort, this was about her.

It was about her, and it was about finding justice for the young woman whose murder had been posted to a website for the express enjoyment of a group of scumbags.

The reminder brought him a minimal measure of comfort, and he only hoped the U.S. Attorney would see the virtue in Ryan's decision to risk himself to stop a killer.

12

A week after Winter and Noah had gifted Dan Nguyen with a bag of chocolate croissants and a mocha latte, Winter held the exact same order in her hands as she approached a couple young women seated on a park bench.

Though the shade of a number of large trees was plentiful, the walking trail and handful of other features throughout the grassy space had seen better days. Then again, the girls were only a few blocks away from their usual place of business. Winter was in an area that some referred to as "the wrong side of the tracks."

One of the two, a petite blonde with large blue eyes, glanced over as Winter approached.

During the Augusto Lopez investigation, the girl had met up with Winter and Levi Brandt—an agent from the Victim Services Division—at a diner. Though she'd introduced herself as Alice, both Winter and Levi had known that wasn't her real name.

Since then, Winter had learned that Alice's real name was Elenore Alice Thompson. She'd always thought that Elenore sounded too old-fashioned and highbrow for her liking, so she preferred to go by Alice.

When Winter thought back to the explanation, the first hint of a smile touched her face.

"I know, I know," Alice had said, waving a hand. "It makes me sound like I should be sitting here in a blue and white dress with a Cheshire cat on my lap, doesn't it?"

Despite the grim nature of their investigation, Winter couldn't help but chuckle at the memory of Alice's tone.

The prostitute was smart, witty, and had a great sense of humor. In all honesty, she reminded Winter of Autumn.

And like Autumn, Alice had been dealt one bad hand after another in her short life.

Where Autumn's father had shoved her headfirst into a coffee table and nearly killed her, all Alice's injuries were invisible. And though Autumn wound up in a foster home run by two kind people who had adopted her at thirteen, Alice's only option to escape her abusive, drug addicted parents had been to run away.

Like so many other runaway teens, Alice had resorted to prostitution to cover her basic expenses.

Pushing aside the cloud of thoughts, Winter raised a hand to wave to Alice and her friend. As the young women glanced over, Winter held up the two lattes and the bag of pastries. Alice's friend tucked a piece of ebony hair behind her ear and smiled.

Levi Brandt and Bree Stafford both had a great deal of experience talking to young women like Alice and her friend. One of the first tricks Winter learned from Levi was to be personable and offer token gestures like food or coffee. It was one thing for her to reassure the girls that she wasn't there to arrest them, but it was another for her to offer them chocolate croissants and a latte as proof that she was there in peace.

Alice's fair face brightened as Winter closed the distance. "Hi, Agent Black. You didn't have to bring us coffee. You're so nice."

Winter shrugged and passed a latte to each of the girls. "It's the least I can do."

The day before, Winter and Noah had swung by the shadier part of the block to ask Alice if she'd noticed anything peculiar during the timeframe when Dakota Ronsfeldt and the other victims had disappeared.

Alice couldn't recall any details, but she said one of her friends might have a better idea. That friend wasn't comfortable speaking to a law enforcement agent on the street where they worked, so they'd agreed to meet up the following day.

Though Noah had parked nearby, Alice had advised Winter that her friend was skittish around men who were, as Alice had said, built like a brick shithouse.

As Winter extended a hand to the dark-haired girl, she offered her a warm smile. "You must be Katya. I'm Special Agent Winter Black with the FBI. You can call me Winter, though."

Despite the flicker of nervousness in her green eyes, Katya managed a smile as she accepted the handshake. "Okay, Winter. It's nice to meet you. Thank you for the coffee, and for the donuts."

With a grin, Alice held up a finger. "Not donuts. Chocolate croissants."

Her trepidation vanished as Katya glanced to the paper bag. "Even better. Wow, thank you."

Winter waved a dismissive hand, a mannerism she'd picked up from Autumn. "It's no problem. I've just got a few questions for you about one of the girls you might've been friends with."

As Winter reached into her pocket for a photo of Dakota, Katya nodded and sipped at her coffee. There was an unde-

niable anxiety that lurked just beneath Katya's curious eyes—
an anxiety that insisted if Winter took one step in the wrong
direction, she would close up like a bank vault.

During the Lopez case, Winter had witnessed just such an
occurrence when the Richmond PD had arrested a potential
witness named Gina Traeger. If they hadn't cuffed her and
brought her in for a minor solicitation charge, they might
have found Augusto Lopez weeks earlier.

Though Alice was happy to cooperate with emissaries of
the FBI, most of the women in her circle harbored a great
deal of mistrust for law enforcement agents.

There were a handful of Richmond City police officers
who came around Katya and Alice's area of business to make
sure the girls were safe, but otherwise, most of the working
girls trusted cops about as far as they could throw them.
Based on Katya and Alice's petite frames, that wasn't far.

Winter kept her expression carefully neutral as she
handed the photo of Dakota to Katya. "Do you know her?"

A shadow darkened Katya's bright eyes as she nodded.
"Yes. That's Dakota. Did…did something happen to her?"

Swallowing past the bitter taste in her mouth, Winter
accepted the photo as Katya handed it back to her. "Yes, we
think something happened to her. When's the last time you
saw her?"

Katya brushed some more hair from her face. "Maybe…
something like three weeks ago? She was from a small town
in Maine, and I just hoped that she had gone back home."

"Can you think back to the last time you might have seen
her? Was there anything unusual that happened, any strange
men you might've seen?" Winter made sure her tone was
confident but gentle.

Fixing her green eyes on the coffee cup, Katya pursed her
lips as they lapsed into silence. A light breeze drifted by,
carrying with it the faint scent of fall. Seasonal changes in

Virginia weren't as dramatic as those farther inland, such as in Chicago or Minneapolis, but Winter still looked forward to the shift.

"Oh." Katya's attention snapped back up to Winter and Alice. "I remember. The last night I saw her, I think it was about three weeks ago, but it's hard to be sure exactly when it was. But I can remember what happened."

Winter retrieved a little notepad from the inside pocket of her jacket before she nodded to bid Katya to continue.

"It was night, but it wasn't that late. The sun hadn't been down for very long. Then, I remember this car pulling up. It was a nice car. And well, it's not really weird for us to see nice cars, but they still stick out, you know?" Katya fidgeted with the cardboard sleeve of her cup.

"Yeah, I know what you mean." Winter offered her another gentle smile. "What happened next?"

"Well, I thought about it, about going to the man in that car, I mean. But I just…like I said, it's not unusual for us to see nice cars, but for some reason, I just didn't like the look of that one. I-I should have said something to Dakota."

Clasping her friend's shoulder with one hand, Alice shook her head. "No, don't say that. You know even if you did, it wouldn't have changed Dakota's mind. That girl's too headstrong for her own good."

A slight smile flickered over Katya's face as she nodded. "Yeah. But, still. I saw it, and I just sort of pretended I was busy with something else so the driver wouldn't notice me. He wasn't there for very long before Dakota went up to him, and then she got in the passenger side and they left. That was the last time I saw her."

"Can you tell me a little more about the car?" Winter glanced up from her notes just as Katya nodded again.

"Yeah. I'm not much of a car person, but it was a nice one. A Mercedes, I think. Black, four doors. Looked new, and it was clean. It had rained that day, but the car still looked spotless. I'd seen it around before a couple times."

Winter jotted down a series of scribbles that looked approximately like the words black Mercedes and four-door. "Did you see the driver?"

Shaking her head, Katya turned her eyes back to her coffee cup. "I didn't really get much of a look at him. It was already dark, and the windows were tinted. He was white, with a short beard and dark hair. Other than that, I'm not really sure."

As she wrote out the description, Winter tried to make the woman feel good about what she'd shared. "This is really helpful. Thank you, Katya. Here," Winter pulled out a white business card, "Alice already has one of my cards, but I'll give you one too. If you need anything, even if it's not related to this case, just give me a call. Even if there's just some creep bothering you, or something like that. Let me know, and I'll do what I can to help out, okay?"

When Katya smiled this time, the expression didn't seem so strained. "Okay. Thank you, Agent Black. It was nice to meet you. If I remember anything else, I'll make sure I call you."

Winter returned the smile as she rose to stand. "Thank you, ladies. Enjoy the croissants."

HEAVING A SIGH, Winter slumped down in the passenger seat of the nondescript sedan.

Midafternoon sunlight glinted off Noah's aviators as he glanced at her. "I take it that didn't go very well?"

As she fastened her seat belt, Winter shook her head. "No, it went well, actually. Alice's friend remembered seeing Dakota get into a black Mercedes on the last night she saw her. She said she'd seen the car a couple times before, and the driver was a white male with a beard and dark hair."

Noah tapped a finger against the steering wheel before he turned the key over in the ignition. "Well, that's more than we had."

Winter barely managed to swallow a groan. "Exactly. It doesn't seem like much, but that's the frustrating part. We've talked to the families of every single victim we identified, and none of them had any idea that they were missing. The only reason there were even missing persons reports was because the other working girls and the cops that come to check on them reported them missing. How do you neglect your children that much as a parent?"

As he spread his hands, Noah flashed her a hapless look. "You're preaching to the choir, darlin'. I don't know. If you wanted a real answer, you could probably ask Autumn."

With a long inhalation of air, Winter leaned her head against the seat. "I miss Autumn. I feel like I haven't seen her in a month. She's been busy with testimony for the Lopez case. It kind of sucks that her first court appearance is one of the biggest trials in Virginia in the last decade. I don't even know if Kent Strickland's trial will be bigger news than the Lopez trial."

Chuckling, Noah shifted the car into gear. "Vigilantes sure do have a way of attracting the attention of the masses. Probably won't be long before Lopez has a book deal. He's going to be living the good life, or at least as good a life as he can behind bars."

Winter's laugh sounded closer to a snort. "For him, I'm sure it'll be pretty good since some of the guards are probably in his fan club. Anyway, you called Dan while I was talking to Alice and Katya, right?"

He nodded. "Right."

"Anything useful?"

"Nothing. He hasn't seen any Jane Does that match the descriptions of our missing girls. He even went back farther than the time they were reported missing, and he still didn't find anything."

Winter pressed a button to roll down her window. "So, whoever our killer is, he's making sure that none of these women's bodies are found. Hopefully, he isn't dissolving them in a fifty-five-gallon drum."

Noah slapped his hand on the steering wheel and laughed so loud it made her jump.

"What?"

Still smiling, Noah glanced to her and then back to the road. "I'm sorry. I didn't mean to laugh at that. That's just literally, word for word what Dan said."

"You know, I don't know a lot about my dad's side of the family. Maybe Dan and I are cousins." Winter offered him an exaggerated shrug.

"Could be. He's from Iowa, though. He didn't move to Virginia until after he joined the Navy and started working on his undergrad."

Winter drew her brows together. "Do you have a copy of Dan's CV or something?"

Noah tapped his ear. "It's called listening, darlin'. When Dan talks about himself, I listen."

"Oh my god," Winter muttered. In spite of her unimpressed tone, a smile crept to her face. "Okay, okay. Seriously, where are we with our voyeuristic stalker turned murderer?"

He tapped the steering wheel as they neared a red light, a mannerism she often noticed when he was thinking. "We were able to set up a rough timeline for each disappearance. Based on everything we've heard from the working girls and the victims' families, they haven't been seen since they disappeared. But their bodies haven't shown up in the morgue, either."

Winter nodded. "So, it's possible that they're not dead, but it seems unlikely considering how long ago the first vic disappeared. She went missing close to a year ago, right?"

"Right. Little more than a year ago."

"And then the exact same MO for the other four victims, until he escalated and recorded himself killing the most recent one. We've got IDs for all of them now, but the only one whose disappearance anyone remembers was Dakota." She glanced down to the little notepad. "Black Mercedes, new, with four doors. It was raining that day, but Katya said the car was spotless. White male driver with a beard and dark hair."

Noah offered her a thoughtful glance. "Well, good work, darlin'. You just found more information about this case than any of us have in the last week."

This time, Winter was unable to suppress her groan.

The most information they'd obtained so far was next to nothing.

Somewhere in Richmond, a psychopath in a Mercedes was abducting women and murdering them, but they had no idea who he was.

13

With one more quick wave to Ryan O'Connelly, Bobby Weyrick tapped the screen of his phone to dial Sun's number. She'd sent him a text a few minutes earlier to say good night, and he had decided to step outside the room to call her. Since she was assigned to keep an eye on Ryan during the day, she and Bobby had only seen one another during their shift changes over the last week.

Regardless of the sudden distance, or perhaps because of it, she had let go of the palpable ire that had simmered in the air after the briefing at the beginning of the investigation.

In the last week, Bobby had learned that Sun wasn't keen on Winter Black, but she still respected the younger woman. She had succumbed to an irrational bout of jealousy after Bobby and Winter had spent a few days wrapping up their previous case in Baltimore.

If he was honest, Bobby was impressed with the way Sun had dealt with the situation.

"Look," she had said. "Just because I don't like her doesn't mean you guys won't get along. And just because I don't like her doesn't mean that you can't be friends with her. I'm sorry I was such a bitch about it."

A week later, thinking of the heartfelt words still brought a smile to his face.

Just as he dropped to sit in a cushioned chair across the hall from a vending machine, there was a click on the other end of the line as Sun picked up.

"Hey," she greeted. "How's babysitting duty going?"

"It's fine. I can't really complain. Ryan's a nice guy, and he's funny. Plus, we like the same TV shows. I could do a lot worse for a protection assignment. Actually, I've done a lot worse. You didn't have to deal with Eric Dalton when we were keeping him at the safehouse so the Russian mob couldn't get to him. That guy never laughed at any of my stupid jokes."

Sun laughed, a light, melodic sound he never thought he'd get tired of hearing. "His loss, then. I love your stupid jokes."

His smile widened. "You know, we've been watching out for Ryan for over a week, and I still haven't asked you about the Presley case. I remember it, but I was working with the counterterrorism people on a terrorist threat at the time, so I didn't pay a lot of attention to it. Which apparently is a shame because that investigation sounds like it was wild."

"It was. Heidi Presley was a lunatic. But she was smart, so she was like a Ted Kaczynski lunatic. Honestly, that's probably the best person to compare her to. Incredibly high IQ, rejection of social norms, complete lack of basic empathy. She was the female Ted Kaczynski in the flesh."

He leaned back in the cushioned chair. "Damn. It took the bureau decades to catch the Unabomber."

"Well, Presley didn't reject technology like Kaczynski did, and that's how we got her in the end. The tech guys in Cyber Crimes cracked open her laptop and found her entire master plan all lined up, including the collar bomb she'd made for

Ryan. Don't get me wrong, she was a really good hacker, but she didn't have access to the resources that the FBI does."

Bobby nodded to himself. "Good thing, then. I like Ryan. It'd suck if he was dead."

Though he expected at least a slight chuckle, Sun sighed instead. "Yeah, I liked him too. Honestly, I think everyone did. He's a charming SOB, no doubt about that. But that's part of his persona, you know? It's how he gets into all these high and mighty social circles so he can steal from people. If I had to guess, I'd say it's how he managed to get enough time alone to slip out from underneath the noses of the cops in Erie."

Even though Bobby had always known Ryan's history, he slumped down in his chair at Sun's assessment.

She was right.

He knew she was right. Ryan O'Connelly had made a life for himself by using his charisma to con his way to luxury. In fact, his trade was precisely what had landed him at the bureau's front door in the first place.

"Yeah," Bobby finally said. "That's true enough."

"I'm sorry, hon." Her words were soft and gentle. "I didn't mean to sound like I was patronizing you or anything. I know you know what you're doing. I guess I just wanted you to know that I get it. I think he might be a good guy, deep down, but he's still looking out for his own interests."

Bobby pressed the heel of his hand into one eye. "Yeah, you're right. I know it, but it doesn't mean we can't watch cartoons on Adult Swim together. If he tries to sneak away from me, I'll personally visit the U.S. Attorney to make sure they throw the book at him."

As Sun laughed, the moment of despondency lifted.

Though Bobby's mood had improved by the time he and Sun's phone call ended, he didn't permit his guard to drop as he let himself back into the hotel room.

Ryan O'Connelly might have been a good man, but Sun was right.

He'd brought them information about a murder they hadn't even known existed, but once he thought his job with the FBI was done, his motives may well change.

The U.S. Attorney had better come up with a good bargain, otherwise the bureau's focus would undoubtedly shift away from the women who were being murdered so they could chase down a fugitive thief.

14

Though Noah was usually among the first to arrive to morning briefings at the office, he was surprised to find that everyone had already taken their seats. He closed the door behind himself and made his way to sit at the table behind Winter and Bobby.

He and Winter had carpooled to the office, but Noah had soon become preoccupied by a battle with a vending machine on the second floor.

In the end, he'd emerged victorious, but the ice-cold can of soda was the reason for his tardiness. There was always a straggler to their meetings, but today was the first time he had been the straggler.

With a pop and a hiss that drew the attention of almost everyone in the room, he cracked open the fruits of his labor.

Ironically, Max was one of the only occupants who didn't look over at Noah when he opened his Mountain Dew.

"This shouldn't take long." The SAC gestured to where Aiden Parrish stood at the edge of the whiteboard. "SSA Parrish has an updated profile for us based on the information that Agents Black and Dalton got yesterday. So, I'll let him start."

Aiden coughed into one hand to clear his throat. "The description of the car and the driver are consistent with what Ryan O'Connelly said when he brought us this information. It was a new Mercedes sedan, and it was spotless even though the witness said it had rained that day. Which means they either went out of their way to wash it, or it had been in a garage all day. Either way, it indicates that they have means."

"What are you thinking for the guy's demographics?" Noah asked.

A couple months ago, he wouldn't have even thought to pose a question to the SSA. But now, though Noah didn't especially care for Aiden Parrish as a person, there was a mutual respect between the two of them.

Parrish nodded and glanced down to a piece of paper in his hand. "Well, based on what Mr. O'Connelly brought us, and based on the fact that he found these leads in the middle of a circle of wealthy aristocrats, the knee-jerk assumption would be that he's a middle-aged man."

Noah lifted an eyebrow. "But you don't think he is?"

As Parrish's eyes met his, he shook his head. "No, I don't. The world is a different place than it was twenty years ago. These days, there are plenty of rich kids around. Trust fund babies or self-made YouTube stars, either way. There are more of them around than there used to be. Based on the way the killer acted in that video, I don't think he's been doing this for long."

Max turned to the Supervisory Special Agent. "What makes you think he's not a middle-aged man who just recently discovered the joys of murder?"

Biting his tongue to stave off a sudden sarcastic chortle at the SAC's candid observation, Noah sipped his can of soda.

Aiden's expression didn't change at the challenge. "Serial killers don't make it to middle age without leaving a trail of bodies behind them. They might just kill animals in that time, but they don't pick up and start killing human beings at age fifty-something without a history of violence. Our killer is wealthy, white, probably between twenty and thirty. Lives in the city, but not near the area where he's been poaching his victims."

"We are dealing with a serial killer, then?" Max asked.

Parrish nodded. "In my opinion, yes. We're definitely dealing with a serial killer. I considered that the videos might have been more of a sick business venture, but even if that's how he rationalizes it to himself, he's a serial killer at heart."

Miguel Vasquez lifted a hand. "Isn't there a way to track the payments back to the guy who made the videos? If this is a business venture for him, wouldn't we be able to follow the money?"

Aiden was shaking his head before Miguel finished. "No. On any website like this, the sellers only accept payment in the form of cryptocurrency. Bitcoins, digital gift cards, things like that. They're all untraceable. Agent Welford couldn't make it to this briefing, but she and another agent in Cyber Crimes are chasing down any lead they can find from this site."

Noah drummed his fingers against the tabletop.

Technology had cracked plenty of cases for them so far, including the Heidi Presley case. But unless they supplemented their technological expertise with good detective work, they wouldn't get far this time around.

So far, the killer hadn't left them a series of clues like Presley had.

He stopped drumming his fingers and returned his attention to Max and Aiden. "Maybe it's time we take a break from the digital trail and see what we can find in person."

Max's gray eyes turned curious. "All right, Dalton. I'm listening."

Leaning back in his chair, Noah spread his hands. "We've still got Ryan O'Connelly in that hotel, right? He's been helping Cyber Crimes monitor that website since he arrived a week ago, and he's sending any leads he finds directly to them. This is a good strategy, don't get me wrong. But maybe it's time he reaches out to the people who told him the rumor in the first place."

After an approving glance, Winter nodded. "Even if Ryan doesn't think his contact in that circle knows the gritty details, they might know more than they think. Just because they don't think it's useful doesn't mean it won't be useful for us."

Max inclined his chin in Winter's direction. "That's good thinking, Agent Black, Agent Dalton. You two go to where Ryan's staying and hash out a plan. Report back to me with it later this afternoon, and we'll get this rolling as quickly as we can. Preferably before this sick bastard kidnaps another girl."

NOAH AND WINTER had called ahead to let Agent Sun Ming know that they planned to stop by to talk to Ryan, but he was still surprised when the door swung open before they even reached it.

Sun's dark eyes flicked from him to Winter as she held open the door. "Agent Black, Agent Dalton. Afternoon. If it's all right with you, I'm going to take a walk around the block while you talk to Ryan. It's beautiful outside, and I've been cooped up in here all day."

With a nod, Noah managed a half-smile. "Sounds good. We'll be here."

Though he expected the shorter woman to merely leave

the room without another word, she returned the pleasant look. "Thank you. I'll be back shortly."

Noah had to fight to keep his eyes from widening. He didn't interact with Sun often, but in all his previous discussions with her, the take no prisoners attitude had been plain to see.

Then again, the woman had been shot. Not only had she been shot, but she'd been front and center for the mass shooting massacre that had been planned and carried out by Kent Strickland and Tyler Haldane. And sure, Noah had seen combat, but the mass murder of innocent civilians in a shopping mall was far different.

As Noah and Winter stepped out of the short hall and into the suite, Ryan O'Connelly's blue eyes snapped up from the screen of his laptop.

"Agents." He pushed himself to stand and extended a hand. "It's been a few days. How's the investigation going?"

Shrugging, Noah accepted the handshake. "We've got some information compiled on a possible profile for the killer, but we haven't found anything solid yet."

"Actually." Winter took a seat on the arm of the couch. "We were hoping you could help us with that. We've been keeping an eye on the forum activity lately, and we appreciate your help with that part of it. But we've hit a digital wall, and now we need to go back to the source to see if we can find a new lead."

A flicker of trepidation passed over Ryan's face. "Go back to the source? Do you mean you want me to wear a wire and go talk to the people I heard this rumor from?"

Winter's expression was calm, but resolute. "Yes, that's exactly what we're thinking."

As he returned to his seat, Ryan combed a hand through his dark hair. "That makes good sense, Agents. But I need to ask you something too."

Noah moved to stand beside Winter. "Okay. Shoot."

"Look, I was serious when I said I came here because I wanted to help you find this sick bastard. And I still do want to help you find him. But it's been a week, and I still haven't heard a word from your U.S. Attorney. I'm not expecting to get off scot-free for everything that happened with Presley, but I need something."

He couldn't fault Ryan for the need to know what his future held. In some capacity, Noah had expected the question. Before he and Winter left for the hotel, they had stopped to double-check with Max about the status of the agreement with the federal prosecutor.

Slowly, Noah nodded. "That's understandable. We talked to SAC Osbourne about it before we headed over here. He has a meeting with the U.S. Attorney to talk about charge reductions scheduled for some time tomorrow. It's in the evening, I think."

"Yeah, evening," Winter confirmed.

As Ryan sank down onto the couch, the shadows beneath his eyes were more pronounced.

Noah moved to sit at the edge of a nearby armchair. "I get that's not what you wanted to hear, or at least that's not what I would have wanted to hear if I was in your position, but we're doing the best we can. We know you're here for a good reason, and believe me, Osbourne will make sure that gets across to the U.S. Attorney."

A slight smile brushed Winter's face. "He's right. SAC Osbourne is a force to be reckoned with. Plus," she paused to hold out her hands, "there's no doubt that doing this will put you even further in the prosecutor's good graces."

The silence that descended over the room was as stifling as the humidity on a summer afternoon in Texas.

As much as Noah wanted to blurt out a list of reasons to motivate Ryan to commit to his role in the investigation, he knew the man needed time to think. A federal agent blabbing about all the ways he could suck up to the U.S. Attorney wasn't conducive to a moment of solipsism.

When Ryan finally dipped his chin in a slow nod, the shadow of anxiety had given way to determination. "Okay. They do dinner parties every Thursday, and my contact is usually the hostess. I'll reach out to her and check to see if they're having one tomorrow evening."

As much as Noah wanted to feel a wave of relief at the agreement, the tension in his shoulders did not so much as lessen.

Though he was a lifelong thief and con man, Ryan O'Connelly wasn't a bad man. Getting him to agree to wear a discrete wire to poke around a group of shady aristocrats was the easy part.

He had a sneaking suspicion they'd only just discovered the tip of the iceberg. For the time being, Noah was glad Ryan was on their side.

15

The family owned restaurant had a certain quaint charm, but the place was a far cry from the establishments to which I'd become accustomed over the years.

My father might have been an asshole, but the man knew good food.

Ever since my sister and I were little, we'd been catered to at eateries so exclusive that the majority of the public would never even get the chance to step inside. With the steep price came quality, and that quality was difficult to sacrifice after I'd honed my palette.

But tonight, I wasn't at the homey Mexican restaurant for food.

I'd only purchased a meal to make sure I didn't stand out. Beside the plate of nachos, I'd cracked open a notebook and a textbook to pretend I was focused on work for a group project in one of my classes.

The course was relevant to my major, unlike the last class that I'd been in with Caroline Peters. Though she'd caught my eye last semester, I hadn't been sure what to do about the intrigue.

Now, six months later, I knew exactly what to do. And thanks to a group project, I had the opening for which I'd been searching.

Caroline and I had sat beside one another since the beginning of the semester, and in the last couple weeks, I'd begun to interact with her more frequently. It started when I leaned over to whisper a sarcastic comment to her, and from there, the conversations became more regular.

When the start date for the group project had rolled around, Caroline was quick to ask if we could partner up for it.

"Hey, Cameron!"

I'd seen her approach, but I pretended to pull my attention away from the text as I flashed her a disarming smile. Though she had expected me, I didn't see any reason to make myself stand out like I was some sort of creep.

"Caroline, hey. What's up?"

With a little shrug, she grabbed my water glass to pour a refill from the decanter in her other hand. "You know, just work. The daily grind. Are you working on our group project?"

As I accepted the freshly filled glass, I pushed the notebook and text to the edge of the table so she could see. "Yeah, I was just jotting down some notes so I could start getting organized for it. I talked to Peyton after class today, and she said she was going to get started on it tonight too. She's going to email us with what she gets done, so I figure I'll do the same."

Even in the dim light, her golden hair seemed to shimmer as she tucked a piece behind her ear. Her crystal blue eyes shifted from me and then to the book as she hunched over to read the writing.

There had been nothing sexual about any of the women

I'd taken captive and killed, but that was as much because those girls were prostitutes as anything.

I'd had plenty of girls since I started college. Being the wealthy, attractive son of a powerful judge did wonders for a person's social circle.

But no matter how kinky the sex was with consenting partners, there had always been a missing element. An itch I hadn't known how to scratch.

As Caroline's bright eyes turned back to me, however, I was sure I'd just figured out how to scratch that persistent itch. Even in the red polo shirt with the restaurant's logo embroidered on the left side, she was beautiful.

I was done with the whores.

Caroline would be mine, and then I would make sure she never belonged to another soul.

RYAN'S vacant stare was fixed in the general direction of the flickering television screen. The episode was a rerun, but that wasn't the reason Ryan had stopped paying attention.

He had never doubted Agent Black and Agent Dalton's sincerity. He'd never even doubted the sincerity of their boss, Max Osbourne. And in another life, he and Bobby Weyrick could have been good friends.

As best as Ryan could tell, all the agents—even Sun Ming—were good people.

He was sure they would do whatever was in their power to ensure the U.S. Attorney followed through with their end of the legal deal.

However, he couldn't help but wonder what aspects of the legal system were in their power.

As a show of good faith, Ryan hadn't asked for his own lawyer. Then again, his mistrust for lawyers was a large part of his motivation for waiving the right to counsel. He'd rather take his chances alone than cast his fate into the hands of a shifty attorney.

Even if every federal agent with whom he'd interacted put forth their best effort to sway the U.S. Attorney, the decision was ultimately in the hands of another lawyer.

After a week, he was no closer to cracking the secret to the sophisticated device attached to his ankle. If he'd been able to peruse the internet, he might have found a remedy by now, but he suspected the laptop he'd been given was outfitted with a keylogger—a type of virus that recorded each keystroke and sent it back to the installer.

He doubted the FBI would be naïve enough to trust someone like Ryan with a computer that couldn't be traced.

Sure, he could grab a pair of scissors and hack away at the strap around his ankle. But the second he cut into the device, an emergency signal would emit to advise the FBI that the monitor had been damaged. Even if he ran as far and as fast as he could manage, he doubted he'd get out of this damn room before they caught up to him.

No, he told himself.

If he cut and ran, he would put Lillian and the kids at risk. A risk that was entirely unnecessary.

Not to mention, by now, the bureau needed him almost as badly as he needed them to forgive his past sins. If the FBI barreled into the midst of the aristocratic circle that Ryan had infiltrated, the killer would slink back into the shadows.

An undercover FBI agent was also out of the question.

The ties that the members had to one another ran deep, and Ryan had only weaseled his way in because he'd stolen from the right people in the past. He'd conned his way in, and he doubted the bureau could replicate the feat without ringing the group's alarm bells.

If Ryan didn't help those women, then who would?

The bureau couldn't pull someone off the street to accomplish the task for them. Whether or not they wanted to admit it, they needed him.

Pushing past the moment of anxiety, he straightened in his seat at the edge of the couch and leaned forward to open the laptop. Though he'd checked the seedy forum a few hours ago, he intended to visit the page now for an entirely different reason—for a reminder.

A reminder that he had made the right decision.

Doing the right thing hardly ever means doing the easy thing. In his mind, the words had been spoken in Lil's voice. The observation had been her senior quote in high school.

Though Bobby Weyrick's eyes flicked up, he made no comment before he returned his attention to his phone.

After a few taps and a couple passcodes, Ryan arrived at the forum.

The layout was basic, and the appearance reminded him of the internet back in the nineties. Whoever had designed the page must have been inspired by old Yahoo GeoCities websites.

As he scrolled down, he expected links to the unsettling videos of the women in captivity just as he'd seen a hundred times before.

When he reached the body of the post, however, his eyes went wide.

"Oh, shit," he muttered under his breath.

There were three new links. All three were labeled as image files, and Ryan's stomach sank.

Bobby's gaze snapped over to him. "What?"

Ryan held his breath as he pulled up the first image. He expected gore or any number of gruesome torture techniques, but the image was unassuming.

From where she'd been photographed on a sidewalk, a young woman's puzzled expression was fixed on her phone.

Her blonde hair was pulled away from her face in a pony-tail, and her outfit was comprised of a red polo and a pair of dark skinny jeans and flats. She looked confused in the first photo, but not frightened.

In the next two, her expression trended in a neutral direction.

The pictures themselves might have seemed innocuous enough, but the comments below the links were anything but.

One offered a sum of cash for the young woman, another listed out a handful of disgusting sex acts they'd like to perform on her, another asked when the photographer planned to post her video, and so on. The English was broken in several of the posts, and the occasional comment in Russian confirmed Ryan's suspicions that the stalker had reached an international audience.

Finally, Ryan glanced to Bobby Weyrick.

He pointed at the screen like he had been asked to select a perpetrator out of a lineup. "You should see this."

16

The legwork of their case had been constant—interviewing family members, friends, exes, and anything in between—and though Winter was glad to have a night to rest her tired brain, her thoughts invariably drifted to her little brother.

To the cryptic messages he'd written on the walls of their old family house, to the equally cryptic email that had led her there in the first place, and of course, to the gruesome sight of the mutilated rats.

Try as she might, she couldn't figure out why he'd butchered four rats and stuffed their innards with Black Cat firecrackers. Though the memory of Justin tossing the miniature explosives at her feet on the Fourth of July had never been significant to Winter, perhaps the experience differed for him. Or perhaps he merely had ready access to fireworks.

She didn't know, and that was the part that threatened to drive her insane.

Squeezing her eyes closed, she rubbed the bridge of her nose as she shook her head. She needed to think about something else, to concentrate on the episode of *Supernatural* she'd been instructed to watch, to solve a sudoku puzzle or a crossword, something.

She needed a hobby.

Stamp collecting, bird watching, photography, something.

Autumn loved video games, so maybe Winter would try to play an online game as a way to spend more time with her friend. Autumn also liked to fish. According to her, the lack of lakes in Virginia compared to Minnesota was what she missed most about her home. Noah was from Texas, so he had to enjoy fishing.

Winter was halfway through composing a text message to ask Autumn for suggestions on fishing rods when a knock on the front door startled her. Noah had used the night off to catch up on laundry, but he'd assured her he would come by when he was finished.

Pushing herself to stand, Winter pocketed her phone and paused the television. "Who is it?" She was sure she knew the answer, but in her line of work, it never hurt to be thorough.

"It's me." Of course it was Noah.

Smiling, she flicked the deadbolt and pulled open the door. The look of contentment gave way to curiosity as she spotted the edginess in his eyes.

She scooted to the side as he stepped through the doorway. "What happened? Your laundry didn't catch fire, did it?"

Though slight, he smiled at the question. "No, thankfully, but I did just get a call from Bobby. Ryan was keeping tabs on that site, and he found three new pictures of a girl. They haven't identified her yet, but they're looking into it."

As she followed him to the living room, she pushed her hair back from her face and pressed her palms against the sides of her head. "Pictures? Just pictures this time, no video?"

Muttering a curse, Noah took a seat in the center of the

couch. "The change is a little unexpected, but hopefully it'll give us a chance to try to find her before anything else happens to her. That's what Weyrick, Parrish, and Ryan are all working on right now. Once they find out who she is, then we can make sure she's okay."

Winter gave an approving nod as she sat at his side. "Then she's in good hands."

With another slight smile, he returned the nod. "That's true. And honestly, I think it proves Parrish's theory about this guy right. If the killer's young, then it means he's still evolving. And we're the lucky sons of bitches who get to tag along for that development."

Winter chewed on her thumbnail before making herself stop. "Lucky isn't the term I'd use, but I'm glad we're there. At least that way, we know there's someone trying to stop it. If he's young, honestly, that's better. It means we get the chance to stop a serial killer before he's racked up a body count in the double digits."

Noah's expression was thoughtful as he nodded. "That's true. I suppose that's a good way to look at it. Man, look at you, being all optimistic over here." He draped an arm over her shoulders.

Rolling her eyes in feigned indignance, she kissed his cheek before she tucked her face in the crook of his neck. "I think I need a hobby," she muttered.

He combed his fingers through her unbound hair. "It's good to have a hobby, but what makes you say that?"

She closed her eyes as he massaged her scalp. "Any time I've got free time, it's like my brain just has to be an asshole and wander off to all kinds of thoughts I don't want to think about. I feel like maybe if I have something to do, then it won't happen as often."

Kissing the top of her head, he pulled her closer. "Maybe. But I don't know. It sounds like maybe there's just something that's really bothering you. And if that's the case, then even a massive stamp collection won't get your mind off of it completely."

A silence enveloped them as she considered her next words. Grasping his upper arm with one hand, she straightened until she met his dark green eyes. A shadow of concern had settled in his visage.

"What's wrong, sweetheart?" His voice was barely above a whisper.

She bit back a weary sigh. "Honestly? I think I'm just worried about my brother. And what's worse, it was almost easier believing he was dead, as terrible as that is to say."

"There are things worse than death," Noah murmured against her hair.

The hair rose on Winter's arms. "Yes, exactly. And I think there are different kinds of dead too. The Justin I once knew is dead, and we don't know what kind of monster has replaced him."

Noah rubbed a hand against the back of her neck. "He'll undoubtedly be traumatized and—"

"No, not just traumatized. If he was, it would still be awful, but at least then he'd be able to get help. But I mean, what if he's as bad as Douglas Kilroy?" She shivered. "Or worse?"

Noah's eyes flicked over to the television as another spell of quiet descended. After the seconds ticked away, he glanced back to her. "I don't know, sweetheart, but I think that's the worst-case scenario, you know? I mean, he's probably going to have some issues. Anyone would have issues if they were in his place. Honestly, it'd be weirder if he didn't."

She managed a smile as she nodded. "Yeah, that's true."

He returned the expression and rubbed her arm. "But there's help for issues. Therapy, medication, stuff like that. Even the big stuff, like schizophrenia. There are meds for that, and therapy helps too. Plus, once we find him, he'll know that he's got a support network."

To anyone else, the thought of their younger sibling being diagnosed with a mental illness like schizophrenia would have been crushing. But to Winter, a schizophrenic diagnosis would mean that there was hope. From what she knew of the disorder, all the oddities about Justin's persona seemed to fit. Paranoia, reclusiveness, the bizarre messages—schizophrenia would explain it all. If she felt the compulsion, she could even run the theory by Autumn.

Though she still worried, a portion of the leaden weight had finally lifted from her shoulders. For the past week or longer, she'd viewed the situation with her brother as black and white. Either he was fine, or he was a maniac like Douglas Kilroy.

Maybe, just maybe he wouldn't be fine, but he could be helped.

17

A iden had stared at the photo printouts of the blonde girl for so long, he was sure he'd be able to draw her face from memory if he was even the slightest bit artistically inclined. However, he had a difficult time drawing anything more complex than a stick figure. His memorization of the young woman's facial features brought them no closer to discovering her identity.

As he glanced to where Ryan O'Connelly sat at a circular table in the center of the conference room, Bobby Weyrick at his side, Aiden bit back a sigh. With their three brains together, they should have come up with a solution by now.

Instead, Weyrick shuffled through missing persons reports, and Ryan pored over the seedy forum. Aiden looked through the state DMV database, but there were thousands and thousands of young blonde women in Richmond.

Right now, they didn't even know for sure that the young woman in the pictures was in Richmond. Ryan had advised them that the forum was used internationally, so for all they knew, she could be in Alaska. Or a different country. The moon.

At the thought, Aiden gritted his teeth. It was already ten at night, but he didn't want to leave the office until he'd at least pinned down the identity of the woman in the photos.

Bobby Weyrick ran a hand through his sandy hair and shook his head. "Didn't see her in any recent missing persons reports. These pictures are brand new, though, so who knows whether or not she's even been reported missing yet."

Aiden nodded. "All we've got are the pictures. We don't even know if the killer has kidnapped her yet. Since there isn't a video of her captivity online at this point, he might not have. Agent Welford is still here looking into the forum posts. She's upstairs so she can use the specialized software in Cyber Crimes, and she said she'll let us know ASAP if she finds anything from tracing the responses to the pictures."

Bobby cursed under his breath. "Maybe one of us should go get some food. Seems like we might be here for a while."

Freezing mid-keystroke, Aiden looked over his shoulder to the photos they'd taped to a whiteboard.

"She's wearing a red polo. It looks like a men's cut. That seem off to either of you?" He shifted his gaze back to Ryan and Bobby as the men exchanged glances.

O'Connelly shrugged. "It's not the most fashionable outfit."

"No, it's not." Pushing to stand, Aiden walked over to the whiteboard and pulled down one of the photos. "Her jeans and her shoes are pretty fashionable, but not her shirt. She's wearing a uniform shirt. Look."

As he set the picture atop the table, he lifted a magnifying glass, peering closer.

Weyrick squinted at the photograph too. "What do you see?"

"A smudge. I think this photo might have been doctored to cover the fact that there's a logo of some sort over the left breast."

After a few more taps, Weyrick turned the laptop for Aiden and Ryan to see. "Here's one that hasn't been doctored, but the angle is wrong." He zoomed in, and he was right. The detail of the image wasn't much help. But it was something.

"I can't read that, can you?" Bobby asked.

As he peered closer, Aiden shook his head. "No, but we can search for businesses in the city that have a logo that's what? Red, white, and maybe green? It looks like there's text in the middle, so we can keep an eye out for that too."

With the instructions clear, the space lapsed back into silence as they went to work.

Aiden pored through the oft overlooked event arena and amusement parks first, then once they'd been ruled out, he switched to chain retail stores. A chain of grocery stores local to the southeast United States caught his eye, but upon closer inspection, the logo didn't appear to match.

Before he exited the grocery store web page, he caught a glimpse of a sale coupon in the part of their site devoted to ads. The deal was good—two brand name frozen pizzas for nine dollars—but the price wasn't what caught his eye.

In the background of the graphic on the front of the box was an Italian flag. Reddish orange, white, and green, just like the young woman's shirt.

"Italian." Aiden glanced from Bobby to Ryan. "Red-orange, white, and green. Those are the colors of the Italian flag."

"Mexican too," Bobby said.

Ryan shrugged. "And Irish."

Aiden had already returned his focus to the screen of his laptop. "How many Irish restaurants do you think there are in Richmond?"

"Could be a pub."

At Ryan's suggestion, Aiden shot him an approving nod. The man might have been a lifelong thief, but he was sharp.

"Good idea. O'Connelly, you look through bars, Weyrick, you look through Mexican restaurants, and I'll look through Italian ones."

After another series of nods, they went back to work. This time, they were interrupted after only ten minutes of searching.

Bobby glanced up and turned the computer monitor to face them. "I think I've got it, boys."

Squinting, Aiden raised the photograph of the woman until it was side by side with the glowing screen. "Super Taco. Yeah, Weyrick. That could be it."

Weyrick spun the laptop around. "Says here that there are two locations in Richmond. Neither are open now, but they open back up tomorrow at ten in the morning. Unless we want to look through the state databases until our eyes bleed, seems to me there ain't much else we can do right now."

Rubbing his temple with one hand, Aiden nodded. "You're right. There isn't. We'll have someone head out there in the morning a little before ten. Otherwise, good work. I'm going home to sleep, and if anything comes up, just give me a call."

With a halfhearted salute, Weyrick nodded back. "'Til tomorrow, Parrish."

Even as Aiden strode out of the building and to the adjoining parking garage, he had already decided he wasn't going home. Not right away.

He hadn't replenished his stash of liquor in some time, and after a sixteen-hour workday, he needed a drink.

As he settled into the driver's side of his car, he unlocked his phone. Before he could think better of the idea, he typed a text message to ask Autumn Trent if she was still awake.

Without pausing to consider how the question would sound at eleven at night, he hit the send button. The woman never turned on the volume for her personal phone, so if she was asleep, the message wouldn't wake her.

Before he dropped the device into the cupholder, the screen lit up with an incoming text message: *I'm awake, what's up?*

If he tried to brush off the text and tell her there was no reason for the late-night contact, she'd see straight through the half-assed fib.

I just worked for sixteen hours and need a drink. Wondering if you want to go to that bar by your place.

He stared at the screen, waiting for the reply. If she said yes, he sincerely doubted their night would end with just a couple cocktails.

18

W ith one last wave to the shift manager of the Mexican restaurant called Super Taco, Noah settled back behind the wheel of his truck. During the first case they worked together, Noah and Winter had alternated driving shifts. But during and after the Douglas Kilroy case some months later, her headaches and visions had increased in frequency and intensity.

Though she'd been opposed to the idea at first, Winter had come to accept that his decision to drive was strictly in the interest of safety. And she also had to come to accept that she fit better in his big truck than he did in her little Civic. Plus, having a handsome chauffeur wasn't half bad, though she'd never admit that out loud.

With a click, Winter fastened her seat belt. "So, no one recognized her from this restaurant. But the prep cook said he thought she looked familiar, and he might've seen her when he was helping their other store a couple months ago."

Turning the key over in the ignition, he nodded. "Finally, something might go right."

She made a tsk-tsk sound with her tongue. "Come on, now. Let's not count our lizards before they've hatched."

Noah shot her a *what the hell* glance. "Beg pardon?"

Winter's blue eyes seemed to sparkle as she smiled and settled into the seat. "Lizards hatch from eggs too."

Shaking his head, he returned his attention to the road as they pulled out of the small parking lot. "You're not wrong, but that sounds weird as hell."

She chuckled lightly. "I got Autumn to start saying it too."

The corner of his mouth tipped up. "I can definitely see her picking that up, yeah."

Their spirits were lighter than they had been all week, and Noah suspected the reason wasn't just the mind-blowing sex from the night before. They were closing in on the bad guy. He could feel it and knew Winter could feel it too.

If they got to the blonde before the stalker, they could post security at her house to keep an eye out for the perp when he came for her. They had the potential to catch him red-handed and toss him in prison before he even thought to lay a hand on another woman.

Then Winter could go back to looking for her brother. Well, until the next bad guy came along.

They'd wrap up their case, and Max would strongarm the U.S. Attorney into offering Ryan O'Connelly a respectable plea deal for all the work he'd done to bring a killer to justice.

That's how cases were supposed to go.

That's how cases went in cop shows, and likely at every other precinct or FBI office in the country. The agents and detectives followed the evidence and caught the killer, and that was the end of the story. There weren't supposed to be fifteen different caveats to every shred of evidence they uncovered. They weren't supposed to have to race against the clock and the Russian mob to locate a corrupt cop.

They were supposed to put away murderers, and he was sure they were about to do just that.

As they pulled into a parking spot at the second, larger Super Taco location, Noah caught the first whiff of Mexican food. He glanced at his watch with a hopeful look that made her smile. "It's almost eleven. Want to grab an early lunch?"

Winter shoved the passenger side door open. "If she's here, then yes. We can sit in the lobby for hours while you shovel tacos into your face and interview her."

He grinned as they walked to the glass double doors that marked the building's entrance.

The silvery tinkle of a bell heralded their arrival, and a young woman glanced up from where she had been studying the touch screen register. A wide smile revealed straight, white teeth. "Hi, welcome to Super Taco. How are you both today?"

Noah returned her smile as he fished out his badge. "Doin' all right, thank you. I'm Agent Dalton, and this is my partner, Agent Black. We're wondering if there's a manager we could speak to."

The overhead light caught the shine of her chocolate-brown hair as she nodded. Though a portion of her welcoming grin waned, her expression was still pleasant.

"That's me. Hi, Agents." She reached across the counter for a handshake. "I'm Morgan Snider, the assistant manager. What can I help you with?"

Winter reached into her black blazer to produce a four-by-six printout of the photo from the shady website. "We're looking for this woman. Does she work here?"

With little more than a cursory glance, Morgan nodded, then glanced up at them both, worry lining her forehead. "Yeah, that's Caroline Peters. She works the closing shift with me every Sunday. Is she okay?"

A sinking sensation made its way to Noah's stomach as he descended back to reality. "She's not here right now?"

Morgan shook her head. "No, she's not scheduled today. She's a student at VCU, and she has classes today."

Noah retrieved a small notepad and a pen. "Do you know if she's in class right now?"

Another head shake. "No, I don't know. I just know that I try not to schedule her too much on weekdays so she has plenty of time to go to class and do homework and stuff. Here, just a second. I'll get you her information and her availability."

Returning the pen and paper to his pocket, Noah nodded. "I appreciate it."

As she disappeared into the kitchen, Winter let out a quiet sigh. "Couldn't be easy for once, could it?"

"Sure couldn't."

Before either of them could make another comment, the assistant manager returned with a couple sheets of paper. Her honey-brown eyes flicked up to him and Winter. "I'm sorry, but our copier is broken, and these are the only two copies we have. You can take them, but I'd need them back."

Noah flashed her a reassuring smile and held up his phone. "No need. I'll just take a couple pictures."

With a nod, Morgan set the papers down and stepped back. "I know that she lives with her parents, and she doesn't have a boyfriend. She's a really sweet girl, and she's a hard worker. When you find her, could you have her send me a text or something to let me know she's okay?"

As he pocketed his phone, Noah nodded. "Of course."

Winter set a business card on top of the availability sheet. "If she swings by or you hear from her, just give me a call. Or if you remember anything else."

"Absolutely," Morgan said, the worry lines on her forehead even deeper now. "Take care, Agents."

Winter offered her a reassuring smile. "You too, Ms. Snider."

As Noah and Winter pushed their way through the double doors, his appetite was pushed to the back of his mind. He'd have plenty of time to eat after they'd ensured Caroline's safety.

Before the doors had even swung closed behind them, Winter had dialed Caroline's number and raised the phone to her ear. As the seconds dragged on, her expression became strained.

Finally, she lowered the device to her lap. "No answer."

"Shit," Noah spat as he pulled open the driver's side door.

"I'm looking up her home address now." As Winter took her seat, her attention remained fixed on the phone as she typed.

Though Noah jammed the key in the ignition, he didn't start the truck. In silence, he waited for Winter to map out their route.

Her blue eyes snapped up to meet his. "Her home address is only a few minutes out of the way on the route to VCU. We can stop there first, and then head to the university." As he opened his mouth to reply, she held up a hand. "Even better, we can head to her house, and I'll call the campus police and have them look for her. Then, if they find her, we can just swing by and pick her up."

They had no idea how long the killer would wait to strike, or if he'd already struck. Every second was precious, and they couldn't risk the lunatic scooping her up off the VCU campus while they were poking around her home address.

Gritting his teeth, Noah nodded. "Yeah. Call the campus police."

She tapped a couple buttons on her phone. "All right, Jeff Gordon. Hope you've still got that lead foot packed away somewhere."

THE CAR RIDE had been quiet aside from Winter's short phone call with the VCU campus police. Her requests were pointed but polite, and her crisp professionalism left no room for debate. Noah couldn't help but be a little impressed by how she'd evolved as a federal agent. A year earlier, she might have cursed the dispatch officer at the first sign of trouble.

In silence, they pulled into a working-class neighborhood occupied by modest, single family homes. According to the little bit of research Winter had managed on the trip, Caroline's mother was a supervisor at a call center, and her father was an auto mechanic.

Though Noah hoped to see a car in the driveway, the block of concrete was empty. Beneath each window beside the porch, a neat row of colorful flowers bloomed. The two-story residence wasn't large, but as he and Winter made their way down the sidewalk, the ambiance was homey and welcoming.

Maybe Caroline didn't have her own car, and maybe she hadn't yet left for class. Or maybe her car was parked on the street after she'd arrived home late the night before to find her usual spot occupied.

And maybe the Cookie Monster would share his Pecan Sandies.

The bizarre saying—one often uttered by his older sister, Lucy—normally brought him some measure of amusement. But today, he felt like an addict who had just gone through the largest comedown of their life.

An hour ago, he'd been certain they would find Caroline Peters and whisk her away in the nick of time. From there, he'd crash-landed back in the real world when they'd learned that her manager hadn't seen or heard from her. Now, he was back in a world where happy endings weren't a given, and where lunatics like Caroline's stalker preyed on the vulnerable.

And too often won.

He shook off the bleak thoughts and glanced to Winter as she prepared to knock on the front door. The crack of her knuckles against the wooden surface rang out through the air with the same force as a hammer against steel. Reflexively, Noah glanced around the quiet neighborhood. Aside from a cat lying on the front steps of the house across the street, the area was still.

"Hello? Mr. and Mrs. Peters? Caroline?" Winter paused and leaned in to listen for a response.

Nothing.

Noah cleared his throat. "Mr. and Mrs. Peters, Caroline, if you're home, this is the Federal Bureau of Investigation. You aren't in any sort of trouble. We're just here to make sure you're okay."

His elaboration was greeted with more silence.

As Noah swore under his breath, Winter knocked a second time, and then a third.

At just before noon on a weekday, it was no small surprise that the Peters weren't home.

With a sigh, Winter stepped away from the wooden door. "Parents must be at work, and Caroline must be in class."

She was either in class, or she was about to be the star of a homemade snuff film. A video clip that would be posted on a dark web forum for creeps worldwide to masturbate over.

At the thought, the taste in his mouth turned bitter. "You've got some units headed over here to keep an eye out for anyone coming home, right?"

Winter's face was cool and determined. "Yeah, they'll be here in a couple minutes."

"Any word from the campus police yet?"

Her expression darkened as she shook her head. "No, not yet."

He flipped the car keys into the air, then caught them in a vicious swipe. "Let's just hope she's on campus then."

19

Ever since she was in grade school, Caroline Peter's music taste had been eclectic. She'd jam out to a Lady Gaga song and follow it with Viking music by a Nordic band whose name she couldn't even pronounce.

By now, at age twenty, she was so used to the bizarre song changes that the difference didn't even register to her unless a friend was listening too.

As she spotted a flicker of movement in her periphery, she glanced up from where she'd been focused on the rubric for a group project. The tall man wasn't bulky, but he'd rolled up the sleeves of his button-down plaid shirt to reveal toned forearms. His dark hair was fashionably messy, and his face was clean-shaven. When she met his pale blue eyes, her lips curved into a wide smile. Pulling out one of her earbuds, she gestured to the seat across the table.

"Cameron, hey, sorry about that. These headphones cancel out, like, all the background noise." For emphasis, she held up the earbuds. "Plus, I hardly even recognized you without, you know." She circled a finger around her mouth.

He mirrored her motion as he took his seat. "Without a

beard?" When he chuckled, his smile revealed rows of perfect white teeth.

Though she couldn't say for certain, she suspected he must have suffered through the displeasure of braces during high school to achieve a smile that flawless. Caroline had been a frequent flyer at the orthodontist from eighth grade all the way until the end of her junior year.

Whenever she'd complain about the trips to the dentist, her father would grin and point to his crooked front teeth. According to him, his genetics were responsible for her messy alignment, so it only seemed right that he be the one to help her fix it.

Caroline's older brother, on the other hand, had inherited their mother's perfectly straight, cavity free smile.

She forced her gaze away from Cameron's teeth, chiding herself to pay attention to what he was saying. "My head-phones are the same way, though. It pisses my dad off all the time. I mean, that's not what I'm trying to do, but it just happens."

With a light laugh, she nodded. "Right? The same thing happens to me with my parents. But, for real, what about the beard? You've had a beard since we were in biology together last semester."

"Last semester? You remember being in class with me last semester?" The mischievous glint in his pale eyes made her pulse pick up, but at the same time, there was an unsettling twinge she couldn't quite place.

For now, she just assumed the discomfort was the product of her own nervousness.

Even during the spring biology course, she'd been quick to notice how attractive Cameron Arkwell was. But back then, she hadn't been anywhere near confident enough to approach someone like him.

Though college social circles weren't the same cliquey

mess as those in high school, Cameron was still considered one of the cool kids.

To be sure, he had friends from virtually every other social circle—the rockers, the athletes, the geeky kids. Caroline had always been firmly in the latter category, though thanks to her job as a server at a local restaurant, she'd gained a great deal of confidence in social situations.

Maybe the day was finally about to come where she would run into Cameron at a frat party.

She was sure she'd just be one of many to someone like him, but according to her brother, that was what college was for.

Sure, the end goal was a degree, but the experience was just as important. In her brother's case, that experience had involved being popped with three minor possession charges in his first six months at VCU.

So far, Caroline had accumulated only one MIP. And since she turned twenty-one in a couple months, she hoped that little minor in possession was the first and last.

Caroline felt her cheeks heat, both at the memory and from being so close to Cameron. "Of course I remember being in class with you last semester. I always sat right behind you."

The unsettling glint vanished as a wide smile spread over his face. "Too bad we didn't get stuck together on a group project then, huh?"

Caroline laughed. "No kidding."

"Speaking of." He set his bag on the floor before scooting forward. "I was wondering if you'd want to meet up at my place after class so we can knock some of it out."

Her heart hammered against her chest, and she could only hope the flush that rose to her cheeks wasn't as noticeable as it felt.

Brushing a piece of blonde hair from her forehead, she

tried to maintain an air of nonchalance as she nodded. "Yeah, that sounds great. Maybe we can just get the whole damn thing done."

Chuckling, he spread his hands. "I wouldn't go that far."

There they were, the stupid butterflies.

As she smiled back at him, she tried to will away the flutter. "Right. Not without Peyton."

He shrugged and reached down for his backpack. "She's been doing a pretty good job all on her own, though."

Well, she thought. There it was.

He might as well have just said outright the real reason for the invitation. Still, there was an aspect of subtlety that she appreciated. Asking a girl to come over to work on a group project sounded much classier than asking the same girl if she'd like to come over to make out or have sex.

"True." Caroline nodded as she tucked her earbuds into a pocket of her canvas jacket. "We wouldn't want to mess up her flow."

Cameron practically beamed at her. "Exactly. You get it."

Though Caroline could swear she caught a glimpse of that same unsettling glint, she pushed the look from her mind. She was just nervous, she told herself. That was why she saw the eerie look in his pale eyes. Her brain was playing tricks on her.

In all honesty, Peyton was the type of girl Caroline could picture someone like Cameron fawning over. Though Peyton was kind, there was a distinctive edge to her dyed black hair, cat-eye makeup and riding boots that told an onlooker she didn't lack confidence.

During a criminal justice class that Caroline and Peyton had been in together, she'd even learned that Peyton's mother was a DEA agent. Apparently, self-confidence ran in the family.

Until a little over a week ago, Caroline had been sure

Cameron wasn't even aware of her existence. When he'd leaned over to crack a joke about an advertisement the professor had just shown the class, she had to do a double take.

At first, she'd been sure he had intended the humorous comment for someone else. When he'd walked down the hall and chatted with her after class, however, she realized she was his intended conversational partner.

From there, they'd made a habit of talking before and after class, and they hadn't hesitated to pair up when the time for their group project rolled around. Since she sat behind Caroline, Peyton had joined them as well.

The sunlight caught the face of Cameron's stylish watch as he took note of the time. "Well, looks like we'd better get to class. Unless..." He left the suggestion unfinished and raised his eyebrows.

Her pulse rushed in her ears, getting the butterflies to fluttering all over again.

She didn't even have to wait for a frat party. If she said yes right now, she could follow him to his car and that would be the end of it. All the flirtatious little comments and looks over the past week and a half would culminate in an encounter she wouldn't soon forget. Caroline wasn't a virgin, but she didn't need both hands to count the number of guys she'd slept with. In fact, she barely needed one hand to count them.

Cameron was a different story.

She didn't know him well, but she knew enough about his reputation to get a clear picture of where he stood in terms of sexual experience.

Caroline decided then that she wouldn't be just another notch on his belt. Though she might not have had the same edgy sex appeal as Peyton Hoesch, she was still pretty in a classic, Marilyn Monroe way.

As she mulled over the idea of skipping class to go home with Cameron Arkwell, she made a show of biting her bottom lip. When she looked up to give the appearance of pensiveness, she noticed that Cameron's eyes were fixed on her. For a moment, she felt like the only woman in the universe.

But she had to be smart.

Slowly, she shook her head. "Skipping class to go work on a project for that class kind of defeats the purpose, don't you think?"

A flash of something—disappointment? anger?—disappeared as quickly as he showed those perfect teeth again. "Fair enough. Off to class we go, then." For emphasis, he swept an arm in front of himself.

She returned the smile in kind.

If he wanted another notch in his belt today, he'd have to work for it.

I HAD HER.

Hook, line, and sinker. I had her.

Caroline Peters had been primed and ready to follow me home after class, but then that bitch Peyton Hoesch had to stick her nose where it didn't belong.

The instructor had given us a few minutes to discuss our group projects amongst ourselves, and that's when Peyton asked about a meetup. Caroline had glanced to me and then to Peyton as she shrugged and told her that we were thinking of getting together to work on our portion of the project that night.

She'd pay for that. She should have kept her mouth closed and let me answer Peyton's question.

For the remainder of the class, I'd occupied myself with

the task of deciding how she'd pay for it. Though the visuals that flitted through my head were enough to put me at ease for a time, my blood pressure spiked again when the instructor dismissed us.

I already knew I could have any girl I wanted, but right now, the only one I wanted was Caroline. And whether or not she was willing didn't particularly matter to me.

Maybe once I was home, I could separate the two of them and take care of Peyton. No, that left the potential for two versus one. And while I stood a full six inches taller than Caroline and closer to a foot taller than Peyton, it wasn't a chance I was willing to take.

"Hey." Peyton's voice cut through the din of voices as the rest of the class rose to leave. When I glanced to the side, her green eyes were fixed on me.

I shoved the irritability down as far as I could manage and smiled. "Hey. What's up?"

"I don't live on campus, and I drove to class today. What's your address? I'd follow you, but I bet we're parked in different garages."

Though the effort felt monumental, I didn't let my façade of nonchalance drop off as I gave her the information, along with my phone number.

For a split-second, I thought that I could just drive Caroline to the lake house. But if neither of us showed up to my house, Peyton would know something was wrong. Even if I'd thought faster and given her a fake address, she wasn't stupid. She would have caught on.

Taking someone I knew personally was risky enough, so I didn't need additional witnesses in the way.

I almost laughed out loud, thinking of all the ways my father would have to cover up for me.

And he would. I had no doubt about that.

As I shouldered my bag, I flexed the fingers of one hand and took in a steadying breath. I'd figure it out.

Once we finished what little work we had left of the project, Peyton would leave, and I'd have my opportunity. In the meantime, I'd use the time to pique Caroline's interest. To make sure she would give me the opening I sought.

With a quick wave, Peyton picked up her messenger bag. "I'll see you guys soon. I had to work the first shift this morning, so I'll swing by somewhere and get some coffee on my way over."

Caroline returned the wave. "Okay. We'll see you soon."

Looking back to Caroline, I shrugged. "Guess we could stop and get some coffee too."

Her blue eyes brightened as she smiled. "Not a bad idea. Thankfully, my restaurant doesn't have a first shift, but I've been up since six."

As we walked toward the door, I chuckled. "Why have you been up since six if you didn't have to work?"

She looked embarrassed. "Nothing."

I offered her a playful jab to the arm. "Come on. Now I really want to know."

When she bit her lip again, my pulse rushed in my ears.

"It's dumb," she said.

"I doubt it."

She sighed as she finally met my gaze. "I have a friend in this online game I play, and she lives in Singapore. Six in the morning is when she gets off work, so I log on so I can play with her."

"That's not dumb. That's awesome. I didn't know you played video games."

Though she shrugged, there was an unmistakable light in her smile. "Just the one, really. It takes up a lot of time. Well, it does if you want to be good at it, anyway."

I understood the desire to be good at something. "Of course. What game is it?"

My dick twitched in my pants. Before the sun went down, Caroline Peters would be mine. As I studied her pretty face, I wasn't even sure I'd put her video online. I didn't need some pervert in the Ukraine whacking off to footage of what was mine.

She opened her mouth to reply, but a black-clad man cut us off as we stepped into the hall.

His steely gray eyes flicked from me to Caroline. "Caroline Peters?" he asked.

I was about to politely ask him who he was, but I closed my mouth as soon as the overhead fluorescence caught the silver of his badge.

Caroline furrowed her brows and glanced up to him as she nodded. "Yeah, that's me. Why? What's going on?"

"VCU Campus Police. I'm Officer Greene, and I need you to come with me." The man's gravelly voice and cold, commanding tone left no room for debate.

Rare were the instances where I was intimidated, but the six-foot-five, broad-shouldered and tattooed man with a military style haircut and a Glock on his hip was almost enough to do the trick. Based on the muscles in the guy's forearms, he could probably bench press me.

And the man wasn't a rent-a-cop from campus security. He was a trained police officer assigned to the Virginia Commonwealth University campus. A matte black service weapon was holstered on one side, a taser on the other.

Shadows moved along Caroline's throat as she swallowed. She must have drawn the same conclusion I had. Though Caroline Peters looked like the girl next door, I could never be completely sure what some people were into during their spare time.

For all I knew, Caroline moonlighted by slinging cocaine in the dark alleys of Richmond.

The thought brought a slight smile to my lips.

A secret double life as a drug dealer might have been a deal breaker for anyone else, but I wasn't anyone else. If Caroline dealt coke by night and attended VCU by day, I'd be so impressed I didn't even think I'd want to kill her anymore. If she was a reverse superhero drug kingpin, I'd be inclined to marry her.

But as I shook myself out of the fantasy, I realized I had a problem. Nudging Caroline with an elbow, I flashed her a reassuring smile. "Hey, I'm sure it's nothing. Don't sweat it. You've got my address, right?"

Swallowing with an audible click, she nodded.

"Just text me when you're done. Don't worry, Peyton and I won't do anything exciting without you." For emphasis, I winked.

As she chuckled, some of the trepidation left her face. "Okay. I'll see you in a little bit."

With a cool, professional nod to Officer Greene, I readjusted my backpack and turned to make my way back out into the sunny afternoon.

First Peyton Hoesch, and now a cop.

The universe must have been conspiring against me and Caroline.

It didn't matter, though. I knew what I was doing, and I knew how to bide my time.

Caroline Peters was mine.

20

Whe Winter got the call from the VCU campus police that they'd found and collected Caroline Peters, she heaved a sigh of relief. Both of Caroline's parents had been contacted, and the couple were on their way to the FBI office. From where she stood behind a pane of two-way glass, Winter crossed her arms and let out a long, quiet breath.

As Caroline sat in a slightly more comfortable room that they reserved for victims and witnesses, she fidgeted with the end of her blonde ponytail. Though she appeared antsy, Winter doubted she knew the danger she'd been in before Officer Greene pulled her aside after class.

Since Officer Greene had first picked her up, he'd tried repeatedly to assure her she wasn't in any trouble. But even now, close to an hour later, the anxiety in Caroline's blue eyes hadn't abated.

Fortunately, Levi Brandt was on his way to the main floor to meet with Winter. Maybe if Caroline heard the reassurance from someone with the term victim in their title, she'd finally relax.

Winter glanced to the side as a shadow appeared in the open doorway. As Levi Brandt stepped into the room, she offered him a quick smile.

"Agent Black." He returned the grin and extended a hand. "Pleasure to see you again." He paused to gesture to the glass. "This is our girl?"

Winter nodded. "Yep. This is Caroline Peters. She was in three different pictures that our suspect uploaded to a dark web forum that our informant found. Whoever took the pictures of Caroline is the same man who recorded himself slitting Dakota Ronsfeldt's throat. It was posted by the same username."

Levi tucked his hands in the pockets of his slacks as he turned to face the two-way glass. "Damn. Lucky you got to her, then. She knows she's not under arrest, right?"

"Of course. The officer who escorted her here told her seven ways from Sunday that she wasn't in any trouble. I guess she's just paranoid."

Levi rocked back on his heels, the calm demeanor never leaving his expression. "There are plenty of folks out there who don't trust cops, and plenty more who just hate them altogether. Believe it or not." His gray eyes shifted to her as he tapped a finger against his chest. "I used to be one of those people. The area I grew up in was all blue collar, working-class people. Any time we saw the cops poking around, we knew they weren't there to do us any favors. As far as we were concerned, cops only ever helped rich people."

"Wow," Winter managed. "So, you became a cop? What inspired that?"

He shrugged. "Well, like I said. We were all under the impression that cops only ever helped rich people, and I wanted to be a cop who helped out the regular Joes and Josephines. So, here I am." Straightening his tie, he took a step toward the doorway. "Let's go make sure Caroline knows we're on her team."

Winter was right on his heels. "Yeah, all right. Fair enough."

With a quick glance over his shoulder, Levi pushed open the heavy door. As she followed him into the small room, she tried to mirror his pleasant smile.

Levi extended a hand to the young woman. "Caroline Peters?"

Her blue eyes flicked from Levi to Winter and back before she nodded. She straightened in her seat on the cushioned bench as she accepted Levi's handshake. "Yeah, I'm Caroline."

"Nice to meet you. I'm Special Agent Levi Brandt with the Victim Services department, and I'm sure you've already met Special Agent Black." He pulled out a chair behind a plain white table and dropped to sit.

Winter followed his lead and sat at his side. Though she'd questioned her fair share of victims and perps since her start with the FBI, she was curious to see how a Victim Services agent conducted an interview.

As Caroline nodded again, her eyes shifted back to Winter. "Yeah, I've met Agent Black. What happened to the other guy, the tall dude with the dark hair and the fancy watch?"

Winter smiled at Noah's description. "Your parents are on their way, and the fancy watch owner, Agent Dalton, will bring them to meet with you when they arrive."

Wrinkling her nose, Caroline looked to Levi. "Why are my parents coming?"

Levi's gray eyes were fixed on the girl, his expression and demeanor exuding a calm that made Winter jealous of the ability. "Well, Caroline, they're coming here for the same reason you're here. To keep them safe."

A portion of the color drained from the young woman's face. "Safe from what?"

"Caroline, have you noticed anyone following you lately?" he asked.

Even though she shot them both a confused look, Caroline straightened in her seat. "Following me? What do you mean? Like a stalker?"

Levi's expression remained calm as he nodded. "Exactly like a stalker."

"You're not here because you're in any sort of trouble," Winter spread her hands but held Caroline's gaze, "but I'd be lying if I said that there wasn't something wrong. Obviously, cops don't just bring people to the FBI office if nothing's wrong, right?"

Though faint, a flicker of amusement flitted behind Caroline's eyes.

"We're asking if you've noticed anyone following you because one of our Cyber Crimes agents found some photos of you online." Winter didn't see any reason to sugarcoat the reason Caroline had been dragged away from VCU and into an FBI interview room.

The girl's eyes snapped open wide. "What? What kind of pictures?" For a moment, Caroline looked like she might faint. "Like, nudes?"

Winter had already started to shake her head before Caroline finished. "No, nothing like that. I don't mean to sound rude, but that's not really the FBI's territory. We didn't find them on Facebook or Reddit or a website like that. The part of the internet where we found them is really specific to a nasty subset of the population."

Caroline's eyes were so wide, Winter thought they might roll out of her head. "The dark web?"

This time, Winter and Levi both nodded.

Raising a hand to cover her mouth, Caroline pressed her

back against the wall. "Oh my god. How? You said your Cyber Crimes people found them? What…what types of pictures are they?"

"The type that the paparazzi might take," Levi replied gently. "They're just you standing on a sidewalk looking at your phone, but it's pretty obvious that whoever took them was out of your sight. That, plus the fact that they were found on the dark web leads us to believe that you and your family might be in danger."

Winter retrieved the little notepad and a pen from her blazer. "Caroline, do you have any idea who might have done something like this? Anyone who would have wanted to hurt you?"

She opened and closed her mouth, but after several seconds of stunned silence, she gave up and shook her head.

Levi shifted his gaze back to Caroline. "Any jealous exes, anything like that?"

Though she looked ready to shake her head in the negative, Caroline froze. "Wait, I do have an ex. We broke up a few months ago, and he was a real dick about it. But, I mean, he cheated on me, so I don't think he'd be jealous, you know?"

Winter could almost hear Autumn say, *oh, honey.*

Instead, Levi shook his head. "That's not necessarily how stalkers work. They don't think rationally. They act based on their emotions, and usually those emotions are incredibly unhealthy. Can you give us his name?"

With a nod, Caroline swallowed. "Yeah, um, his name is Brett Chaplain. He's a business student at VCU, or at least he was, last I knew. I don't talk to him anymore. I try to keep my distance."

After she jotted down the young man's name, Winter pocketed the notepad and stood. "Thank you, Caroline. I know this is a lot to deal with right now, but you're doing great. Keep it up, okay?"

Before Winter could worry if the encouragement had been too childish, Caroline dropped her face in her hands. She inhaled and exhaled several times, clearly trying to gather herself. Then, as if the breaths had been fortifying, she raised her head, appearing much more calm. "Thank you, Agent Black. Take care."

Even Levi's face brightened with a smile as he gave Winter a little salute.

She pulled open the wooden door and stepped into the hall. In the back of her mind, she already knew the ex-boyfriend wasn't responsible for the kidnapping videos, but they had a duty to follow every lead.

As she made her way past the door to the area behind the interview room, a flicker of movement drew her attention.

"Aiden?" She stepped into the small space. "What are you doing over here?"

His pale eyes met hers, and she noticed right away that he seemed...peculiar. Though only slightly, he looked off-kilter. If the man didn't come across so polished and poised all the time, she doubted she would have noticed such a slight variance. But with Aiden, anything less than perfection was bizarre.

Unfortunately, she didn't have time to delve into the various scenarios that might have thrown someone like Aiden Parrish off-balance.

Turning back to the glass, he stood ramrod straight as he gazed into the room. "Just checking in on the investigation. You know it's not Caroline's ex, right? We're looking for a serial killer, not a jealous ex-boyfriend."

After his assessment of Justin's mental state, her knee-jerk reaction was to disprove anything he said. If he was wrong about one perpetrator, then he could be wrong about someone else.

"Sometimes those two things aren't mutually exclusive," she said. "It's a lead, and I'm going to follow it. If nothing else, we rule out a possibility."

He gave her a stiff nod in response. "Fair enough. Don't spend too much time on it, though. Ryan O'Connelly has a dinner party to go to later tonight, and you and Agent Weyrick are his chauffeurs."

Even as she nodded, she realized that in the rush to get from one place to another to find Caroline before her stalker, she had all but forgotten about the plan to send Ryan undercover.

Grinding her teeth, Winter turned to step out into the hall without a word of farewell to Aiden. Though failure to follow up on Caroline's ex would be a rookie misstep, Winter already knew she was about to chase down a dead end. Statistically speaking, women were more likely to be stalked by someone they knew as opposed to a perfect stranger, so Brett Chaplain couldn't be ignored.

On the off chance that Brett was involved with the stalker photos and the kidnappings, Winter could hit two birds with one stone. She could prove that Aiden was fallible, and she could get a violent offender off the street.

But she knew better than to raise her hopes.

Caroline Peters was only one piece of the puzzle, and they still had many more to find.

21

Ryan pinched the American flag pin between his thumb and forefinger to hold it up to the light. Even though he knew what he was looking for, an up-close examination of the unassuming recording device belied no hint of the pin's true function. The stars and stripes were outlined with a silver border, and the light glinted off the polished flag.

Prying his focus away from the pin, he offered a half-smile to the man at the other end of the circular table. "You know," Ryan paused to chuckle as he fixed the pin to his lapel, "I remember the days when you'd pat a bloke down looking for a wire. And you were looking for an actual wire some primitive caveman tech taped under his shirt with a battery pack the size of a Walkman."

Bobby Weyrick snorted out a laugh. "Glad I wasn't in the bureau back then. These things were a little clunkier when I started a few years ago, but I think I missed the worst of it. Everything's wireless these days."

"Ain't that the truth." Ryan readjusted his black tie, hating how nervous he felt.

The agent glanced down to his nondescript watch.

"Winter should be here soon. She's on her way back from Brett Chaplain's place."

Ryan lifted a curious eyebrow. "I take it she and Agent Dalton didn't find anything."

With a shake of his head, Bobby leaned back in his seat. "No, they didn't. Just like Parrish said. We're looking for a serial killer, and Chaplain was just a regular ex-boyfriend. Winter said he'd been out of town until the night before last, and between his roommates and his job, there's someone to vouch for where he was almost every hour of the day."

"Couldn't be that easy, could it?"

The corner of Bobby's mouth twitched. "Easy stuff like that is what the city cops get to deal with. When they get a doozey like this," he shrugged, "that's when they get the bureau involved. Ain't a lot of cases that come through our office that are cut and dry like a crazy ex-boyfriend or girlfriend."

Ryan nodded his understanding. Over the past week, he'd discovered more about Federal versus State jurisdiction than he ever thought he'd learn outside of a college classroom. Bobby was right. In the old adage about pulling out the big guns, the Federal Bureau of Investigation was the big gun.

Neither Ryan nor Bobby got a chance to expound on their stinted conversation before the glass and metal door swung inward with a light creak. The newcomer's vivid blue eyes flicked from Bobby to Ryan as she let the door fall closed. Tucking a wayward piece of ebony hair behind one ear, she pulled out the chair to Ryan's side and took a seat.

As he made his best effort to appear amiable, Ryan nodded. "Agent Black. Nice to see you again."

Her mouth moved in what might have been a slight smile, though Ryan wasn't quite sure. "You ready for this?"

Biting back a sigh, Ryan spread his hands. "As ready as I'm going to get, I'd imagine."

With a reassuring smile, Bobby gestured to Agent Black. "We'll both be right outside if you need us. Do you have any reason to believe there's the potential for a violent confrontation?"

Ryan shook his head. "No, I don't think so. They're a bunch of shady arseholes, but they aren't like the mob or something. They watch each other's backs and cover up each other's skeletons, make sure all their kids get into the best schools, screw over poor people to make a few bucks, but they aren't about to go from door to door busting kneecaps if they think something's off."

"Right." Agent Black still looked serious, or like she had the makings of a headache coming on. "If they need something like that done, they'd hire someone to do it, right?"

Ryan rang a pretend bell. "Bingo. These dinner parties aren't anything extravagant. They're exclusive, but they aren't 'knock on an alleyway door and give a secret password' exclusive."

Agent Weyrick scooted his chair closer to the table. "Still. We ought to have a few code words or phrases in case you run into trouble."

The thought made Ryan's heart pound against his chest. The men and women who attended the dinner parties might not have even been capable of throwing a punch, but he was sure they knew how to find someone who could. If they discovered that he was spying on their little club for the FBI, he might be able to make it out of the house, but he wouldn't make it far beyond that.

Even though there would be no attendees who had the gall to confront him themselves, they had more than enough money to pay an actual mafioso to find and deal with Ryan's disloyalty. And if the members of that elite circle knew that he was there to air their dirty secrets to the world, there wasn't much that two FBI agents could do to help him in the days that followed.

That was the beauty of their type of power. They never dirtied their own hands. They never had to worry about how they'd deal with a potential threat. They just located a capable third party, pointed them in the direction, and fired them at their adversary like they were a Howitzer.

Ryan had learned long ago that knowledge, though powerful in its own right, was not power. Only power was power.

"Once you get there, you'll just find your contact, same as you normally do." Winter Black's voice cut through his grim thoughts.

Mechanically, Ryan blinked to clear his vision. "Her husband used to be a major player in their weird little social circle. The only women other than her that I usually see around there are the wives. Honestly, I don't even think that Mrs. N is real keen on being part of this thing. But she's a political figure, so she needs the donations and the endorsements."

Agent Weyrick's mouth had become a hard line. "Everyone's got a price, don't they?"

The pit in Ryan's stomach was more noticeable at the agent's grave expression. He knew firsthand how an attempt to walk with one foot in the darkness and one in the light ended. Eventually, no matter how hard a person tried to maintain a balance, everyone had to choose.

Living in both worlds wasn't just a tightrope walk—it was impossible. And for someone like Mrs. N, a time would eventually come where she would fall onto one side or the other.

But Nicole Nichols's fate wasn't his concern. She'd made her bed, and she'd become adept at maneuvering through the underworld of the wealthy elite without staining her hands too extensively.

Ryan was here for his sister and his niece and nephew. He'd asked himself if he wanted one foot in the dark or one in the light, and he'd made his decision. But just because he'd chosen the light didn't mean the decision wouldn't come with a price.

As he pulled himself from the reverie, he glanced back up to the two agents. "Before we start figuring out these code words, you know I've got to ask. Any update on the U.S. Attorney?"

Winter Black nodded. "Yes, though we're still waiting to hear the results. SAC Osbourne is meeting with him tonight. We ought to know more by tomorrow morning, and as soon as we do, we'll let you know."

Weyrick's eyes shifted from Agent Black to Ryan as he tapped a finger against the polished table. "He's going to tell them about what we're doing tonight, about how you're helping us with it."

Swallowing the sting of bile that had risen up the back of his throat, Ryan managed not to puke. "Okay. That's all I can really ask for, I guess."

He'd hoped to know more about the deal the U.S. Attorney planned to present to him before he attended the dinner party. After all, if an opportunity to escape existed, it would be in the short window of time he was relieved of the high-tech ankle monitor.

However, he still didn't know what the U.S. Attorney intended to heap onto his plate. And unless he knew that the man intended to well and truly screw him over, he wouldn't run. He owed that much to Lil. The kids. Himself.

Coughing into one hand to clear his throat, Ryan nodded again. "All right. Well, let's figure out these code words then."

22

When Peyton Hoesch glanced up from her phone, her first instinct was to look back down and pretend she'd seen nothing. Cameron Arkwell was an amiable enough guy on most days, but she'd always seen a different persona that lurked beneath his pale blue eyes.

He was intense, but she was sure he was harmless. After all, plenty of friends and coworkers had told Peyton she had the same sort of intensity too.

"Caroline isn't going to make it." Peyton wasn't sure why she felt the need to vocalize the words. Cameron was looking at the same group text message conversation as she.

Shadows shifted along his clean-shaven face as he clenched and unclenched his jaw. The seconds of silence ticked away, and the only sound was the quiet drone of the refrigerator to Cameron's side. His eyes were fixed on the screen of his smartphone as he slowly nodded. "Looks that way."

Shifting in her seat at the massive kitchen island, Peyton looked back to her phone and pulled up her and her mother's text history.

Peyton's mom had been an agent in the Drug Enforcement Agency for the past twenty years, and even though the work didn't often follow her home, Maryann Hoesch made a point to pass some of her law enforcement knowledge down to her daughter.

To be sure, Peyton didn't want to be a federal agent like her mother. Her major was sociology, and the marketing class she took with Cameron and Caroline had been more of an accident than anything. She'd added the course to her schedule at the last second, needing the three credit hours to remain a full-time student. Unless she maintained full-time status at VCU, she wouldn't be eligible for scholarships or financial aid.

The marketing course was one of the few that hadn't filled up during Peyton's last-minute scramble to throw together her schedule, and it had been a placeholder until she found a course that actually interested her.

Marketing strategies might have been intriguing to people like Cameron Arkwell and Caroline Peters, but Peyton had to fight to keep her eyes from glazing over during each class period.

By the time she remembered to swap the class to something less mind-numbing, she would have had to pay a nominal late enrollment fee. To avoid the seventy-five-dollar charge, she decided to tough out the marketing class.

I should have paid the seventy-five bucks, she thought as she glanced back to Cameron.

The unsettling anger had dissipated, but the glint in his pale eyes was still present.

As his gaze met hers, Peyton shrugged. "We could just set up a different night to work on it. I've got a paper due tomorrow for one of my other classes, so I can just head home and work on that."

With a slight smile, Cameron waved a dismissive hand.

"No, don't worry about it. We can work on something, make the trip out here worth it, you know?"

In that moment, the irascibility seemed so distant that it might have been a figment of Peyton's imagination.

It might have been, but she still couldn't shake the nagging sensation in the back of her head. Rather than leap out of her seat to collect her car keys and leave, Peyton stayed where she was, silently consenting. But she wasn't consenting at all.

One way or another, she was going to leave the awkward air that had settled over the kitchen.

Breaking her gaze away from Cameron's, her fingers flew across the virtual keyboard of her phone.

Hey Mom, favor? I'm at a classmate's working on a group project and it's getting kind of awkward. Could you call me so I can leave without seeming rude?

Tonight wouldn't be the first time she had asked a friend or family member to help nonchalantly extract her from an unwanted social situation.

Sure, honey. Give me a sec and I'll call and say something about the dog we don't have.

In spite of the palpable discomfort that hung in the air, Peyton smiled to herself as she locked her phone. They had three cats and an iguana, but no dog.

All the while, Cameron's blue eyes had been fixed on his own smartphone. As if he'd been snapped out of a trance, he looked up to her before gesturing to the fridge. "Do you want something to drink?"

Just as Peyton was about to shrug and make an effort to brush off the offer, the screen of her phone lit up as the device buzzed against the granite bar.

Eyes wide, she feigned surprise as well as she was able. "Oh. That's my mom." She didn't wait for a confirmatory gesture before she picked up the phone and swiped the screen. "Hey, Mom. What's up?"

"Hey, sweetie," her mom said. "I just got word from my boss that I'm going to have to stay late. Charlie's been cooped up inside all day, and I hoped I'd have been home by now to let him out. Could you do me a huge favor and head home to let him out before he pisses on the living room carpet again?"

Peyton suppressed a chuckle. Their fake dog's name had always been Charlie. "Yeah, I can do that."

"And, honey, please. I know you're working on something for one of your classes, but he's probably ready to piss himself right now." Her mom's voice was level with just enough of a hint of panic that Peyton almost had to ask herself if they really did have a dog.

They didn't, of course. Peyton was deathly allergic.

"Of course, Mom. I'll head over there now." Painting an apologetic expression on her face, she shrugged as she met Cameron's curious stare.

"Okay, thank you, honey. I'll see you later. Love you."

"Love you too, Mom."

As she locked the screen and returned the phone to the back pocket of her jeans, she spread her hands. "I'm sorry. My mom got roped into working late and she needs me to go home and let out our dog before he pisses on the floor."

Cameron leaned back against the counter and crossed his arms. "Your dog? I didn't know you had a dog."

Shouldering her handbag, Peyton blinked. "Yeah, we've had him for a few years."

Cameron arched an eyebrow, suspicion alight on his face. "Really?"

What was going on? Why was he skeptical of her sudden need to leave?

Even if he'd put two and two together and realized that she'd concocted an excuse to escape, there wasn't any reason for him to care. He and Peyton were just short of perfect strangers.

She swallowed the sudden rush of anxiety and forced an amiable smile to her lips. "Yeah, his name is Charlie."

Partly because of her mother's line of work and partly because of the activism she'd done on campus, Peyton was well aware of sexual assault statistics for young women in college.

By the time they graduated, one in five college girls would have been sexually assaulted at least once. The number had held steady since at least the 1980s, and it didn't seem to be in decline.

Peyton also knew that the most likely perpetrator of such an assault was a man who was a friend or acquaintance of the victim.

Women were rarely assaulted by someone they didn't know.

By the time she'd run through the disturbing knowledge, her heart hammered in her chest. She'd been down this road before, and only quick thinking and a convincing line of dialogue had gotten her out of the scenario unscathed.

She was confident she would be able to say the same for tonight. Thanks to her mom, Peyton had an unquestionable way out of this damn house.

If Cameron and Caroline wanted to work with Peyton on any more of their project, they could meet up in the student commons in the middle of the day.

There was no way in hell Peyton was ever coming back to Cameron Arkwell's house.

He'd mentioned earlier that his father was home, but the man wouldn't be able to hear a thing from his upstairs office.

For the first chunk of Peyton's visit, she'd been comforted by the flickering light of the television in the nearby great room. But when Cameron's sister, Maddie, had flicked off the screen and left, Peyton had gone on guard.

"Charlie, huh?" Though he'd donned a smile, the sly glint in his eyes remained.

Before Peyton could elaborate on her and her mother's fake dog, Cameron chuckled.

"You know." He leveled an index finger in her direction. "I love that name for a dog. I love it when pets have people names, you know? You can say things like 'dammit, Kenneth, stop drinking out of the toilet,' and it just sounds hilarious."

Peyton could only hope her smile was convincing.

With a laugh that sounded more nervous than amused, she tightened her grip on her handbag and nodded. "That's almost exactly what my mom said when we named him."

There was some truth in the statement. Two of their three cats were named Mavis and Greg. They'd named the other one Almond Joy, and Peyton had named her iguana Geico.

Whenever her mom walked by the terrarium, she'd always coo at the lizard about how she wished he could save her fifteen percent on her car insurance.

At the fond memory, Peyton dug up the remainder of her fortitude.

It was time to leave. When she got home, she could tell her mom all about the uncomfortable encounter with Cameron Arkwell. Maybe one of her law enforcement friends had heard the young man's name mentioned in connection with a crime.

Or maybe, the entire unnerving look in Cameron's pale eyes had been manufactured by Peyton's imagination. Maybe Cameron was a perfectly normal, albeit intense, twenty-two-year-old man.

Either way, Peyton didn't intend to stick around to find out.

She squeezed the handle of her purse. "Well, thank you for hosting this group study thing. Sorry we didn't actually get anything done."

His smile widened as he shook his head. "It's okay. It happens, you know?" He straightened to his full height and gestured to the hallway at the end of the kitchen. "Here, you can go out this way. I'll follow you so I can open the garage door. The front entrance is usually all locked down after the staff leave."

The effort to maintain her nonchalant smile had turned monumental.

Just as she was about to turn to make her way to the hall, he held up a hand. "You're going to go let your dog out, right?"

His stare didn't waver.

Swallowing against the sudden roiling in her stomach, Peyton nodded. "That's right."

Though the corner of his mouth turned up in the start of a smile, the look wasn't content or amused. Between the smirk and the devilish glint in his eyes, Cameron Arkwell looked like a lion circling the antelope that was about to become its next meal. The subtle warning signs in her head blared now, and she fought the urge to turn around and run to the door.

"You don't have a dog." His voice was so matter-of-fact, so cool and sharp, that the chill of adrenaline clawed its way up her spine.

"I-I'm sorry?" She managed to furrow her brows to flash him a confused look.

With a nonchalant shrug, he stuffed his hands in his pockets and took a step toward her. "Last week in class, remember when we were talking about being mindful of allergies in marketing campaigns? Professor Marshall asked for examples, and you told him you were allergic to dogs."

Oh, no.

Her throat all but closed up, and the glance over her shoulder was all but involuntary. When in doubt, just tell them the truth. In her thoughts, the words had been spoken by her mother.

Heaving a defeated sigh, Peyton tucked a piece of ebony hair behind her ear. "Well, considering that I didn't even remember that, I didn't think you'd remember it."

His smile didn't reach his eyes. The expression was wooden and icy, just like everything else about him.

"Look, I..." She rubbed the bridge of her nose. "I didn't want to be a jerk, but it's just weird. I've just about reached my limit for social interaction for the day, and I want to go home."

The seconds ticked away as he kept his pale eyes on hers. His expression shifted from thoughtful to understanding, but for the duration of the change, the look in his eyes remained the same.

Finally, after what might have been an eternity, he chuckled, a deep ha-ha sound that raised goose bumps on her arms. "Yeah, all right. I get it. I've always been pretty extroverted, but I guess there are a lot of people out there who don't really look at social interactions the same way I do. My sister, she's pretty introverted. So's my dad."

Peyton's muscles were so tense that her neck creaked as she readjusted the handbag on her shoulder. With a half-smile, she nodded.

He spread his hands and took another step. "You didn't have to have your mom call to make up some excuse for you, you know? You could've just told me the truth."

For a moment, she didn't think she'd be able to speak. *Fortitude, dammit.* "I'm sorry about that. It just...it seemed like the truth was too rude, I guess. And it's not you, not at all. You've been a great host. I'm just really not much of a social butterfly, or at least if I am, my quota for it fills up pretty fast."

Somewhere in the house, a clock tick-tick-ticked the seconds by. Peyton thought she might scream before he raised both shoulders. "Understood. All right, come on, then." He waved to the hallway again. "I'll open the garage door for you. There's a keypad that we use to open the door out there. My dad's a little crazy about security, so he doesn't want us giving the code to anyone. Even though, you know, it's inside the house."

Of course he had to accompany her to the exit. This house was a fortress.

With as much of a smile as she could manage, Peyton turned to the hall. She slipped on the flats that she'd discarded in the mudroom, unlocked the deadbolt, and stepped into the shadowy garage.

As soon as she set foot on the concrete floor, she caught the flicker of movement in her peripheral vision. She couldn't be sure what it was, but the paranoia that had weighed down her mind since she arrived insisted that she should duck away from the shadow.

But whatever it was, it moved too fast for her to avoid.

Rather than strike her square on the temple, the heavy blow landed closer to the top of her head. A series of starbursts exploded in her left eye, and white-hot pain lanced through her brain. The blow was so disorienting that she hardly heard the sickening, dry crack as the unknown object met her skull.

As she careened to the floor, she didn't have to ask herself what had just happened, or who was responsible for what had just happened.

She already knew the answer. Cameron Arkwell was a psychopath.

The world moved in slow motion as she continued her

descent, and at the last possible instant, she tucked her hands beneath her face to brace against the force of the fall. Rather than faceplant into the concrete, her nose smashed into the back of one hand.

All at once, the pace of her reality sped back up to normal.

Though she couldn't be sure in the darkness, she felt the warm trickle of blood against the back of her hand as the fading bursts of light danced along her vision. The world around her spun, and she had to gasp for a much-needed breath of air.

Darkness threatened to engulf her limited vision, but she squeezed her eyes closed and clenched one hand into a fist. She'd been punched before, but she'd never experienced a blow like this, never been struck so hard that the force threatened her consciousness.

Swallowing down the threat of nausea, she gritted her teeth together.

Not like this, she told herself.

She wouldn't let herself lapse into unconsciousness and leave her body to the mercy of a lunatic like Cameron Arkwell.

His grip iron, Cameron clamped a hand around each of her ankles. The fabric of her t-shirt rode up as he dragged her along the floor, but the cool touch of the polished concrete against her stomach was shocking enough to snap her back from the edge of unconsciousness.

She needed to fight. She needed to do something.

As she forced open her eyes to take stock of the situation, Cameron muttered a string of curses.

Whatever he'd used to hit her, he had intended for the strike to knock her out.

With one arm, she pushed herself the rest of the way to her back. Cameron's six-foot, well-toned form was silhouetted against the doorway by the warm light from the distant kitchen. Had he held a butcher knife, the scene would have been a picture-perfect poster for a horror film.

Before she could consider the strategic pitfalls of where she lay half in and half out of the doorway to the garage, she snapped up one leg to ram her shin into Cameron's balls.

She felt a grim sense of satisfaction when his eyes widened, and he took in a sharp breath. Hunching over, he let out a grunt of pain.

Peyton didn't pause to bask in the glory of her successful hit. Yet another wave of adrenaline surged through her as she pushed herself to stand on legs that felt as structurally sound as gelatin. A wave of dizziness rushed up to greet her, but within two rapid beats of her heart, the adrenaline stilled her vision.

Cameron stood in the center of the doorway, and she knew her window of opportunity to make it past him was about to slam shut. She knew better than to think she could coax him to cough up the code for the garage door. She knew better than to think she could get out of this house alive if she didn't make her move right then.

With as much strength as she could muster, she shoved him back into the mudroom to make room to slip past. She caught a glimpse of the pale shade of his eyes as she rushed into the hallway.

When she reached for her handbag to retrieve the pepper spray she always carried, a leaden weight dropped in her stomach.

The purse had slipped off her shoulder when she'd fallen to the floor in the garage.

The purse, her pepper spray, her car keys, her phone.

She cast a panicked glance around the kitchen, and that's when she spotted the knives. Only the adrenaline with which she'd been overcome kept her from vomiting all over the ceramic tile.

Peyton Hoesch wasn't a killer. She was a sociology student at Virginia Commonwealth University because she wanted to obtain a Master's in Social Work. She was active in a handful of student organizations that reached out to the vulnerable members of the VCU student body to offer them aid when the pressure of the world seemed too much to bear.

Though the moment of contemplation felt like an eternity, only a split-second had elapsed. She didn't have to kill anyone, but she had to defend herself.

Her footsteps were quiet as she hurried over to the wooden knife block, and she could hear little over the rapid cadence of her heartbeat. With one trembling hand, she took hold of the butcher knife and pulled the blade free.

At the same time the overhead light glinted off the metal, a hand clamped down on her ponytail. The sting of the strands ripping free of her scalp accompanied the rough motion as Cameron pulled her back to him.

Tightening her grasp on the knife, she barely managed to turn to face him and stop her body's momentum before she crashed into him.

As his eyes met hers, his iron grip clamped down around her wrist. Though she resisted, the fact remained that Peyton was a five-foot-two, one-hundred-pound woman who avoided the gym like the plague, and Cameron Arkwell had the muscular build of a professional athlete.

He forced her arm out wide, but she didn't let her grip on the knife falter. With the other hand, he grabbed her by the throat.

The cry for help that she tried to make was crushed into little more than a squeak as he tightened his grasp. A dull pop sounded out, followed by a sharp pain that lanced all the way to her collar bone.

Not like this.

She wouldn't die as she stared into the eyes of a man whose countenance was overcome with a morbid sense of satisfaction, whose eyes were alight with a predatory glint she'd never before seen any human being wear. She wouldn't let this prick win. Not when she still had one free hand.

Digging her nails into his wrist, she started to lean forward. The less distance between them, the less leverage he could utilize to strangle her. Though the pain in her throat was almost unbearable, she forced the sensation to the back of her mind.

Beneath her nails, she felt the first warm trickle of blood. Rather than try to best his strength by shoving his arm away, she tightened her grip and twisted his wrist.

As soon as the hold loosened, she rammed a knee into his gut and jerked her other arm out of his grasp.

Right then, she could end the entire ordeal.

If she drove the finely made kitchen knife through his eye, through his heart, even through his throat, she would be free.

But then what? Then his father would rush downstairs to find his son dead, Peyton with blood covering her hands and clothes, and…what?

With a swift step backward, she held out the knife. "Don't move, Cameron." She wanted the command to be a shout, but due to the damage to her esophagus, she was lucky he heard her at all.

His eyes flicked up to meet hers as he clutched his damaged wrist. There was unabashed venom in his expression, a sentiment she could only classify as one step short of a murderous rage.

"I'm leaving." The words were closer to a normal speaking volume, but far from the imposing tone she wanted. "You stay right there, or I swear to god, I'll stab you in the heart."

Though his eyes followed each and every movement as she stepped backward, he didn't respond.

The house was a maze to her—she'd never lived anywhere with more than two-thousand square feet of space. Compared to what she was used to, Cameron Arkwell's palatial residence might as well have been a labyrinth.

She would have to turn around if she wanted any chance to figure out where she was going, but she couldn't let him out of her sight.

Glancing over her shoulder, she angled her body to the side, but kept the knife trained in Cameron's direction. For what felt like an eternity, she sidestepped across the expansive kitchen to the arched doorway. The dining room was beside the kitchen, and then after that, the hallway to the foyer. At least, that's what she remembered.

Once she was beneath the arch, she dared another glance to the shadowy hall. She barely had a chance to glimpse the distant foyer before she snapped her attention to the flicker of movement in her periphery.

In a blur of motion, Cameron was gone.

The short hall at the other end of the kitchen led to a great room, and she could only assume the route was an alternate method for him to close the distance between them. Rather than pause to scope out his location, she turned and sprinted through the dining room and into the foyer.

With every step, she half-expected a landmine to detonate beneath her feet, or a masked man to emerge from the darkness to tackle her to the floor. She thought to shout for help, but she doubted the strangled vocalization would be heard in the next room, much less the next floor.

She was, very clearly, on her own.

Even with the evil lurking so close, she'd never felt so alone.

The moment the front door was in sight, she forced herself to look over her shoulder.

Nothing stirred. She still had time. Hope seeped into her heart as she reached for the deadbolt with one shaking hand.

Clutching the knife with fingers that felt numb, she nearly cried in relief as the lock disengaged with a metallic click. One more. She moved to undo the lock on the door handle, praying this one turned just as easily.

The hair on her arms raised as the tiniest sound she'd ever heard penetrated the heavy sound of her breathing. A small squeak of rubber on floor, and she knew he was behind her.

She felt him like a rogue wave coming from nowhere.

Fumbling with the lock, she refused to look back, afraid she'd freeze in horror if she did. Afraid Cameron Arkwell would have transformed into a monster with drool dripping from pointed teeth, sharp claws reaching out to scrape down her back.

At the same time she turned the little lever to the left, another noise, this time an explosion of sound, shattered the eerie spell of quiet that had fallen over the house. White-hot pain ripped through her back, and she thought for a second that she'd been set ablaze.

Even as she watched crimson droplets spatter against the dark wood of the door, the series of events hadn't entirely registered in Peyton's head.

Her arms were cold, and even though she couldn't recall loosening her grasp, the butcher knife slipped out of her fingers to clatter to the floor. Her vision swam as she sank to her knees.

With all the energy left in her body, she looked down at her shirt. In the center of the black fabric, a splotch of darker darkness spread. As she tried to take in a breath, her lungs seemed to fold in on themselves with a wet sucking sensation. Warmth spread along the back of her throat, followed by the taste of metal.

She was cold. Not just her arms, but her entire body had gone cold.

As she completed her final slump to the floor, her cheek met the smooth tile. By then, she couldn't feel much of anything.

"Mom!"

As she did when she was a child, she called out for her mother, though the sound got lost in a gurgle of blood.

Peyton knew she was supposed to fight, but she no longer had the energy. All she wanted to do now was sleep. When she woke, everything would be better, she knew.

Yes, better.

When sneakered feet entered her field of vision, Peyton closed her eyes.

She just wanted to sleep.

23

A s the plastic wrapper in Winter's hand crinkled, Bobby Weyrick's eyes snapped over to the quiet disturbance. Pausing midway through opening the fun-sized candy, she slowly lifted her shoulders.

With a light chuckle, Bobby returned his attention to the laptop he'd claimed in their makeshift workspace.

"Whose idea was it to put a bowl of Halloween candy in the FBI surveillance van?" Even as she posed the question, Winter popped the chocolate and caramel candy into her mouth.

Bobby flashed her a grin. "Someone who knows we like to snack when we're bored, I bet."

Leaning back in her seat, Winter reached for another candy. "Well, so far, the great mystery of who gave us this Halloween candy is probably the most interesting part of this entire night." For emphasis, she unwrapped a Twix.

Stretching his arms above his head, Bobby nodded. "You're not kidding. There's only so much tennis talk I can handle, and I'm getting close to my breaking point."

Winter grunted out her agreement and took a bite of the

delicious treat. So far, Ryan O'Connelly's undercover venture to collect information about their mysterious internet stalker turned murderer had been a big fat bust.

"I bet it was Vasquez."

When Winter returned her attention to Bobby, his eyes were fixed on the orange bowl of candy. "Vasquez? What makes you think that?"

As he glanced back to the laptop—the device that had recorded more than an hour of inane conversations so far—he shrugged. "That dude's got a sweet tooth. He used to work the night shift, and every year, like clockwork, he'd go out to the store on the day after Halloween, or Easter, or Christmas, any one of those candy holidays and buy shitloads of the stuff. So, if you think this is a lot right now, just wait until November first."

Winter licked her fingers. "My friend does that, but with food she cooks. She'll practically beg us to come over and eat the leftovers so they won't go bad."

He reached for a candy bar too. "Sounds like a good friend."

In the quiet that followed, Bobby's attention shifted back to the laptop. Ryan had just greeted a man named Oliver Jacobs, and the two were discussing the attendees of the dinner party that evening.

Straightening in her seat, Winter wiggled the mouse of her own laptop to bring the screen to life. As soon as she opened a blank notepad file, her fingers flew along the keyboard to type out the names mentioned by the two men. Though the names were being recorded, she decided to turn her and Bobby's boredom into a bit of productivity.

Jacobs's voice came through the speakers fainter than Ryan's, but his words were still clear. "Mario Reyes and his wife are here tonight. Have you seen them yet, Tom?"

The alias Ryan used for his dealings with the secretive

group was Tom Wells. According to Ryan, the name was conceived in homage to Tom Petty. Ryan had admitted to taking on so many fake names that he needed a method to keep them straight in his head.

After she copied Mario Reyes's name, Winter minimized her notepad and pulled up one of the FBI's databases for personal records.

"What've you got?"

Winter kept her focus on the screen as the results populated. "Mario Reyes, sixty-four, lived in Richmond for the last twenty years, according to public records. He's a fairly successful venture capitalist, married to his high school sweetheart, three kids, all of whom are grown."

Bobby's chair squeaked as he leaned back. "Venture capitalist? Like *Shark Tank?*"

Though she didn't break her focus, she nodded. "Yeah, exactly like that. There's nothing unusual in his record, but…" Out of curiosity, she opened the link to his oldest son's records. As she scanned the page, she took in a breath.

Without speaking, Bobby rose from his chair to stand behind her. "Wow. Arrested twice for cooking meth? How is he not in prison?"

Clicking her tongue, Winter switched back to Mario Reyes's page. "Probably because his dad is a billionaire."

Bobby whistled through his teeth. "Meth is some nasty stuff, no doubt there, but people high on meth tend to be erratic. The guy we're looking for is calculated. There's no way the man in the videos we've seen was high when he recorded those. Not high on meth, at least."

Winter had to agree.

As Ryan and Oliver Jacobs's discussion shifted to horse racing, Bobby returned to his seat. "You know, I get that O'Connelly's a thief, but compared to the guys and gals we've looked up so far tonight, he's practically a saint."

After storing the results from Mario's search in a folder designated specifically for her research into the group, she glanced to Bobby. "No, he's really not a bad guy."

Bobby's smile turned wistful. "Yeah, I don't think he's a bad guy, either. I think he was dealt a pretty bad hand, and he bluffed his way through it. You remember that spunky old woman from Heidi Presley's hotel heist? Charlotte, right?"

"Right." Winter smiled as she thought of the woman. "Heidi wanted Ryan to kill her, but he didn't."

"He risked his life for Miss Charlotte, and he risked his freedom to come help us find this guy who's been kidnapping and murdering girls here in Richmond. Even if he's a thief, I don't really see how someone like that can be a genuinely bad apple."

She rested her back against the chair, lifting the hair off the nape of her neck. "Yeah, I think you're right. I never got the impression that he was a malicious criminal."

He gestured to the laptop. "I just hope that this is enough to get the U.S. Attorney to see that too."

As the space lapsed into silence, Ryan and Oliver Jacobs's conversation finally moved away from horse racing.

"Have you seen Nathaniel Arkwell yet tonight?" Jacobs's question was calm and conversational.

"Judge Arkwell? No, I don't think I have," Ryan replied.

Winter and Bobby exchanged knowing glances before she turned back to her laptop. As the men's discussion continued, she typed Arkwell's name into the database search tool.

Jacobs made a "hmm" sound. "I've been trying to get him to bring his son in to meet us, but Nathaniel says he's still too young, maybe a little too wild. He's only twenty-two."

Ryan chuckled. "I remember what it was like at that age. It's all parties and girls."

In a couple more clicks, Winter pulled up the information. "Nathaniel Arkwell. Virginia State Supreme Court judge for the last five years, and a city judge before then, defense lawyer before that." She narrowed her eyes at the screen. "Well, that's interesting. Even though Mr. Arkwell is a judge, he seems to be a pretty savvy investor. He made it through the recession in 2008 without much of a financial loss, and since then, he's almost tripled his net worth by playing the stock market."

Bobby snorted. "My guess is that this group facilitates more than a little bit of insider trading. Sounds like Ryan'll have his work cut out for him after we find our killer."

As Ryan and Jacobs parted ways after promising to meet again soon, Winter stashed the information from Nathaniel Arkwell in the digital folder along with Mario Reyes. "SSA Parrish says that he thinks the killer is young."

Lips pursed, Bobby nodded. "And so far, everyone here has been in their fifties and sixties. What are you thinking? Do you think the SSA's profile is off?"

Winter shook her head. "I'm not sure."

With a thoughtful look in his eyes, Bobby shrugged. "Maybe we ought to widen the net a little bit. Like with Mario Reyes. Mario's squeaky clean, but his son's a meth cook."

"Right, yeah, that's a good point. When we get back to the office, we can take a look through the names we've gotten so far. But this time, we focus more on their kids."

When Winter reached back to the candy bowl, Ryan's voice came through the laptop speakers.

"Nicole." Despite the distance, the audio was almost devoid of static. "Nicole Nichols, it's so nice to see you again, love. How are you doing?"

Winter sat up straighter. The notorious Mrs. N.

Winter had already done her due diligence on Nicole Nichols, and the woman's records were unassuming. Though Ryan had provided them with a couple names before tonight, he hadn't committed all the members of the group to memory. Their secretive circle kept no records of its members, so the dinner party was the best way for them to compile background information on the potential pool of suspects.

The woman's voice came across almost as clear as Ryan's. "Oh, I'm hanging in there. How about you, Tom? How are you?"

"I'm doing well, thank you. It looks like we're short a few people tonight," Ryan said. "I haven't seen Nathaniel Arkwell yet. Do you know if he plans to be here?"

"Judge Arkwell? No, I don't think he could make it. He's got quite a bit on his plate right now, work wise. He said he planned to stay at home and catch up."

Ryan made a sound that roughly equated to "ahh" over the microphone. "I was wondering if we'd have a chance tonight to talk a little bit more about that business venture you mentioned a few weeks ago. The videos of those girls, I mean. It seems like an easy way to make some quick cash."

"Easy?" Nichols echoed. "What do you mean?"

"Well, just find a few girls that need a job, get them to pretend they've been kidnapped on camera for a few days, and then give them part of the profit. I don't even think it's illegal, is it?"

A spell of quiet settled in after Ryan's question, and if it hadn't been for the occasional voice in the background, Winter might have thought they'd lost the connection.

When Nicole Nichols spoke again, her voice was hushed. "That's the thing, Tom. I...don't think those videos are fake."

"You don't?" Ryan's tone quieted to match Nichol's, but there was a distinct edge of panic in his voice.

"No. I know you told me you were sure they were fake, but, well." Another uncomfortable pause. "You're new here, and I don't want you to get the wrong impression about our members. Most of the folks here are decent, and I don't want you to think we're some group of crazed serial killers. We do what we can to help one another financially, and maybe some of the methods we use aren't completely legal, but no one's getting hurt. That's not what we do here."

"Of course not. Do you…well, do you have any idea who might've made the videos? Should we go to the police or tell someone else who's here tonight?"

Nichols sighed. "I'm not sure that'd be a good idea. I don't know who it is, and if the videos are real, I don't want anyone to know that we're snooping around about it."

Turning to Bobby, Winter lifted an eyebrow. "She's worried about a serial killer ruining the reputation of her fancy club, not necessarily about the fact that they're killing people. Is that how you took that?"

With a scowl, he nodded. "Yeah, that's about how I read it. I guess at least we don't have to worry about the videos being part of a bigger conspiracy. We've got a rogue killer to find, which is better than trying to infiltrate the Illuminati."

Better, maybe. But if Ryan's dialogue so far that night was any indication, it wouldn't be much easier to track them down.

No one in the group knew the specifics because no one wanted to know. They'd rather pretend their black sheep didn't exist than face reality.

As long as reality didn't hurt their bottom line.

24

Nathaniel took the steps two at a time as he hurried downstairs. Even through his noise cancelling headphones, the gunshot had rung out clear as day. He hadn't seen Cameron return home before he retired to his office, but as soon as he heard the gunshot, he knew his son was involved somehow.

Panic welled up in the back of his throat, so visceral and raw that he felt like he was being strangled.

Cameron had finally snapped and had taken out his years of anger and rage on Maddie. Nathaniel knew it. His son had killed Maddie, and Nathaniel had done nothing to prevent the confrontation.

He should have known. Should have seen the signs.

The emotional distance, the blatant manipulation, the lack of empathy. Since he was old enough to talk, lying had come just as easily to Cameron as telling the truth. Whenever he was caught in the midst of a wrongdoing, he showed no emotional reaction unless it suited his master plan.

Though Cameron had always been outgoing, Nathaniel had long suspected that his son's friendships and romantic relationships were superfluous. One dimensional. Fake. The only reason he maintained social connections was because he could manipulate them to his benefit.

Nathaniel didn't have to guess that manipulation was the motivator behind his son's outgoing personality. Cameron had told him as much.

During his senior year in high school, the boy had gone off on a tirade about how unfairly he was treated in relation to his sister, and he'd included all the questionable thoughts that had flitted through his head on a routine basis.

At the time, Nathaniel had brushed off the admission. He'd assured himself and his son that Cameron was just angry. After he admitted that he'd harbored a twinge of favoritism for his daughter, he was sure they'd be able to turn around their strained and awkward relationship.

But, like he so often was with his son, Nathaniel had been mistaken.

He and Katrina hadn't been the best parents to Cameron when the boy was little. Nathaniel knew it, but he'd never dream of besmirching his late wife's memory by advising Cameron that she'd given birth to him well before she should have. He'd never tell his son that she'd ignored his cries and pleas for attention because she suffered from a severe bout of postpartum depression, or that she would be diagnosed two years later with bipolar depression.

Nathaniel knew his son's upbringing had been rough, but until now, he'd been convinced that there was an answer to the distance between them. He'd been sure they could mend the bridge.

He'd been sure until he heard that gunshot.

Heart hammering against his chest, Nathaniel gasped for breath as he hopped off the final landing and rushed into the foyer.

Even as he stepped into Cameron's field of vision, those

steely blue eyes didn't stray from where they were glued to the front door. Though Nathaniel knew he needed to look over to confirm his fears, he held out a hand as he approached Cameron. He wasn't about to turn his back on the kid when he held a stainless steel forty-five in one hand.

"Cameron." His voice was calm but forceful. It was the same tone he used in court. "Cameron, give me the gun."

Cameron's pale eyes stayed on the door. Just as Nathaniel opened his mouth to make the request again, his son grasped the weapon by the barrel and extended the handgun to Nathaniel, grip first.

As he reached for the forty-five, he noticed the smears of red along Cameron's wrist. Scratches. Defensive wounds from whoever he'd just shot. Without hesitating, Nathaniel pried the weapon from his son's hand.

Jaw clenched, Nathaniel turned to the object of Cameron's fascination—a fascination that was comprised of equal parts anxiety and curiosity.

Nathaniel's neck felt like it was made of stone as he moved to look at the foyer. But when his gaze fell on the crumpled body in front of the wooden door, he heard himself take in a sharp breath. He knew right away that the young woman wasn't Maddie.

His gaze was transfixed on the woman, but no matter how hard he tried, he couldn't will his legs to move.

If she wasn't Nathaniel's daughter, Cameron's sister, then who was she?

All at once, a rush of adrenaline surged through his body to break the spell that had rooted him to the spot. Without another glance to Cameron, Nathaniel hurried over to the young woman's side. He was careful to avoid the pool of syrupy blood as he knelt to press his fingers against her neck.

The seconds ticked away in silence as he willed her pulse to return.

His effort was for naught. The girl was dead.

Nathaniel snapped his head up to look at his son. "Cameron. Cameron!"

As if he'd been ripped away from a trance, Cameron blinked before he met his father's stare.

"Cameron, who is this? And what happened down here?" The gold overhead light glinted off the frame of the handgun as Nathaniel held up the weapon for emphasis. His hand shook with each rapid beat of his heart, but he ignored the tremor and forced his attention to Cameron. "Who is she, and why...why...in the fuck did you shoot her?"

Though he wanted to launch into a string of obscenities, to ask his son what had possessed him to retrieve a hidden, semiautomatic handgun and fire a round into the back of a young woman who had been clear across the room, he bit his tongue.

After all, wasn't it Nathaniel's fault this had happened in the first place?

If he'd just paid attention to his son when he was little, they wouldn't be standing here. He was sure of it. If he and Katrina had just waited another couple years until her mental state had been stabilized with the help of antipsy-chotic medications. If he hadn't been so laser-focused on his career at the time. If he'd gotten the boy help when it was clear that he needed it. If he hadn't been so worried about how having an unstable child would affect his goals.

If...

If...

If...

He could romanticize the past and think about how he'd follow the right path if he had it to do over again, but the truth was, he and his wife had been kids. Nathaniel was twenty-three when his son was born, and Katrina had only been twenty.

They thought they could handle it. They wanted to start a family someday, anyway, right? What did it matter that they'd gotten a few years jumpstart? Having a family was their dream, and there was no way a dream would be the wrong path.

But the path had been wrong. Very wrong.

They should have waited. If they'd waited, then the girl in the pool of blood on the tiled floor would still be alive. Her parents wouldn't receive the news that every parent dreaded.

Her death was on the father's hands just as much as it was on the son's.

A father who was a judge. A father who should have known better.

He had to fix this.

As he jerked himself back to the present, he glanced over to Cameron's blank stare. Aside from handing Nathaniel the weapon, he hadn't moved.

"Cameron." Raising one hand, Nathaniel snapped his fingers until his son's pale eyes flicked over to him. "Cameron, snap out of it. The cops are probably already on their way, and if they aren't, they will be soon."

Cameron's brows drew together. The kid looked genuinely confused. "The cops? What? Why?"

He bit back an impatient retort. "Because this is a quiet neighborhood, and this is a loud weapon. I need you to tell me what the hell happened."

A silence settled in between them as Cameron opened and closed his mouth, his eyes wide. "I don't, I don't know, Dad."

Dad.

Cameron never called Nathaniel something so familiar. He called him Nathaniel or Judge Arkwell, but never Dad. Not unless he was making an effort to come across as condescending.

Nathaniel narrowed his eyes. "Dad?"

Cameron blinked a few times, appeared to be physically taken aback.

Teeth clenched, Nathaniel held his son's gaze. "What happened, Cameron? I'm going to help you, but unless you tell me the truth, there won't be much I can do. You understand me?"

The sharpness returned to Cameron's pale eyes, and the feigned look of forlorn regret vanished. "She was trying to steal something." His voice was flat, almost robotic.

If he was lying, Nathaniel had no earthly idea how to tell.

"She was trying to steal something?" he echoed. "What was she trying to steal?"

With a long exhale, Cameron shrugged. "I don't know. I went to the bathroom, and when I came out, I saw her looking through the pantry. She was about to put something in her purse. It looked like cash, but I wasn't sure. I confronted her about it, and she hit me with her purse." He gestured to the faint marks on the side of his face.

Nathaniel guffawed, a single loud barking sound of disbelief. "She hit you with her purse, so you shot her?"

Throwing both arms up in the air, Cameron took a step back. "What do you want from me, Nathaniel? I saw that she was trying to steal from us, so I confronted her. She attacked me, and I just..." eyes wide with clear exasperation, Cameron spread his hands, "I just reacted. I defended myself."

Though Nathaniel wasn't sure he believed the succinct explanation, he wanted to believe it. Desperately. He wanted to believe that the only reason Cameron would harm another human being was in the defense of his home. As his thoughts veered in the direction of the flash drive and the unsettling video of the young blonde woman's grisly murder, he clenched his jaw.

"How'd it escalate from her hitting you with her purse to

you shooting her in the back?" As Cameron opened his mouth to offer a rebuttal, Nathaniel raised a hand. "I'm not asking because I don't believe you. The cops are already on their way here, and I need to know what happened if I'm going to help you."

Shadows moved along Cameron's face as he gritted his teeth. After a few seconds of silence, he nodded. "Okay. She hit me with her purse. That was in the kitchen. You know how you keep that stash of cash in the coffee can in the pantry? I think that's what she was going for. That's what it looked like, anyway. She was about to take it, but she saw me and tried to put it back. When I confronted her about it, that's when she smacked me with her purse."

Nathaniel was motionless as he waited for his son to continue.

Cameron heaved another sigh. "She turned around, and I thought she was just going to run out through the garage. She must have realized she'd gone the wrong way, so she decided to come back in through the hall behind the kitchen. I was standing in her way, and she kicked me in the balls so she could get past."

The kid's face was as unreadable as a slab of granite. It was a trait he'd picked up from Nathaniel. The ability to remain stone-faced was worth its weight in gold in a courtroom.

"By the time I made it into the kitchen, she was holding that butcher knife. I tried to take it away from her, but she broke away and made a run for the front door. I remembered that forty-five, and I just went for it. I mean, for god's sake, she tried to kill me! What the hell was I supposed to do?"

Jaw clenched, Nathaniel didn't respond.

Cameron jabbed a finger at the knife. "She was going to kill me! You see my wrist, right?" For emphasis, he held up his hand. Sure enough, there were streaks of crimson that ended halfway down his forearm. "Was I supposed to let her get away and tell someone that I was the person who started it all? Have her press charges against me? Because you know that's what would happen!" He sneered. "How would that look to your precious voters, Dad?"

Cameron's tone was just below an outright shout when he finished. It was the most emotional display Nathaniel had seen from the kid in years, maybe even an entire decade. Either he was telling the truth, or he'd perfected the art of lying.

"Okay." Nathaniel's voice cut through the silence like a razor through butter. "Okay, you're right. Even though I understand what you were doing, that doesn't mean the cops will. Here's what I need you to do. And Cameron…"

In the split-second of silence, he willed every bit of vitriol into his gaze as he could manage. This was the expression he used on criminals just before he handed them their sentence.

Cameron swallowed.

"I need you to listen to every single word I tell you, and I need you to follow my instructions to the letter. Do you understand me."

The young man nodded. "Yes."

"Go take a shower and change your clothes. Fast. Make sure you put on something that'll cover the wound on your wrist. When the cops get here, all you need to say to them is that you had gone to your room for something, and you don't know what happened. That's all I need you to say. Absolutely nothing more than that. Do you understand me…" Nathaniel's voice broke, "son?"

Another nod. "Yes, I understand."

"Good." Nathaniel gestured to the stairwell. "Now, go get it done."

Without another word of acknowledgement, Cameron turned and sprinted up the stairs.

Nathaniel didn't have time to contemplate how much of his son's story was true, if any of it was true, or if all of it was true.

He had a son to protect. A reputation to protect.

He knew what he needed to do.

As he approached the fallen girl, he raised the forty-five and took aim at the side of the door. Even if he presented the police with a story of self-defense, they'd likely still test his hand and his clothes for gunshot residue. If the tests came back negative, their curiosity would be piqued.

And right now, the last thing Nathaniel needed was a cop's curiosity.

With a quiet sigh, he squeezed the trigger. Splinters exploded from the heavy door, but even the powerful round from the handgun didn't pierce through the barrier. It didn't matter. All that mattered now was that, when they tested him for gunshot residue, the results would be positive.

He pressed a small lever on the weapon's frame to release the magazine, and then he pulled back the slide to release the chambered round. As he set the handgun atop the end table where he had initially hidden the weapon, he handled the forty-five with the same tender care he would give to a newborn kitten.

Once the weapon, the loose round, and the magazine were arranged neatly on the smooth driftwood, he headed to the kitchen.

From the same coffee canister his son had mentioned, he retrieved a wad of twenties. The canister had started out as a secret hiding spot for his fund to buy Katrina birthday gifts, but once she died, he hadn't been able to bring himself to get rid of the stash. Each year, he added more to it just like he had when she was alive. He wasn't sure the value of the wad of money, but it was at least several thousand dollars.

For how long he stood with his vacant stare fixed on the cash, he wasn't sure.

The money was never meant to be used to cover up a young girl's death. He should have been able to use it to buy his wife jewelry or home improvement supplies.

Blinking away the sudden blur in his eyes, he closed the pantry door. "I'm sorry, Kat," he murmured.

He almost lost his nerve when he saw the way the girl had crumpled to the floor. The dark crimson pool beneath her had started to thicken and coagulate. This wasn't the first body he'd seen—after all, he'd been a defense lawyer before he was a judge.

But this was the freshest body he'd ever seen. All those before now had been on a silver table in the basement of the medical examiner's office.

I wonder what Dan Nguyen will think about this.

The thought was inane. Stupid. Pointless.

As he tucked the cash into the young woman's back pocket, he swallowed the sting of bile and stared at the butcher knife lying on the tiled floor. Without pausing to give himself time to hesitate, Nathaniel took out a handkerchief and used the snowy white cloth to pick the knife up by the handle.

He cursed as he dragged the blade along his forearm once, and then a second time, and gritted his teeth before stabbing the tip into his bicep. Hands trembling violently now, he carefully replaced the weapon in the young woman's hand.

Gritting his teeth against the sudden, searing pain, he rose to stand. From a back pocket, he produced his cell phone to dial 911.

He needed to do this. He had to do this. There was no other choice.

"I'm so sorry," he said, his face raised to the heavens as he spoke to his dead wife. "This is my fault. I'll fix it, I promise."

Entering the three digits, he made the call.

He was the reason that girl was dead, and he would pay whatever price the state saw fit.

Plus, maybe in prison, he'd finally find some peace.

25

At first, Aiden thought the buzz on the nightstand by his head was an alarm. He opened his eyes a slit, and he wondered why his alarm had gone off before the sun had even crested the horizon.

Blinking against the harsh light of the screen, he mentally shook the cobwebs from his brain. No, that wasn't his alarm. It was a few minutes before five in the morning.

He was receiving a phone call.

With a quiet groan, he plucked the device from its resting spot on the wireless charger and squinted at the screen. His early morning caller was none other than Detective Jordan Ramsey of the Richmond City Police.

Swiping the answer key, he raised the phone to his ear. "This is SSA Parrish." His voice was thick with sleep, but at five in the morning, he wasn't worried about how the tired slur made him appear.

"Parrish, hey," the man replied. "This is Detective Ramsey. Sorry to wake you up, but we just got an urgent request to pass one of our homicide cases over to the bureau. Well, we aren't technically sure if it's a homicide yet."

He had to suppress another groan. "Then why is it being passed to the bureau? And why are you calling me instead of Max Osbourne?"

The detective ignored the second question. "The victim is Peyton Hoesch. She's the only daughter of a decorated agent in the DEA. You might've heard of her, Agent Maryann Hoesch?"

"Maryann Hoesch?" Aiden sat up in bed, his mind working at full speed now. "As in, the Maryann Hoesch who ran point on the takedown of the De Luca family in D.C.?"

"Yeah, that Maryann Hoesch."

Aiden slid out of bed and paced to the window. "Does Maryann know her daughter is dead?"

The detective cleared his throat. "Yeah. She...she asked me to call you specifically. Well, not you-you. But an SSA or above. You just happen to be my contact."

"Jesus," Aiden breathed. "Okay. I'll head into the office. I'll be there in about an hour. I'll call you when I'm there."

"Roger that. Talk to you soon."

After he returned his phone to the nightstand, he shifted to face the woman in his bed. Her back was to him, and the meager city lights outlined the shape of her body beneath the sheets. As he reached out to run his hand along the curve of her hips, she groaned softly.

The faint scent of citrus still lingered on her even after the lengthy night they'd spent together in this bed. Her bed, not his.

Before he could be tempted to crawl back under the sheets for another round, he said, "I've got to go."

Fabric rustled as she moved to lay on her back and smiled sleepily at him. "I had fun."

Pulling on his pants, he returned her smile. "Me too."

In the dim light, her honey-brown eyes were darker, and her dark brown hair looked almost ebony. He was ashamed of how badly he wished they'd been the hair and eye color of another.

"Goodbye, Aiden," she murmured.

He grabbed his jacket, trying to remember her name. "Bye, Hannah." At least he thought that was right. "I'll talk to you later."

26

By the time Noah reached the Arkwell residence, Peyton Hoesch's body had already been taken to the medical examiner's office. Glancing around the foyer, he took a drink of the seasonal latte he had stopped to order on his way to the scene.

They had all been called in to the FBI office bright and early that morning, and since Caroline was safe and Ryan O'Connelly's undercover effort had yielded little and less, they'd been tasked with the investigation of Peyton Hoesch's death.

The homeowner, a state supreme court judge named Nathaniel Arkwell, claimed that Peyton had been caught stealing from him, and that she'd become violent when he confronted her.

Noah turned his attention to a man with dark blonde hair brushed straight back from his forehead. The first rays of daylight that filtered in through the foyer windows caught the gold badge around his neck.

With a slight smile—the best Noah could manage at six-thirty in the morning—he inclined his latte in the detective's direction like it was a glass of beer.

"Morning, Detective Ramsey." He followed the greeting with another long swig.

"Morning, Agent Dalton," the man greeted. From the inside of his black suit jacket, he produced a small pad of paper and a pen. "Well, let's take a walk through the scene then, shall we?"

Swallowing the gulp of coffee, Noah nodded. "Yeah. Even this early in the morning, I have enough wit to gather that this is where Peyton was shot?" He gestured to the dark stain on the tile just in front of the wooden door.

With the pen, Detective Ramsey pointed to the dried blood. "That's right. Based on a preliminary look at the spatter, she was standing in front of the door when she was shot. We'll know for sure once the ME gets a chance to look at her, but right now, it looks like she was shot in the back."

Noah lifted an eyebrow. "In the back? Didn't Arkwell say he killed her in self-defense?"

The detective spread his hands. "That's his story, Agent. Don't shoot the messenger. We're on the same team."

As he glanced down to the blood and then back to Detective Ramsey, Noah slowly shook his head. "That doesn't make sense. Why'd he say he shot her in the back?"

"He claims she used that knife right there. Or, I should say, the knife that was right there. We already photographed it and bagged it up as evidence. It's on the way to your lab, if it's not there already. But he claims that she came after him with a butcher knife when he confronted her about stealing a wad of cash out of a secret stash in a coffee canister."

Noah wrinkled his nose. "A coffee canister?"

Detective Ramsey scratched the side of his face with the pen as he looked to his notepad. "Yeah, there's something here that feels a little off to me too. I asked Arkwell how she'd know it was there, and he went on a spiel about how thieves know all the good hiding spots, and they know where to look for valuables. Some people hide cash in the freezer, some people stash it in empty boxes of cereal, and some stuff it in a canister in the back of their pantry."

With a glance to the dried blood stain, Noah nodded. "That makes a weird sort of sense, I suppose. If she was about to leave the house, then why'd he shoot her?"

The detective returned the pad of paper to his pocket. "According to him, he was still afraid for his life at that point. He said that she was coming after him again and turned just before he pulled the trigger. Virginia's got a version of the Stand Your Ground law, or the Castle Doctrine. Under that, it's still likely to be treated as a self-defense case."

Noah circled the blood stain and glanced over to the short hall that led to the dining room and then the kitchen. "How tall is Peyton Hoesch? How much does she weigh?"

From the corner of his eye, he saw the detective pull out the notepad. "Little over five foot, somewhere in the neighborhood of a hundred pounds."

"What about Nathaniel Arkwell?"

"Little shorter than you, about one-ninety. It looked like he was in decent shape."

"So, Arkwell's trying to tell us that a six-foot something grown-ass man in good physical shape was scared that a petite, five-foot tall, twenty-some-year-old girl was going to kill him?" He paused to gesture to the edge of the hall where Ramsey stood. "He was standing right about where you are, and he was afraid that, even though he was holding a semiautomatic handgun, the petite twenty-something was going to kill him? He was so scared that he pulled the trigger from a good ten to fifteen feet away? At the end of that hallway there?"

Detective Ramsey pursed his lips and nodded. "Yeah, like

I said, I see where you're coming from. But, just to play devil's advocate, remember that Arkwell's a judge. He has to deal with death threats all the time, and he's got to be on guard more often than not. He might have thought she was high on PCP or meth or something. I'm sure he's seen plenty of violent crimes committed by meth heads in his career."

Noah nodded. "Right, I suppose that makes sense. We've got to remember that we're not dealing with just an average civilian. Have y'all dusted for prints yet?"

The man pointed down a hallway. "The CSU is still here, but they're in the garage right now. Arkwell says that's where the confrontation started. What are you thinking you'll find by dusting for prints?"

"Arkwell said she was stealing some cash out of a canister in the pantry, so let's start there. Dust to see if she even touched the pantry, or the coffee can. Who else was in the house when it happened?"

"Just the son. Arkwell said he was upstairs in his room. Hoesch was over to work on a group project with his son, and the son went to grab something. According to Arkwell's statement, that's when Peyton Hoesch decided to start snooping through their pantry. He was watching television, but when he went into the kitchen to grab himself another beer, she was digging around in the pantry with a wad of cash in her back pocket." Detective Ramsey gestured in the direction of the kitchen.

With a quick nod, Noah started off down the short hall, Detective Ramsey close behind.

"Arkwell says he asked her what the hell she was doing, and that's when she bolted. She tried to run out through the garage, but as soon as she realized the door was locked with a keypad, she kicked him in the nuts and went through the kitchen. That's when she picked up the butcher knife."

Noah's eyes drifted to the wooden knife block, and he swallowed yet another disbelieving snort.

This case just got weirder and weirder.

As he paused to stand in front of the granite island, Detective Ramsey leaned against the counter.

"I'm not saying I think the guy's lying, not necessarily, anyway," Noah said. "But the whole reason I'm here is because Peyton Hoesch is Maryann Hoesch's daughter. The same Maryann Hoesch who headed up the task force to take down the De Lucas in D.C. I'm just having a real hard time believing that her kid would be sneaking around a rich judge's house looking for hidden cash, you follow me?"

Detective Ramsey nodded. "I follow you. Okay, but suppose that Peyton is a good kid, and suppose that Arkwell is lying. Why? The guy's a judge, he's got to know what'll happen if we find out."

Noah glanced to the knife block and shook his head. "That's the million-dollar question, isn't it? Honestly, Detective, we live in a fucked up world. Might be that Arkwell has a predilection for girls quite a bit younger than himself, and when she turned him down, he decided to shut her up for good."

The detective's mouth turned down in a look of distaste. "That's one explanation for it."

"It's just a theory, but I know for sure that something here stinks. Something about this whole situation doesn't sit right with me, and I'm willing to bet that the rest of the bureau will feel the same way when I bring this back to them." He tapped his finger against the paper sleeve of the cup.

He understood why the bureau had issued an all-hands notice for the murder of a fellow federal agent's daughter, but until now, he'd assumed that the statement of a judge would be a reliable account of the events that had transpired the night before. Now, however, he had more questions than answers.

The story itself read like testimony from a drunk witness, not a state supreme court judge.

After another swig of coffee, Noah nodded at the detective. "Thanks for the walk-through. Like I said, have the CSU dust the pantry and garage for prints. And, for the time being, leave the crime scene tape up. I know that Arkwell claims this was self-defense, but for right now, you and your people treat this like the scene of a homicide."

Detective Ramsey's expression turned grim. "Roger that. We'll send everything to the FBI lab, and I'll let you know if we get word of anything new on our end."

"Much appreciated. Take care." With a lift of his hand, he turned to make his way back outside.

Now, it was time for him to figure out whether or not Peyton Hoesch was the degenerate thief that Arkwell made her out to be.

And if she wasn't, then they'd have a brand-new heap of shit to add to the investigation into Caroline Peter's stalker.

A heap of shit with a judge on top.

27

Leaning back in the rickety chair, Winter crossed both arms over her chest. There were no silver bracelets around Nathaniel Arkwell's wrists. As of now, the man was merely in the interview room for routine questioning in a self-defense case. He wasn't even under arrest, and so far, he'd been cooperative.

To her side, Bobby stifled a yawn with one hand. She knew her fellow agent well enough to realize a strategic gesture when she saw one.

Nathaniel Arkwell's light brown eyes shifted over to Bobby, though his expression changed little. "Something wrong, Agent Weyrick?"

With a pleasant smile, Bobby shook his head.

Ever since his arrival at the field office, Nathaniel Arkwell had been unusually keen on using their names in his dialogue. The oddity was so striking that Winter wondered if he'd been implanted with a subdermal recording device, or if he was a cyborg altogether.

Feigning hesitance, Winter raised a hand. "I've got something, Mr. Arkwell. I was wondering if you could tell me what exactly it was about this five-foot-two, one-hundred-pound college student that made you fear for your life. No disrespect intended. I'm just trying to make sure we get a deep understanding of what happened. Maryann Hoesch has been a DEA agent for more than twenty years, and she wants answers. You're a veteran of the armed forces, aren't you?"

Jaw clenched, the man nodded. "I am. United States Navy, five years."

Winter wrote down the number, even though there was no need. She already knew everything about his military career. The logistics of it, anyway. "Five years. What did you do in the Navy?"

Beside the glint of indignation in his brown eyes, there was a flicker of a darker sentiment. Was it shame? Guilt? Anxiety?

"I was a mechanical engineer," Nathaniel said.

"For five years. And during that time, you saw combat, didn't you, Mr. Arkwell?" Winter raised her eyebrows and turned her attention to Bobby. "Agent Weyrick, you were in the military, weren't you?"

Bobby's mouth was a hard line as he nodded. "Sure was. Army. Did two tours in Iraq and Afghanistan."

Winter fixed Arkwell with a look of fake intrigue, but she didn't address the man when she spoke. Her and Bobby's hope was that a little bit of pressure would get the judge to come clean in the event he was lying to them. "So, Agent Weyrick, what would you do if you saw a petite college girl trying to steal a few grand out of your secret stash?"

Bobby feigned a pensive expression as he shrugged. "Well, I'll tell you what I wouldn't do. I wouldn't grab my service weapon and shoot her in the back when she was trying to run away."

Arkwell narrowed his eyes. "You didn't see the look in her eyes when—"

Winter raised a hand. "Neither did you, Mr. Arkwell. You shot her in the back. You shot the daughter of a DEA agent in the back. And during your statement, you mentioned, and I quote, 'The crazed look in her eyes,' and how you'd seen it before in people who were high. What are you going to say if we get the tox screen results back and it says she was completely clean and sober?"

Shadows moved along his face as he clenched and unclenched his jaw. "Then there was something else wrong with her. Clearly, the girl was unstable." He pushed up his sleeve and gestured to the bandage on his forearm. "She attacked me, Agents. She was at the door to try to leave, but I fully believed that, when she turned, she was going to come after me again. I wasn't willing to risk it."

In the seconds of quiet that followed, Winter pinned the man with a scrutinizing stare. All the little aspects of his story lined up with the evidence they'd collected so far. The shell casings for the forty-five were collected right where Nathaniel claimed he'd been standing when he fired the two rounds—one of which hit the door.

He'd agreed to provide a sample of his DNA in case they needed the analysis later in the case, and he'd volunteered for them to swab his hands for gunshot residue. But no matter how cooperative the man was, she couldn't shake the itch in the back of her head that insisted something was wrong.

Finally, Winter nodded. "Okay. What about the second shot? According to the neighbor who called the disturbance in, there were two shots fired, and one was fired at least a minute after the first. Could you explain that for us, Mr. Arkwell?"

With a weary sigh, he rubbed his eyes. "I fired the first shot as a warning. I thought it would be enough to scare her into leaving. We...exchanged some unpleasantries, and then she finally turned around. I've already told you what happened next."

Winter wanted to smack the man and curled her fingers into fists to keep from doing so. A petite, twenty-year-old girl armed with nothing more than a butcher knife had simply stood there while a round from a semiautomatic handgun splintered a chunk out of the door at her back, and that hadn't been enough to make her run? That made exactly zero sense.

However, no matter how much the act seemed to be inconsistent with reality, the physical evidence corroborated Arkwell's story.

Glancing to Bobby, she pushed to her feet before she said something she didn't need to say. "All right. Thank you, Mr. Arkwell. If you'll give us a little more time, we need to double-check a few things."

Without waiting for a response, she pulled open the heavy door to step into the hall. Before the latch had clicked into place, a familiar twinge of pain lanced through her temples.

Squeezing her eyes closed, she pinched the bridge of her nose.

"Whoa, you all right? You need me to grab you something?"

Before Bobby had finished the concerned query, she was shaking her head. They'd had a few conversations about their respective headaches. While Winter's were the result of the traumatic head injury she'd suffered at Douglas Kilroy's hands, Bobby's migraines were largely the result of bad luck in the genetics department. Either way, he had assured her he could sympathize with the sudden onslaught of unanticipated pain.

Though she knew better than to tell him the truth of her

headaches, she was glad to have another person with whom she could commiserate.

"I'm all right," she finally said, digging in her pocket for the tissue she always kept on the ready. "Give me just a second. I'll be right back."

With a quick nod and a concerned glance, Bobby stepped into the room behind the pane of two-way glass. Winter was surprised to see Aiden in the shadowy space, but she didn't have time to puzzle over his unexpected appearance. She needed to make it to the ladies' room before she collapsed into a heap, or before blood started to gush from her nose.

Groaning, she hurried down the hall and shoved her way into the bathroom. At quarter 'til seven in the morning, she wasn't surprised to find the space unoccupied.

As if the headache was a living creature that could sense the close proximity of relative privacy, another sizzle of pain flashed through her head.

By now, closing and locking the stall door, wadding up toilet paper to press to her nose, and slumping down in the corner where her feet wouldn't be visible was a bizarre sort of routine. In a strange way, the familiarity of the whole process was a comfort.

Back during the Kilroy investigation, the visions had literally and figuratively brought her to her knees. But now, although the headaches were less intense, she had learned to spot the signs that told her to find a quiet place to succumb to her strange sixth sense.

Pressing the tissue to her nose, she slid down the cool tile wall to sit. As she squeezed her eyes closed, she half-expected to lose consciousness.

Instead, she felt as if she'd closed her eyes just to teleport through the void of space and time. Either she'd teleported, or she'd stepped onto the set of a movie.

In the depiction her mind presented to her, she was at the

intersection of a rundown industrial neighborhood. Ruddy orange streetlights glinted eerily off the worn asphalt. The dilapidated buildings looked familiar, though she couldn't place the scene at first.

A couple young women milled about, and when Winter spotted a petite blonde with large, blue eyes, she realized why the area looked so familiar. The blonde was Alice, and the intersection was where she and a few of her friends conducted the majority of their business.

A less familiar blonde emerged from the shadows of an alley as a spotless black sedan approached. The engine was little more than a quiet hum, and the ruddy streetlights glinted off the Mercedes emblem affixed to the front bumper. Though Alice gave the car a cursory glance, she turned around and made her way back to the entryway of a tall building as the blonde approached the driver.

Alice might have looked young, but she'd been around the streets long enough to recognize a sketchy situation when she saw one. Sometimes, she tried to talk the younger, inexperienced girls out of putting themselves in a potentially harmful situation, but she wasn't always successful. As she'd told Winter, "Money talks and bullshit walks."

As Winter closed the distance between herself and the blonde who'd approached the Mercedes, she took in a sharp breath.

She recognized the silvery shade of her hair, the hue of her pale blue eyes. Only Winter's most prominent memory of those eyes was watching them glaze over as the last of the life left the young woman's body.

"Dakota," she heard herself say.

Those hauntingly familiar eyes snapped over in Winter's direction, but the driver of the vehicle stretched out an arm to beckon her closer.

With a sharp intake of breath, Winter sat bolt upright as

she was ripped out of the unnerving scene and deposited back into the ladies' room in the heart of the FBI field office.

"Oh my god," she murmured to herself.

Unsurprisingly, the tissue in her hand was splotched with red.

A black Mercedes, spotless, even though it had rained that day. Just like Katya had said. And who drove a black Mercedes? Whose name had been mentioned by both Ryan O'Connelly and Oliver Jacobs during the dinner party?

"Shit, shit," she spat as she pushed herself to stand.

Nathaniel Arkwell drove a black Mercedes sedan, and Nathaniel Arkwell was a member of the same group that Ryan O'Connelly had infiltrated.

Spitting four-letter words every step of the way, Winter shoved her way back into the main part of the bathroom, tossed her bloodied tissue, and washed her hands. Before all the droplets of water had even been displaced, she was back in the hallway.

She breathed a sigh of relief when she opened the door of the small office just off the interrogation room. Aiden's pale eyes shifted over to her as the door fell closed. As soon as the latch clicked into place, she flicked the lock on the lever handle.

"What?" Aiden barked before concern transformed his features. "What's going on?"

Though the initial edginess might have been her imagination, she could have sworn he had been annoyed by her sudden appearance at first. Biting back a smartass response, she took a step forward and gestured to Nathaniel.

"That's him. That's our guy."

Aiden gave his head a little shake. "He is? For what?"

She paused to arrange her racing thoughts before she spoke. "For Caroline Peters and Dakota Ronsfeldt. Katya said there was a black Mercedes that picked up Dakota the last time she and Alice saw her. A black Mercedes sedan that was clean even though it had rained that day. I saw it. I watched him pull up to Dakota, and I watched her get into that car."

"A vision?"

Her nostrils flared as she nodded. She still wasn't sure how she felt about that word. "Yes. A vision. Just now."

"Damn," he spat. "Nathaniel Arkwell? Did you see him? Or just the car?"

"It's not a coincidence. You know it's not, and I know you don't believe in coincidences. What are the odds that Nathaniel just happens to be associated with a dead girl who matches our demographic? A dead girl killed by a guy who drives the same type of car that was seen picking up Dakota Ronsfeldt less than a week before a video of her murder was posted on the dark web?"

Aiden kept his eyes on hers as the seconds of silence ticked away. Finally, though the gesture was slow, almost reluctant, he nodded. "How do we prove it? We'd need a warrant to search anything that wasn't in plain sight around where Peyton was killed. Not to mention, I'm sure Arkwell owns some other properties. We'd have to search those too, if we wanted to be thorough. And the car."

Winter pursed her lips as she mulled over his assertion. As it stood, despite the holes in Arkwell's story, they hadn't collected enough damning evidence to secure a warrant for the rest of the house, much less any other property in his name. If they went to a judge with the theory that Nathaniel Arkwell also happened to be the voyeuristic murderer they'd sought for the past week and a half, they'd be laughed out of the chambers.

Not only was Nathaniel Arkwell wealthy, but the man was a state supreme court judge. If they wanted a warrant, the order had to be ironclad.

For the remainder of the investigation, their steps had to

be carried out according to a strict, specific plan. A plan that would give the defense attorney zero room to wiggle or produce a legal loophole or technicality.

Finally, she returned her gaze to his. "We could get a forensic psychological evaluation of him."

To her surprise, he shook his head. "I don't see how that'd help us get closer to a search warrant."

More often than not, he was the one to suggest that they bring in Autumn's expertise—or the expertise of Shadley and Latham, according to official documents.

As he returned his attention to the glass, Winter pressed her fingertips against her eyes. "Well, what else do we have to go on right now?"

"Once the tox screen results get back to us, and once Dan has a chance to write up the official cause of death, we'll have more to go on." The twinge of irritability was back in his voice.

She crossed her arms. "You know that probably won't be enough for a warrant. Besides, wouldn't it be better to have more information rather than less?"

With one hand, he rubbed his eyes and sighed. "We can't just call Autumn whenever we're not sure how to proceed in an investigation."

Winter studied his face. "Yes, we can. That's literally her job. When we're running low on leads, we call her and her firm, and they help us figure out a new lead based on psychological evidence. You know, evidence that we're not qualified to produce."

Though the gesture seemed grudging, he turned to meet her unimpressed stare. As much as she wanted to prod him for more details on his sudden reluctance to reach out to a person he normally didn't hesitate to contact, she pushed aside the nagging curiosity. "Look, if anyone will be able to tell us whether or not Nathaniel Arkwell matches the profile we've come up with, it's going to be Autumn. At the very least, it can't hurt."

Jaw clenched, he nodded. "Fine. I'll contact Shadley and Latham."

Winter knew Autumn's capabilities, and she knew the woman would be able to tell with just a handshake whether or not Nathaniel Arkwell was the serial murderer they'd chased after for the past week and a half.

Because if Nathaniel Arkwell wasn't the man who had murdered Dakota Ronsfeldt, then there was still a serial killer running amok in Richmond.

28

When Autumn Trent arrived at the FBI field office, she was surprised to be greeted by Noah Dalton. According to the tall man, Winter and Bobby were preparing to question Nathaniel Arkwell, and Aiden Parrish was attending to business in the BAU. Though she was glad to see her friend, the absence of Aiden Parrish—her usual FBI escort—struck her as odd.

However, she didn't give the oddity much thought as she followed Noah to a briefing room to discuss the Nathaniel Arkwell case. What appeared to be a straightforward instance of self-defense had quickly devolved into a murky web of lies and half-truths.

And then, there was Winter's vision.

Though the piece of insight wasn't part of any official FBI record, she and Noah both knew that Winter's visions were just as reliable as any piece of physical evidence they might have uncovered.

Nathaniel Arkwell was, in some capacity, responsible for the disappearance of Dakota Ronsfeldt. Now, all they had to do was prove it.

As they headed to the interrogation room, Autumn half-expected Aiden to wander into their path. But other than a vaguely familiar forensics tech, they encountered no one.

Noah's green eyes flicked to her as he gestured to the pane of two-way glass. "Well, that's him. State Supreme Court Judge Arkwell."

The door swung closed behind Autumn as she moved to stand at her friend's side. "He shot Peyton Hoesch?"

Noah shrugged. "Shot her in the back, as best as we can tell. The ME should be wrapping up his evaluation here soon."

She glanced back to the glass. "He hasn't asked for a lawyer? Why?"

With yet another shrug, Noah crossed his arms over his chest. "Not really sure. Probably because he's a judge, if I had to guess. Might be that he's just representing himself."

Autumn studied the man through the glass a moment longer, her finger tapping her bottom lip, before turning her attention back to Noah. "Guys in positions of power like this don't usually take their fate into their own hands. Even if he's passed the Bar, especially because he's passed the Bar, he would be smart enough to get some high-priced defense lawyer in here to argue on his behalf."

Eyebrow arched, Noah flashed her a curious glance. "Why do you think he's in there by himself, then?"

The tapping continued. "Guilty conscience, maybe. He might feel bad about what happened to Peyton, and now he's facing the consequences himself because he feels like it's what he deserves."

Noah didn't appear convinced. "That doesn't sound like something a serial killer would do."

"That's not necessarily true." She returned her scrutiny to the man on the other side of the glass. "Jeffrey Dahmer confessed to all his crimes after he was caught. I don't know that he necessarily felt guilty, but he just accepted that the jig was up and that it was time to face the music. If Arkwell is the guy who killed Dakota, then that might have something to do with why he hasn't asked for a lawyer."

Stuffing his hands into his pockets, Noah rocked back on his heels. "Everything we've got so far is circumstantial at best, but the more it piles up, the more suspicious this whole thing gets. Ryan O'Connelly, our informant for this case, remembered Arkwell from the group of wealthy elite he infiltrated. We've got someone out looking for our witness, Katya. She said she didn't get a good look at the guy, but we'll see if she recognizes Arkwell."

As Autumn scrutinized the judge's vacant stare, the interview room door swung inward to admit Bobby Weyrick and Winter. Arkwell jerked to attention, almost as though he'd been in a trance before the interruption. When his eyes shifted to the two agents, there wasn't the usual spark of defiance or glint of determination. The man looked defeated. Worn down.

Narrowing her eyes, Autumn took another step closer to the pane of glass. The shadows beneath Nathaniel Arkwell's brown eyes were more pronounced, and he looked like he hadn't slept in days. He was harrowed, but beside the worry was a familiar, albeit unexpected, flicker.

"He's scared." She pulled her gaze away from Arkwell as she glanced to Noah.

Noah lifted one broad shoulder. "Well, he finally got caught."

Autumn had been called to the FBI office because her friends thought they'd come across a serial killer, but Autumn wasn't so sure that Arkwell was the subject of their query. She didn't even need to touch him to feel that certainty. She just knew it.

"Look, I'll just come out and say it. Based on my first

impression, I don't think that's your guy. Maybe he shot Peyton Hoesch, and maybe he didn't, but I don't think he's your serial killer. The guy who recorded himself slitting a woman's throat isn't the haggard-looking father of two in there."

The silence that enveloped them dragged on for several long seconds before Noah finally spoke. Autumn was prepared to defend her stance, to go on a tirade about the common traits of sociopaths. She was well-versed in playing devil's advocate.

Instead, he merely nodded. "They're in there to get his official statement. Whether or not you think he's the guy who killed Dakota Ronsfeldt, there's no doubt that he's full of it about what went down with Peyton Hoesch."

Jaw clenched, Autumn returned the nod. "Agreed."

"So." Winter's voice cut through the awkward moment of tension that threatened to overtake them. "Mr. Arkwell, let's go through this one more time. You said that Peyton Hoesch was in the pantry snooping through your coffee canister looking for cash, right?"

"That's right."

Autumn drew her brows together and flashed Noah a look as she watched her friend through the glass. "A coffee canister?"

"That's exactly what I said." Noah inclined his chin at the glass. "Peyton Hoesch was the daughter of a DEA agent. She was an LGBTQ advocate at VCU, and she was studying sociology so she could get her Master's in Social Work. When Peyton was ten or eleven, her mother, Maryann Hoesch, started taking her with her every week when she went to help out at a no-kill cat shelter."

"Jesus," Autumn breathed. "And a girl like that just goes pilfering through pantries hoping to find some cash?"

Noah didn't answer. He didn't need to. The story was ridiculous.

In the other room, Winter's intent stare was fixed on Judge Arkwell. "Mr. Arkwell, you shot the daughter of a federal agent in the back from about fifteen feet away while all she was holding was a knife. I'd like to implore you to consider how that must sound from our point of view. You said that she was stealing from you, but I'm not so sure that's exactly how it all happened."

Arkwell opened his mouth to interject, but Winter cut him off with an upraised hand. Autumn had never witnessed her friend in action, and between her steely expression and her calm, icy tone, the sight was impressive.

Rising from her seat, Winter propped both hands atop the table and leaned in to glare at the judge. "I'm going to give you one last chance to tell us what really happened. Castle Doctrine or no, if you keep lying to us, I'm going to get a warrant to rip apart your house. After that, I'll take every single piece of information they find, and I'll hang you with it."

Glancing to Noah, Autumn nodded her approval. Damn impressive.

The judge's countenance changed little as he shook his head. "I've told you everything."

Noah heaved a sigh. "Guess he's not ready to come clean. I was hoping you'd get to weigh in on his statement, but it looks like he's going to feed them the same line he's been spouting since he got here."

With an upraised brow, Autumn turned to her friend. "What now, then?"

He reached into the pocket of his dress pants to produce a key ring. "Come on. Let's talk to the ME. Maybe if we get some more information from him, we can use it to get Arkwell to talk."

"What about the other girls? The whole serial killer angle?"

Noah looked on the verge of laughing but kept his mouth carefully closed. "That's your territory, darlin'."

Great.

Autumn knew she'd be able to tell whether or not Nathaniel was the man who'd killed Dakota as soon as she shook his hand, but she wasn't sure how she'd justify her conclusion to anyone other than Winter.

For the first chunk of her life, Autumn had grown up in an impoverished neighborhood in Minneapolis, and another in Minnetonka, Minnesota. In the shady area where she'd come of age, people didn't trust cops. They all knew how the city police were inclined to tunnel vision, how they honed in on one person to the exception of all others.

Even though Autumn knew better than to think her friends at the Federal Bureau of Investigation had the same propensity for dishonesty, her old misgivings were difficult to assuage. She didn't doubt that there was more to Nathaniel Arkwell's encounter with Peyton Hoesch than he let on, but she wasn't so sure he was the man who had abducted five young women and recorded himself slitting the throat of one.

To be sure, she didn't have a soft spot for Nathaniel Arkwell's fate. By all accounts, Peyton Hoesch was a genuinely good person, and if she hadn't been killed by the jackass in the interview room, she could have gone on to help people in need, just like her mother. If Arkwell was responsible for her death or had a hand in covering up what had really happened to her, then as far as Autumn was concerned, he could rot.

But tunnel vision didn't just mean an innocent person faced imprisonment for a crime they didn't commit.

Tunnel vision—in this case—meant that there was a

murderer on the loose. A murderer who would undoubtedly strike again.

29

I hadn't managed to take much with me when the cops shooed me out of the house. Aside from the clean clothes on my back, I had my wallet, keys, and my school backpack. Even then, the cops rummaged through my bag before they let me leave. Apparently, based on the suspicion in the detective's eyes, they weren't completely sold on the good judge's rendition of events.

I knew why he'd fired the second shot, but I had no idea how he intended to explain it to the cops. They'd look for defensive wounds, and when they didn't find any, their curiosity would be piqued. There was blood beneath Peyton's nails—my blood. Not my father's.

Unless Nathaniel gave them a believable story to discourage the need for DNA testing, they'd eventually find out that the man was full of it. Then, well…

Then they'd come for me. And when they came for me, part of me knew that it would only be a matter of time before they discovered the bodies. I was confident in my ability to avoid detection, but I wasn't naïve or delusional.

Just because I knew they would come for me didn't mean I had to let them find me.

If I ran now, I'd have enough of a head start that I could disappear. I could fly to Panama or another country that didn't have extradition laws, and I could live out the rest of my days in a tropical paradise. With the money I could pull from the bank and from the secret stashes in the lake house, I'd be set for years.

The plan seemed foolproof, but I couldn't shake a nagging sensation in the back of my head.

Even though Nathaniel had all but leapt at the opportunity to take the fall for me—to throw himself in the line of fire to redeem himself in his own eyes—it was his fault I was in this mess to begin with. If he hadn't been such a bad parent, none of this would have happened.

I grated my teeth as I flicked on the turn signal to merge onto an on-ramp.

If I left now, I knew the failure would follow me no matter where I went. Whoever I pretended to be, Nathaniel's shadow would always loom over my life like a storm cloud.

Before I left, I had to make sure he'd remember what he had done. I had to make sure he knew that his last-ditch effort to mend the canyon between us was folly. I wanted him to know that I was aware he hadn't done any of this for my benefit. In his eyes, he'd only ever had one child.

Soon, however, he'd have none.

Since Maddie was under eighteen, she'd been sent to stay with Nathaniel's sister and her husband after the cops had hauled Nathaniel off for questioning. Though I was headed east—the opposite direction of my aunt and uncle's house—I would be back soon enough.

I knew Nathaniel wouldn't care if I disappeared, but he would care if Maddie did the same.

Though there were a few other handguns stashed

throughout the house, I knew better than to think I'd be able to sneak through the crime scene tape to retrieve one of them. A year ago, I'd stashed a couple rifles and a semiautomatic handgun at the lake house.

The same lake house where I'd taken Dakota Ronsfeldt and the other four hookers. Nathaniel hadn't been there in years—ever since he bought a beach house in Newport News—and he had no idea what I'd done with the basement. Even if he thought to visit, I was the only one with a key to the lowest level of the place.

I'd pay a visit to the girls before I left.

It was the least I could do.

NOAH HAD BEEN eager to speak to Dan Nguyen about Peyton Hoesch's injuries, so he skipped the usual pit stop to buy the man pastries and coffee. Besides, he and Winter had been to the medical examiner's office less than a week ago. Dan's monthly quota of free baked goods had been filled.

As Autumn shoved the car door closed, Noah glanced over to her. "You ready for this?"

"Ready for what? You haven't told me what this little field trip is all about."

His laugh sounded closer to a snort than a chuckle. No, he hadn't told her that they were heading to the medical examiner's office to look at a dead body. He didn't want to give her a chance to chicken out.

"You're right…it's a surprise."

She waved a dismissive hand as they started toward the entrance to the nondescript building. "Let me guess. This is a skating rink. I'll have to murder you if you say yes."

Noah grinned, even though he knew he'd be skating on

thin ice with her the second she realized what it really was. "Not quite."

He beckoned for Autumn to follow him past the reception area. "Come on, we need to head downstairs."

With a wordless nod, she stayed behind him as they walked to the end of the hall and down a short flight of steps. Pushing open a set of swinging metal doors in the middle of the downstairs hall, he glanced back to Autumn.

Her expression was calm and collected, but as she stepped into the exam room after him, a cloud settled in to darken her bright eyes. Noah snapped his head around to follow her line of sight.

From where he'd been focused on a clipboard, Dan opened his mouth to greet them as he glanced up from the piece of paper. When his gaze settled on Autumn, whatever salutation he'd been about to utter died before it left his lips.

He recovered from the moment of awe in short order, but the mixture of surprise and irritability had lasted long enough to raise Noah's curiosity. Autumn had been a student of Dan's at VCU, and Noah couldn't help but wonder what had transpired in the time they'd known one another.

"Afternoon, Dan," Noah said, breaking the trance.

The medical examiner's dark eyes shifted to him, and he nodded. "Afternoon, Agent Dalton. Miss Trent."

"*Doctor* Trent." The annoyance in her tone was unmistakable.

Now, in addition to asking Autumn about her disdain for roller skating, he'd have to ask what had transpired in her and Dan's history to sour their attitude toward one another.

"Right. Sorry." Dan took in a breath and waved his clipboard. "You two are here about Peyton Hoesch, right?"

Noah nodded. "We are. What can you tell us about how she died? Arkwell doesn't deny shooting her in the back, and based on how the cops found her body, that's the only possible angle he could have shot her from."

The misgivings dissipated from Dan's face as he glanced to the clipboard and then the body at the other end of the room. "That's right. Point of entry was her back, at the bottom of her right lung. Based on the amount of internal damage, her death would have been nearly instant. The bullet shredded her lung and nicked a couple major arteries. Much of the bleeding was internal, but she bled out and suffocated at the same time."

Noah looked to the sheet that covered Peyton's body. "Jesus. What about defensive wounds, signs of a struggle, anything like that?"

Dan nodded as he took a step toward the silver exam table. With a cursory glance to Noah and Autumn, he pulled the sheet from Peyton's face. Her skin was ashen, her eyelids dark, and her ebony hair was splayed out behind her head.

She didn't look real. They never did.

With the pen, Dan gestured to the side of her head. "She sustained a pretty heavy blow to the back of her head before she was killed, and bruising around her throat suggests that she was strangled."

Noah met Autumn's gaze. "What can you tell us about the blow to the back of her head? How much damage did it do?"

Dan cast a pensive look at Peyton's body. "It was a solid blow, but it didn't knock her unconscious. She would have been a bit disoriented, maybe a little lacking in hand-eye coordination."

Nathaniel Arkwell's self-defense explanation was losing more credibility with each passing second. If any more circumstantial evidence piled up, they would have enough for an arrest warrant even without irrefutable physical evidence. Though conviction in a trial required proof beyond a reasonable doubt, arrests were made based on the rule of probable cause.

"Sexual assault?" Noah asked, and the medical examiner shook his head.

"No. The girl was sexually active, but no tears or other marks of forced penetration."

Thanks to Dan Nguyen's thorough examination, Noah was sure they'd crossed the probable cause threshold.

"Arkwell claims he killed her in self-defense," Autumn said. "He claims he feared for his life."

Dan's brows furrowed. "So, he shot her in the back?"

Noah shook his head. "There's a lot about his story that doesn't make sense. He didn't say anything about strangling her or hitting her on the back of the head."

As Dan tucked the pen back into his pocket, he looked thoughtful. "We found some evidence underneath her fingernails too. Your perp will have defensive wounds somewhere on his body. I'd say the location of those defensive wounds ought to tell you quite a bit about what he was doing before he had to 'defend himself.'"

Noah scowled. "Considering we haven't seen them yet, I'd say that about answers the question."

Even as he nodded his agreement, Dan's expression darkened. "To be absolutely sure, we'll run the DNA under her nails against Nathaniel Arkwell's DNA. There are no wounds on her body to indicate she might have scratched herself. Have your agents strip him to look for defensive wounds. If you need a court order, you ought to have all the evidence you need now. But based on the injuries to the victim's neck and head, it's safe to rule out a self-defense theory. Agent Dalton, Dr. Trent, I'm ruling Peyton Hoesch's death a homicide."

30

As soon as Winter got the call from Noah about Dan's findings, she hurried to the forensics lab to personally request a rush on the DNA they'd collected from Nathaniel. Specifically, she asked the forensics team to compare Nathaniel's DNA to the skin cells taken from beneath Peyton's fingernails. She was also interested in all the places the girl's fingerprints had been found.

When she arrived back downstairs, she made her way to the closet-sized space behind the interview room. The makeshift office turned storage area had become their forward operating base for the questioning of Nathaniel Arkwell, and she wasn't surprised to see that Bobby Weyrick and Aiden Parrish were both present.

"You checked him for defensive wounds?" She posed the question before the door had even latched closed.

Bobby nodded, but his expression was grim. "We checked, but there was nothing there aside from the cuts from the knife. He's got a bruise on one knee, but it's small and looks a couple days old. Probably just from smacking it into a desk or something."

Winter turned her attention to Aiden. "No scratches? How? Dan said that she didn't scratch herself, so who did she scratch?"

"Not Nathaniel Arkwell," Bobby muttered.

Glancing back and forth between the two men, Winter held out her hands. "You checked his whole body, right?"

Bobby nodded again. "Had him strip down to his underwear. Believe it or not, he agreed when we asked him to do it. There was nothing. No scratches."

Aiden's intent stare was on the pane of glass. "Maybe he had an accomplice. Someone who got away before the cops arrived."

Winter's phone pinged, and when she opened the file sent by the forensic team, she let out a breath. "Peyton's fingerprints were found in the kitchen but nowhere near the pantry," she told the men. "Well, gentlemen, looks like self-defense is out the window. This is officially a homicide case."

As he rested both palms atop the table, Aiden leaned forward, his pale eyes laser-focused on Nathaniel Arkwell. "Go read him his rights. Let him know we aren't buying his self-defense explanation anymore and turn up the heat. Make sure he knows he won't get special treatment just because he's a judge."

Though Winter was tempted to implore Aiden to conduct the interrogation, she kept the request to herself. During the investigation into a corrupt Baltimore detective, Aiden had managed to crack a Russian mafia foot soldier. She could only imagine that getting a confession from a wealthy judge would be a walk in the park for him.

But no matter how proficient the Supervisory Special Agent was at interviewing a suspect, Winter wasn't about to ask the man to do her job for her. After all, it had been her and Bobby's combined effort that had elicited a confession from the corrupt detective himself.

Rising to his feet, Bobby combed a hand through his hair and nodded at her. "All right. Let's go see what this dickhead has to say for himself."

Without a knock or announcement, Winter shoved open the door to the interview room and strode into the dim space. Once he closed the door, Bobby retrieved a pair of silver handcuffs and held them up for Nathaniel to see.

"Nathaniel Arkwell," he paused to open the silver bracelet, "you're under arrest for the unlawful killing of Peyton Hoesch. You have the right to remain silent. Anything you say can and will be used against you in a court of law."

Nathaniel's eyes went wide as Bobby snapped the handcuff around one wrist. The agent then threaded the bind through a metal loop on the table and attached it to the other wrist.

As he straightened to his full height, Bobby crossed his arms as he continued the Miranda warning, making sure each and every word was precise. This was a freaking judge, after all. He, more than anyone, would know which hoops he could jump through. He finished with, "Do you understand these rights as I have read them?"

The judge shifted his wide-eyed stare from Bobby to Winter and then back. "I-I do. What, what do you mean? Murder? I told you what happened. It was self-defense! She was going to kill me with that knife!"

Winter leaned down until they were eye to eye. "Doubtful, Mr. Arkwell. You see, we got her tox screen back, and she was..." She narrowed her eyes. "She was as sober as a judge."

Resting both hands on the table, Bobby pinned Arkwell with a venomous stare. "So, that right there is enough to poke a few holes in your story, don't you think? You see, Mr. Arkwell, I was in the military for six years. We're about the same height. And honestly, I might be a little thinner than you. You're in pretty good shape, especially for someone your age."

Winter pulled out a rickety chair and moved to sit. Arkwell's eyes darted from one agent to the next as he struggled to decide where to place his focus.

"Even if a girl Peyton's size had a butcher knife and she was facing me," Bobby straightened to his full height, "I wouldn't have gone out of my way to pick up a gun to shoot her. One solid punch to the head would've knocked her out cold, don't you think? She's only a hundred pounds. I could probably bench press her, and I'm sure you could."

Winter didn't give Nathaniel time to insert a word edgewise. "Not to mention the fact that she was already injured by then, right?"

Waving an appreciative index finger at her, Bobby nodded. "Right. Because someone had actually punched her in the back of the head. Or, if they didn't punch her, they hit her with something. The cops didn't see anything at the scene, but we'll see what we can dig up after we get a warrant for the rest of the house."

As best as Winter could tell, the cloud of confusion on Nathaniel's face was genuine. "Sh-she was injured in the scuffle. I told you that I followed her into the garage when she tried to leave. That's when I tried to just knock her out, like you said. But she didn't go down, and then she kicked me."

Anger burned in Winter's veins as she scooted forward. "There's something you're not telling us, Mr. Arkwell."

Nathaniel started to shake his head, but before he could speak, Bobby cut him off. "You want to hear what I think happened?"

Winter turned to her fellow agent and nodded, playing along. "I'm interested."

As he scratched the side of his face, Bobby made his way

to stand behind Nathaniel. "You said your son was upstairs, right? In his room, looking for something?"

"That's right." The judge's voice was a croak.

"And you were in the living room, watching some TV. I think your son went upstairs, and you took the opportunity to make your move. You propositioned this pretty young girl, threatened her, probably. You wanted her to come to your room with you for a little fun. I mean, it's been quite a while since your wife passed, hasn't it? Got to fill that void somehow."

As Bobby went on, Winter kept her scrutinizing stare on Nathaniel Arkwell. Anger clouded his light brown eyes as he clenched his jaw and shook his head.

"No. None of that happened. I'd never do that to a-a young woman, to a girl." Anger rolled off the man in waves. Either he was deep in denial about his shameful predilection, or he was truly offended by the idea that a couple FBI agents would assume he was a rapist.

She and Bobby exchanged vehement glances, and he nodded. They were on the same page.

Arkwell's outburst was unexpected, and truth be told, it was bizarre. Inconsistent, even. Until now, the man had been as cool as a cucumber.

Taking on a friendly countenance, like an old friend posing a question, Bobby leaned against the far wall. "Why'd you strangle her then?"

Though the expression was fleeting, a measure of unabashed shock flitted over Nathaniel's face. The rise and fall of his chest had quickened, and a flush had risen to his cheeks.

And then, as if it had never been there at all, the ire vanished. The cadence of his breathing was still rapid, but the ire that had been about to boil over had dropped down to a simmering irritability.

Nathaniel laced his fingers together. "I grabbed her by the throat to push her away from me after she'd grabbed the knife." His voice was cool and calm, his body language impassive and almost unreadable.

This was the judge in him, Winter knew. The training that forced him to remain neutral during the most heinous of trials.

Winter lifted an eyebrow. "Why didn't you tell us that to start with?"

Shaking his head, he turned his eyes down to his hands. "Didn't cross my mind. I figured that more or less went with the territory of self-defense."

As she looked back to Bobby, Winter gritted her teeth.

In one moment, the man had seemed ready to stammer out a confession, and the next, he was made of stone.

If she wasn't so sure of what she'd seen in her vision, she would have doubted herself now.

She'd double-checked the DMV records to be sure that Nathaniel Arkwell owned a black, new model Mercedes sedan, and the database confirmed that he did. Though she hadn't caught a clear picture of the entire license plate, she could swear that the first couple letters matched what was listed in the DMV database.

But now, she wondered. She wondered why Nathaniel was so defensive, and why the idea that he'd tried to molest Peyton Hoesch seemed to offend him such a great deal. Much more than shooting her in the back.

They had a clear picture of how Peyton had been killed, but at the same time, they knew nothing about the events that led up to her death.

31

Aiden didn't think he had been consciously avoiding Autumn that day, but when she and Noah Dalton entered the briefing room, he felt an unmistakable pang of guilt. Though he half-expected her to ignore his presence altogether, her face brightened when her green eyes met his. As Noah took his spot behind Winter and Bobby, Autumn picked her way over to where he stood on the other side of the room.

Silver was threaded through the teal fabric of her button-down shirt, and the color made her eyes seem brighter. Though the matching silver flats and black slacks weren't as dressy as the designer heels he'd seen her wear a few times, she looked every bit the successful professional.

"No Louboutins today?" He couldn't help the smile that crept to his face when she chuckled.

She shook her head. "No, not today. How do you know so much about women's fashion, anyway?"

The smile was still on his lips as he shrugged. "The red sole makes them pretty distinctive. My ex used to wear them too."

Her eyes flicked to Sun Ming, and he had to fight to keep from cringing.

"Different ex," he said.

As she returned her attention to him, her smile took on a sarcastic edge. "Well, she had good taste then." White light glinted off the band of her silver watch as she raised her wrist to check the time. "Looks like we've still got a few minutes. I was hoping to get your take on Nathaniel Arkwell so far. I've got an interview scheduled with him in a little bit, and I'm curious to hear your impression."

He should have been glad she cut right to business, but to his continued surprise, he was disappointed. With a quick glance to the rest of the room, he was satisfied that no one was paying special attention to their conversation. Though he had no intent to hide his thoughts about Nathaniel Arkwell from the rest of the agents in the room, he also didn't want to start a debate with any of them regarding the likelihood of Arkwell's involvement in the disappearance and potential murder of five young women.

"I think he's lying about what happened to Peyton Hoesch." Aiden lowered his voice, and her expression turned curious. "But I don't think he's the serial killer we're looking for. I think if he was, then there would be a history of behavior to back it up."

Autumn nodded. "I agree. But how thorough was the investigation into his background?"

This time, it was his turn to fix her with a sarcastic smile. "That's your territory, Dr. Trent. It's why you're here."

Leaning against the wall at his side, she shrugged. "Fair enough. What's your theory on what happened to Peyton?"

He crossed his arms and glanced around the room again. "He might not be a rapist or a serial killer, but I think he made a move on Peyton, and she didn't take it well. He was probably surprised, and he overreacted, so the confrontation turned violent. He might *think* he acted in self-defense, but he's actually the one who instigated the whole incident in the first place. That's why he acted so offended when Winter accused him of assaulting Peyton."

Her eyes met his as she nodded. "Because he wasn't trying to assault her, at least not in his mind. He wanted consensual sex, but she wasn't having it. It's plausible."

"Plausible, but there are still holes in that story too." He held up a hand. "The blood and skin cells the ME found under her fingernails. That wasn't from an old confrontation, and Nathaniel didn't have any wounds that matched. Also, her fingerprints weren't on the pantry where he accused her of stealing money. Then, of course, the fact that he shot her in the back. But part of that is explained by the theory that she turned him down."

"He might not have wanted her to tell anyone else about the encounter, and that might have biased his assessment of how much danger he was in. In a way, he was looking for a reason to turn the incident into a self-defense situation." She tapped a finger on her chin. "Huh. Interesting."

He arched an eyebrow at her. "Interesting? What do you mean?"

Shaking her head, she waved a dismissive hand. "Nothing. I'll find out after this briefing."

As if on cue, Max Osbourne strode into the room and closed the door behind himself. He nodded a greeting to Aiden before he took his place behind the wooden podium. "Ladies and gentlemen, we've gotten some news back from the chief medical examiner." He paused to gesture to Winter and Noah. "Agents Black, Dalton. You're the leads on this case, so I'll let you take it from here."

As Winter rose to her feet, Aiden felt a twinge of pride. They might not have been on the best terms after he provided her with such a blunt assessment of her brother's mental state, but he was still impressed by how far she'd come over the last year.

Clearing her throat, Winter glanced down at the little notepad she carried. "This is a new development, but based on Nathaniel Arkwell's actions and the inconsistency of his recount of Peyton Hoesch's death, we have reason to believe that he's involved in the disappearance of five young women, including Dakota Ronsfeldt."

Six months earlier, Aiden might have succumbed to a bout of panic at the announcement. The lead had resulted from one of the strange visions she sometimes had about cases they worked, and he would have worried that she couldn't sufficiently explain the reason for her hunch. But over the past year, she had learned to hone her bizarre ability and use it to her advantage. By working backward from the vision, she knew where to look for evidence that supported her theory.

"What do we have that connects those murders to Nathaniel Arkwell?" When Max Osbourne posed the question, there was no accusatory undertone to his voice. Apparently, he'd also realized that Winter Black was a cut above a typical investigator.

She flipped back a couple pages. "Judge Arkwell drives a black Mercedes sedan, which is the same make and model that a witness saw pick up Dakota the night she disappeared. Our informant for this case, Ryan O'Connelly, recognized him from the group where the rumor of the deaths originated. With that, plus the suspicious behavior he's exhibited so far in our investigation of Peyton Hoesch's death, I think there are too many coincidences to ignore."

Max nodded. "Agreed. Do we have enough to get a search warrant for the rest of his house?"

Winter glanced around the room, but she didn't let her eyes linger on any one person. "We believe so. Agent Vasquez is on his way to the courthouse to present the evidence to a judge right now. We'll have the warrant in hand within the hour."

"What about Arkwell's motive for killing Peyton Hoesch?" Max asked.

When Noah Dalton spoke, their collective attention shifted to him. "He might have been trying to kidnap her. The medical examiner said she sustained a heavy blow to the back of her head. When that didn't knock her unconscious, it's possible that Peyton tried to flee, and Arkwell killed her before she could make it out of the house."

As Aiden shook his head, he could feel Autumn's stare on the side of his face. "His son was home at the time. Why would he try to abduct one of his kid's classmates? The son said Peyton was there to work on a group project with him. All the previous victims were prostitutes. There's no indication any of them had a connection to Cameron Arkwell, so why would Arkwell Senior change his MO so suddenly?"

Winter and Noah exchanged glances. Aiden might not have been keen on Noah Dalton's company, but he could admit the Texan was just as high caliber an investigator as Winter. His question wasn't borne from a desire to discredit their theory. Aiden retained his skepticism because he wanted to find the *right* answer, not just the easy answer.

"It could have been out of convenience," Winter said as she pocketed her notepad. "She was there, and he found her attractive, so he decided to try to abduct her before his son could catch on to what was happening."

"Forty-four-year-old serial killers don't change their MO that quickly." Aiden's voice was so matter of fact, he sounded like he'd just announced the solution to a simple math problem.

When the time came to debate the value of circumstantial evidence versus the value of behavioral analysis which was backed by decades of experimental, empirical data, he didn't pull his punches. There were still too many who thumbed their noses at the study of human behavior—those who referred to psychology as a "soft science" or who insisted that behavioral analyses ought to take a back seat to virtually any other type of evidence.

As long as he was still barraged with the same lines of tedious questioning in a courtroom, he would hold his ground, even if he respected the agents against whom he argued.

To Aiden's surprise, Max Osbourne turned his attention to Autumn. "Dr. Trent. Thank you again for being here. You have an interview scheduled with Mr. Arkwell, don't you?"

Autumn's expression was all but unreadable as she nodded. "I do." She glanced down to her watch. "In about twenty minutes."

The SAC swept his steely gaze over the room. "Right now, we've got two credible theories for what happened to Peyton Hoesch. In either case, we're confident that Nathaniel Arkwell is lying or omitting information. Our first goal is to find out what happened to Peyton, and then we can put the pieces together to determine whether or not he's the serial killer we've been looking for over the past week and a half."

Though part of Aiden hoped that Nathaniel Arkwell was indeed the voyeuristic murderer they sought, he reminded himself of all the good that hope did in this job.

32

I t might have been my imagination, but I thought the grass was greener toward the back of the yard. According to most farmers and gardeners, decomposing organic matter was the best fertilizer.

The entire area was lush and green, and the shade from a number of lakeside trees kept the sun from scorching the grass and shrubbery beneath. There wasn't much I liked these days, but I'd always liked my family's lake house.

My father had abandoned the property in favor of a more modern residence on the beach in Newport News, but I still preferred the lake to the ocean. There was a certain tranquility that came with the relative isolation an hour outside the city. I could hear the birds chirp, the woodland animals chatter at one another, and the calm drone of the afternoon breeze.

I'd entertained the idea of just staying here, but I shot it down in short order. I hadn't expected my father to take the blame for Peyton Hoesch, but I wasn't delusional enough to think that the man would be able to maintain his façade for longer than a day or two. Eventually, he'd crack, and he'd tell them the truth. He'd tell them about the flash drive. About the knives.

It was just a matter of time.

They'd find me if I stayed put at the lake house, but I didn't intend to stay. I'd come here to say goodbye, and to retrieve a rifle I never thought I'd have to use. The weapon was a last resort, a final option if the walls closed in around me. When I bought the rifle from a sporting goods store on the outskirts of town, I'd both hoped and dreaded the day that I'd be forced to use it.

Nathaniel had a couple AR style rifles, but I knew better than to try to nab one from under his nose. If there was one thing that man was diligent about, it was his firearms. But Virginia's gun laws were lax, and I'd picked up my own semi-automatic rifle not long after I turned eighteen.

My intent had been to defend myself from law enforcement if and when they came for me. Today, I'd allocated a different purpose to the fearsome weapon in my arms.

"I'm sorry, ladies."

To an onlooker, it might have looked like I'd just spoken to the empty yard behind the rustic house. But I knew better.

"I don't think I'll be back to visit you all again. I've got a few things I've got to take care of, and then I'll be leaving the country. It's looking like Panama right now, but maybe the Ukraine. I can speak a little Spanish, but I don't know any Russian, so we'll see."

I readjusted the messenger bag on my shoulder and heaved a sigh. I'd been skimming cash from Nathaniel for the past ten years, and even though he was diligent about his firearms, he'd never noticed the couple hundred dollars that went missing every so often.

This whole mess was Nathaniel's fault, so it seemed fitting that he ought to pay for it. I only regretted that I wouldn't be able to turn the rifle on him.

I couldn't physically reach Nathaniel, but I could still hurt him.

And just like he'd ruined me, I'd ruin him before I left this country. I'd take everything from him, just like everything had been taken from me when my mother died.

Nathaniel was in the custody of the police, but Maddie wasn't. Maddie, my aunt, uncle, and nieces were all still within my reach. And before I left the United States, I'd kill them all.

I returned my attention to the unmarked graves of the five women I'd killed.

Dakota Ronsfeldt.

Anastasia Mitchell.

Cassi Coleridge.

Thaisa Glendower.

Constance Wolsey.

It was a shame I wouldn't have the time to bury the rest of my family out here. Personally, I couldn't think of a better resting place. These women had been hookers when they were alive, and I knew there was no way they'd ever be buried in an area half as nice as the lake house. I did them a favor, and there wasn't a single one of them who had been grateful for it.

If Katrina Arkwell was still alive, I was sure all our stories would have ended differently. Maybe not the women buried beneath the massive elm tree, but for the rest of my family.

Nathaniel never should have let my mother drive that night. She'd been prescribed a new medication, and the start of a hurricane poured rain onto the city streets. One of the side effects of her medicine was blurred vision and dizziness. She hadn't seen the flood waters until it was too late, and I was sure the medication was at fault.

Well, the medication and Nathaniel. If he'd stopped her, if he'd insisted that she didn't need to go to pick up my sister before the full force of the hurricane hit, she'd still be alive.

Her death had been ruled an accident, but I knew better.

I knew who was to blame, and now he would pay.

NOAH GLANCED up from his phone as the door to the interview room creaked open. A teenage girl with dark brown hair pulled back in a ponytail stepped in ahead of the middle-aged woman at her back. The girl's green eyes flicked around the small room as the woman thanked the agent that had escorted them through the FBI building. When the woman's attention shifted over to Noah, he offered them both a pleasant smile.

Moving to stand, he extended a hand to the pair. "Maddie Arkwell, Susanna Arkwell, I'm Special Agent Dalton."

With a nod, Susanna accepted the handshake as her niece pulled out a chair. "Agent. Could you tell us why we're here? I was with Maddie last night when she answered the detective's questions. What is it that the FBI needs to know that the Richmond PD didn't?"

Noah's smile was unfaltering. He'd expected a certain level of obstinance from the sister-in-law of a judge, and so far, he wasn't disappointed. "That's a good question. Please." He waved to the chair beside Maddie. "Have a seat."

Her expression was begrudging, but Susanna accepted his offer.

Maddie glanced from her aunt to Noah. "Can I see my dad?"

The hopeful glint in her eyes was enough to elicit a pang of trepidation, but he shoved the sentiment aside. "Not quite yet. We've still got some information to get from him, but then you'll be able to talk to him."

The teenager responded with little more than a grim nod. "You think he killed that girl, right? Peyton Hoesch? That's what my brother said her name was. If my dad killed her, it was self-defense."

There wasn't so much as a sliver of doubt in her eyes. She spoke with the same certainty he'd expect from a chemist, a doctor, a mathematician.

Not what he'd expect from the frightened daughter of a predator.

Leaning back in his seat with a light creak, Noah folded his hands on the table. "Why do you think that, Maddie?"

She laughed, but the sound was mirthless. Despite the confident visage she put forth, the light glimmered on the first hints of glassiness in her eyes. "Because he doesn't even kill spiders when he finds them. If they're too big, he catches them and puts them outside. Otherwise, he just leaves them alone. He doesn't even *like* spiders, he just doesn't want to kill them."

He'd anticipated a flash of defensiveness, but the pain and worry behind Maddie's green eyes was above and beyond the Stockholm Syndrome type traits for which he'd prepared.

As he regained his focus, Noah straightened. "Were you at home when Peyton was shot?"

Shaking her head, Maddie picked at a piece of fuzz on her t-shirt. "I was at my friend's house."

"When you left for your friend's house, where was Peyton? What was she doing?" Though professional, he made sure to keep his tone amiable.

Maddie shrugged. "She was in the kitchen with my brother. They were waiting for their other classmate to get there so they could work on some group project."

Noah's next question was perfunctory. "Who was the classmate? Do you know their name?"

She glanced to her aunt, and Susanna shrugged.

"I'd never met her or anything." Maddie's eyes were back on him. "If that's what you're asking. I'd never even heard her name before then."

"What was her name?"

The teenager paused to look thoughtful. "I heard them say it a couple times while I was in the kitchen texting my friend. I think her name was Caroline? I don't think I heard them say her last name though."

The effort to keep his eyes from widening was monumental. Clamping his teeth together, he pushed past the rush of surprise.

Caroline Peters, the young woman whose pictures had been posted on the dark web forum used by the killer responsible for the disappearances of five other young women was supposed to have been in that home at the same time Peyton Hoesch was killed.

Circumstantial or not, there was no way they could ignore the newest piece of evidence. There was no feasible way to write the Arkwells' connection to Caroline Peters off as circumstance.

He swallowed and returned his focus to the room. "Was your father home at that time?"

"Yes. He was upstairs in his office."

With a nod, Noah moved to stand. "Okay, ladies. Those are all the questions I have for now. I need to step just outside and make a few phone calls, but I won't be far, I promise."

"Agent Dalton." The woman's voice stopped him just short of the door.

He forced a neutral countenance as he faced her. "Yes, Mrs. Arkwell?"

"What exactly happened to Peyton Hoesch?" The haughtiness had dissolved from her expression, and now her blue eyes were weary.

"Well, Mrs. Arkwell." He cast a quick glance to Maddie. "Peyton Hoesch's death has been ruled a homicide."

To her credit, Susanna moved past the shock almost as soon as it settled in on her face. "A homicide? Why is this a federal case?"

He clenched his jaw. "Because Peyton Hoesch was the daughter of a DEA agent, Mrs. Arkwell, which makes it a federal case automatically. Your brother-in-law's statement is inconsistent with the forensic evidence we've collected so far, and right now, we're trying to figure out why he's lying to us."

"Lying?" Maddie echoed, her eyes wide. "Why...why would he lie?"

Noah held out his hands. "I don't know. That's what we're trying to find out. Thank you again for answering my questions. You've both been very helpful so far." He gave them the most genuine smile he could manage. "Sit tight while I make those calls. I'll be back in a few minutes."

33

Autumn didn't need the newest information Noah'd just texted her to know for certain that Nathaniel Arkwell was a liar. As soon as the judge accepted her handshake, she knew. He was lying to protect someone, and there was only one person who that *someone* could be.

Now, she just needed him to say it.

Clicking the pen in her hand, Autumn glanced over to the two-way mirror before she offered Arkwell a smile. "Mr. Arkwell, I just want to make sure you understand that this interview is being monitored, and that anything you say here can be used against you in a court of law."

His light brown eyes were fixed on hers as he nodded. "I understand."

She renewed her smile. "Good. Now, Mr. Arkwell, in your own words, I'd like you to tell me what happened last night, step by step. I know it might seem tedious, but it is often the smallest detail that turns out to be important."

With another nod, he launched into the same recollection Autumn had already heard from Winter, Noah, and Aiden. She scribbled out a couple notes, but the writing was merely to make herself appear busy. By the time he finished, his expression had hardly changed.

But it *had* changed. A less keen observer might not have noticed, but Judge Arkwell was nervous. And next to the trepidation was weariness. Like he'd been maintaining a façade for too long, and the effort had sapped his mental resources.

As he finished the story, she rested one hand on the yellow legal pad and fixed him with an inquisitive look. "What did you hit her with?"

He drew his brows together. "Beg pardon?"

Autumn didn't let her stare waver. "You said you hit her in the back of the head in the scuffle. What did you hit her with?"

His brown eyes darted back and forth before he finally shook his head. "I...I think it was a tool or something. I didn't really look at it, I just grabbed it so I could defend myself."

She glanced to the pane of glass, but Arkwell hardly noticed. "I'm sure you saw it afterward, right?"

He opened and closed his mouth, but he didn't speak.

"Mr. Arkwell, do you *remember* the fight you had with Peyton Hoesch?" As much as she wanted to ask him why he was lying, she reminded herself that she was conducting a clinical interview, not an interrogation.

Asking about his memory was relevant to an assessment of mental illness, though she sincerely doubted that the judge had experienced a dissociative episode. There were no signs of schizophrenia or any similar disorder in his family's history.

She didn't need to touch him again to know he was just a liar.

As he stammered out a nonsensical response to her question, the realization struck her. Nathaniel Arkwell didn't fit

Aiden Parrish's psychological profile of the serial killer from the dark web forum, but *Cameron* Arkwell very well might.

She nodded absentmindedly as she set the pen on the pad of paper. "Could you tell me about your son? What's your relationship with him like?"

A wave of anxiety spread over the judge's face. "M-my son? Why?"

Autumn folded her hands. "Interpersonal relationships are a key component to a person's mental health. I'd like to know a little bit more about your family so I can get a better picture of what your life is like."

The shadows shifted along his throat as he swallowed. Between the wariness and the stubble that darkened his cheeks, he looked like he'd aged ten years since she walked into the room.

Slowly, he nodded his understanding. "My son is…he's smart. He's been on the Dean's List for almost every semester he's been at VCU."

"What about his mother? What happened to her?" Though she worried her tone might sound too crisp, the faraway look in Nathaniel's eyes made her wonder if he would have noticed had she shouted the question.

"She was in an accident about eleven years ago. She was on her way to get Maddie, our daughter, from a friend's house. It was dark, and a hurricane was about to make landfall. We'd just gotten hit with the edge of it by that time, but it was enough to cause quite a bit of flooding." He shook his head and rubbed his eyes. "She didn't see the flood water until it was too late."

More than a decade later, and the loss of his wife was still an open wound. Though Autumn thought to prod him for more information about the status of his marriage before Katrina's death, she didn't need her sixth sense to know that Nathaniel had cared deeply for Katrina.

"We went to high school together, but we didn't start dating until we were in college. We're both from Kansas, but she followed me out here when I joined the Navy. She found out she was pregnant a few weeks after we got to Norfolk, so I guess it's a good thing she did." His eyes were glassy by the time he paused.

Autumn couldn't help but wonder if he'd ever sought counseling or help after the loss. Based on the pain in his face, she thought the answer was a definitive no.

Before she composed another question, he went on. "I got my first assignment while she was pregnant, and I felt terrible when I had to leave. She was really great about it, though. She was excited. It was a little earlier than we'd planned, but we knew we wanted to have a family. She was only twenty at the time, and I was twenty-three, but we figured we'd be okay."

As Nathaniel paused to swallow, Autumn made no move to interject.

"After Cameron was born, it...changed. We'd both been excited before, but then, once he was there." With his vacant stare fixed on the corner of the room, he shrugged. "It was like it turned real for her. Don't get me wrong, she loved Cameron, but I just don't think she was ready. The doctors diagnosed her with postpartum depression but having a diagnosis didn't make it any easier."

Just below the nonsense she'd scribbled out earlier, Autumn jotted down Cameron's name. Beside it, she wrote *neglect?*

The lack of attention during a small child's critical development stages was associated with an increased likelihood of antisocial personality disorder, a disorder present in many serial killers and other violent offenders.

She glanced back to Nathaniel just as he returned his

focus to her. "Mr. Arkwell, do you know where your son is right now?"

He shook his head, and she watched as the stony facade settled back into place. "No. The police wouldn't let him stay at the house, so he probably went to stay with a friend."

Though his composure was admirable, there were cracks in the veneer that hadn't been there before. Beneath his show of invulnerability and exasperation, he wanted to talk to her. He'd demonstrated as much when he opened up about Katrina Arkwell.

At the same time, there was a powerful mental force stopping him from doing so.

The sentiment was so pervasive, she didn't have to touch him to feel it. Nathaniel Arkwell was motivated by guilt.

34

As Miguel Vasquez presented the search warrant to the uniformed officers posted just inside the Arkwell residence, Winter glanced around the spacious foyer. The ceiling was two stories high, and a sleek chandelier hung over the entryway. An arched doorway to her left led to the dining room and then the kitchen, and the short hall directly in front of the foyer led to the great room. On the right, a set of stairs ascended to the sunny second floor.

"I had a friend who lived in a house like this when I was in middle school." Stella Norcott's voice drew Winter from her silent contemplation.

Winter fished out a pair of nylon gloves as she turned to the forensics expert. They'd already donned their protective Tyvek jumpsuits and paper booties, and all looked like giant snow bunnies milling about. "It's massive. It makes executing a search warrant for the entire place into a full-time job."

As she produced her own gloves, Stella smiled. "That's why my team and I are here. Now that we're fairly sure that the person who posted those videos on the dark web is the same person who killed Peyton Hoesch, it was easy to get a whole team assigned to search this place."

Glancing to the side, Winter gestured to the stairs. "From the looks of it, the bedrooms are upstairs. The second story wasn't accessible without the warrant, so I was going to head up there first to see if I could find the son's room since SSA Parrish's profile indicated that the perp was younger." Looked like Aiden's profile might be spot on...dammit.

With a nod, Stella picked up her kit. "Okay. Let's go see what we can find. I've got two people designated to the garage and the car, and the rest will spread out to go through the rest of the house."

"I'll be in the garage with them," Miguel Vasquez said. He snapped his blue gloves into place and made his way to where a crime scene tech stood beneath the arched doorway.

Winter flashed him a quick thumbs-up before she turned to follow Stella upstairs. She had volunteered to help execute the search warrant in hopes that her sixth sense might help her pick up on a clue that might have otherwise been over-looked. Even as she and Stella walked up the stairs, Winter's eyes darted back and forth as she looked for any hint of a red glow.

"Nathaniel Arkwell's son is a suspect now, isn't he?" Stella pushed open a closed door to reveal a pristine bedroom.

Based on the colorful bedspread and the poster for the newest *Wonder Woman* film, the room belonged to Maddie Arkwell. Beside the open doorway to the walk-in closet, a modest aquarium bubbled quietly. A wooden carving of the letter M sat atop a matte black computer desk, and beside it were a couple succulent plants.

With a nod to Stella, Winter stepped back into the hall. "Cameron Arkwell is a suspect, but Maddie Arkwell isn't. We'll still look through her room if we need to, but we should start with father and son's."

Stella nodded, and they made their way to the next door in line. The décor for the second room was minimal, and the space was every bit as tidy as Maddie's room. Gray-blue walls complemented the navy bedspread, and the only items on the wall were a couple Tarantino movie posters. If it hadn't been for a neat stack of mail at the edge of the computer desk, Winter wouldn't have been sure whose room they were in.

Glancing to Stella, she pointed to the envelopes. "These are addressed to Cameron Arkwell. This must be his room."

Stella's green eyes went from curious to determined as she did a full three-sixty of the room. "I'll start with the closet."

Winter pulled the sheet of paper from the topmost envelope. The letter was dated a little over a month ago, and the text merely advised that Cameron's tuition had been paid.

Must be nice. Winter replaced the envelope and shuffled through the remaining pieces of mail. Each was from VCU, and each had already been opened.

She rifled through the top drawer on one side of the desk, but all she found was a stash of basic office supplies. A stapler, a stack of blank paper, a box of mechanical pencils, a couple HDMI cables. When she opened the larger bottom drawer, her heart pulsed, nearly taking her breath. Atop another stack of printer paper, a spiral notebook glowed like an ember.

With a quick glance to the closet door, Winter reached down to grab the notebook. When she flipped to the first page, she forced herself to exhale the breath she'd been holding. She knew the page was blank, but the ghostly handwriting was outlined in the same angry shade of red as the cover had been.

It should have been Nathaniel who died that night, was the first sentence that jumped out to her.

Before she could read through more of the text, movement flickered in Winter's periphery as Stella poked her head out from the closet door. "Did you find something?"

Angling the paper at the sunlight that streamed in through the picture window, Winter nodded. "I think so. This page is blank, but there was something written on top of it." She met Stella's curious glance. "Do you have a pencil?"

As Stella held up a finger, she ducked back into the closet to reemerge with her kit in hand. "I found something like this a few years back, and ever since then, I've always carried a piece of graphite with me just in case. Here, set it on the desk."

Nodding, Winter set the notebook down and stepped aside and waited while Stella took the prerequisite "before" photos of the seemingly blank page. Though she tried to peek over Stella's shoulder as she gingerly rubbed the graphite along the paper, she couldn't make out any details.

"Oh my..." Stella set down the graphite before she turned her wide-eyed stare to Winter. "You should look at this."

Winter's expression was grim as she looked down to the faint, white writing. The start of the diatribe referenced Nathaniel Arkwell's shocked reaction to something Cameron had given him, but there were no specifics listed. They might have been on a different page, but Winter had no way to know for sure.

After the writing speculated on Nathaniel's various weaknesses, Winter was certain the musings had been written by Cameron Arkwell.

Nathaniel should have been the one to drive through that hurricane to pick up his precious little girl. She's the only kid he's ever given a shit about. He should have died for her. It should have been Nathaniel who died that night. Someday, I'll make sure he knows that. I'll make sure it's the last thing he ever hears from me.

Though ominous, none of the statements were a direct

threat of harm to any one member of his family. However, what was clear was that the kid carried a chip on his shoulder. Winter didn't have to stretch her imagination to envision Cameron Arkwell as the perpetrator of a violent crime.

Nathaniel Arkwell was a different story. According to his daughter and his sister-in-law, the judge didn't even like to step on bugs in his own home. He collected firearms, but he'd been adamant that the weapons were strictly for self-defense.

Winter could feel Stella's eyes on the side of her face. "What are you thinking?" she asked. The good humor had vanished from her tone, and her visage was steely.

Lips pursed, Winter shook her head. "Cameron's got a grudge against his dad and his sister, that's for sure. By itself, none of it's necessarily incriminating. But when it's taken in context with Peyton Hoesch…"

Stella nodded her understanding. "It changes the narrative."

As she retrieved her phone from a pocket to take her own picture of the paper, her pulse rushed in her ears. "It changes everything, and it means that Aiden Parrish was right. It means that there's still a serial killer on the loose, and it means we've been looking into the wrong person."

She gritted her teeth.

Aiden was always right.

35

Though Aiden wondered at first why Autumn had delved into the subject of Nathaniel Arkwell's son, he didn't take long to put two and two together.

The Richmond police had asked Cameron the usual series of questions about what had happened leading up to the time when Nathaniel Arkwell allegedly shot and killed Peyton Hoesch. They'd swabbed his hands for gunshot residue, but they hadn't looked for defensive wounds.

At the time, they hadn't known that they *needed* to look for defensive wounds. At the time, Nathaniel's story didn't involve a physical altercation. And at the time, they had no reason to doubt the Honorable Judge Arkwell's recount of events. When a suspect provided a weapon and claimed that they had fired the fatal shot, the first question on the detectives' minds wasn't whether or not they were covering for someone else.

After Nathaniel told Autumn what had happened to his wife, the man pulled up his stone-faced façade. But this time, there were cracks in the stone. If Aiden noticed the judge's weariness, he knew for certain that Autumn had noticed.

"Why are you so interested in my son all of a sudden?" Nathaniel asked. The defensive undertone to his question was plain to hear. Autumn was close to a nerve.

Her expression was blank as she met Nathaniel's accusatory stare. "Your family life is relevant to this interview, Mr. Arkwell." Her tone was as unreadable as her face.

The judge narrowed his eyes. "How so?"

Autumn didn't flinch. "Does it bother you to talk about your son?"

When the start of a flush crept to Arkwell's cheeks, the corner of Aiden's mouth turned up. It really was a shame Autumn hadn't accepted a job offer at the FBI. With the uncanny knack she had for seeing straight through a person, her interrogations would have been a thing of beauty.

Arkwell pressed his fingertips together. "It doesn't *bother* me, Ms. Trent. I just don't see how it's relevant. I've told you and the Feds what happened, and I don't see what asking me about my kids could possibly accomplish."

Her green eyes flicked down to the yellow legal pad as she scrawled out a few words. Nathaniel's intent stare followed each and every movement of her wrist, but she rested her hand over the paper as she regarded him.

"What are you writing?" Arkwell jabbed a finger in the direction of the legal pad. His stone-faced visage was about to crumble.

He was sure Autumn knew it, but she belied no hint of her intent. Her bright eyes were calm, her movements easy and unassuming, her tone cool and professional. Now more than ever, he understood why she'd landed a position at a firm as lofty as Shadley and Latham.

And now more than ever, he wished she had accepted his invitation the night before last. He could have woken up to the soft scent of apples and vanilla on her skin when Detective Ramsey called him at five in the morning instead of with a woman he barely knew.

He brushed away the thoughts. This wasn't the time or the place to mull over his missteps in the realm of interpersonal relationships. Not when Nathaniel Arkwell was so close to cracking.

Autumn slowly shook her head. "I'm not trying to make you uncomfortable, Mr. Arkwell. This is a clinical interview to establish your state of mind before and after Peyton Hoesch was killed."

The judge leaned forward to fix her with a withering stare. "You're trying to figure out if I'm lying? If I'm crazy? Is that what this is? I've already told you and the FBI what happened. How many times do I need to say that?"

Rather than shift away from the intimidating glare, she folded her hands and scooted to the edge of her seat. "Then why are you suddenly so reluctant to elaborate on it? Do you feel guilty about something, Mr. Arkwell?"

Before Arkwell could reply, Aiden's phone buzzed against his side. With another glance at the judge, he retrieved the device from an interior pocket and unlocked the screen.

"Of course I feel guilty," Nathaniel said.

As Aiden's eyes fell on the photo that Winter had group texted to him and Noah Dalton, Nathaniel Arkwell might as well have been on the moon. He zoomed in to read the handwriting that had been outlined on the sheet of lined paper, and the familiar twinge of adrenaline rushed up to greet him.

Pocketing the phone, he strode out of the room. He rapped his knuckles against the heavy door, but he didn't wait for a response before pushing down on the lever and nudging it open.

He made a note of the judge's harrowed expression before he turned his attention to Autumn. "Dr. Trent, if you could, I need a word with you."

A flicker of curiosity flitted over her face, but she nodded as she picked up her pen and paper to stand. "Sorry, Mr. Arkwell. This will just take a minute."

As the door latched closed, he beckoned her into the observation room. She opened her mouth to speak, but he cut her off.

"You need to see this. I know he was about to give you something, but trust me." He retrieved his phone and unlocked the screen before he handed it to her. "This is a major development."

Wordlessly, she accepted the device from his outstretched hand.

He studied her face as she read through the rant that Cameron Arkwell had scrawled. Pursing her lips, she glanced up to him and then back to the screen. The shadows casted by the harsh white light lent her face an ethereal glow.

"Cameron Arkwell wrote that?" Her tone insisted that the question was as much a statement as a genuine inquiry.

He nodded. "Yes. Winter said she double-checked the handwriting against Nathaniel Arkwell's, and it didn't match. She found it in Cameron Arkwell's room."

Rubbing the bridge of her nose, she handed the phone back to him. "Shit. *Shit.*"

Aiden nearly reached for her but kept his hands at his sides. "What?"

When her eyes met his, there was a split-second of anxiety in her otherwise polished demeanor. "Arkwell's daughter and his sister-in-law are here, aren't they?"

"They are. Dalton was with them, last I knew. Why?"

"Okay, good. If he didn't know before, Cameron knows by now that we'll figure out who really killed Peyton Hoesch, and he knows we'll figure out that he's killed before. This..." She gestured to the phone. "This is sort of like his manifesto. There might not be anything incriminating on that page, but it spells his intent out pretty clearly."

Aiden ran a hand down his face. "He's going to kill his sister."

Her expression was grim as she nodded. "His sister, and potentially the rest of his family. She's staying with them, so I doubt he'd have a moral issue killing them all to get to her."

"I'll tell Winter. We still need something solid from the father." He gave her an expectant look, but to his surprise, she shook her head.

"I can't interrogate him. I could lose my license. I'll get ahold of Winter while you take that picture to Nathaniel Arkwell and get him to talk."

Though his first thought was to protest, he knew she was right. She couldn't stroll into the interview room to present a hateful rant that had been written by Nathaniel's son. She couldn't, but Aiden could.

"Okay. I'll deal with the judge, you call Winter." He held her gaze as he gestured to the room. "Stay here, though. I might need you."

Her expression was unreadable as she snapped a hand to her forehead in a crisp salute. "Aye-aye, Captain. I'll be right here."

He tried to suppress his sarcastic smile, but the effort was for naught. "At ease, Trent."

With a half-hearted release of the salute, she pulled out a chair and dropped to sit.

The good humor and the moment of levity were miles away as he pushed open the door to the interview room.

Nathaniel's attention jerked to him, and the man narrowed his eyes. "Where did she go? Who are you?"

As Aiden produced his badge, the movement was just short of reflexive. "I'm Supervisory Special Agent Parrish."

He paused to slide his phone across the table. "Do me a favor and take a look at that, will you?"

Nathaniel set his mouth in a hard line, but the handcuffs clattered as he pulled the phone closer. When he peered down at the image, Aiden wasn't sure what to expect. He wasn't sure if the judge would snap at him, if he'd toss the smartphone off the table, or if he'd launch into a string of obscenities.

But the longer Arkwell stared at the screen, the more the resistance in his eyes dissipated. By the time he pried his gaze away from the picture of Cameron's letter, he'd been thoroughly deflated.

Arkwell slid the phone back to Aiden. "Where'd you get this?"

"Your son's room. Your daughter is here, along with your sister-in-law, but we have good reason to believe your brother and your two nieces are in danger. I've been in the BAU for a long time, and I've seen men like your son snap before. He knows we'll find out he was the one responsible for Peyton Hoesch's murder, and he knows we'll find out about the other women he's killed."

All the color drained from Arkwell's face. "The other women?"

Aiden nodded. "Five in total, six if you count Peyton. His initial target was a classmate named Caroline Peters, but we got to her, so we think he decided to target Peyton when he realized he couldn't get to Caroline. Did you know anything about this, Mr. Arkwell?"

The man started to shake his head before Aiden even finished. "Jesus, *five*? Five women? Oh my god." He dropped his head into his hands, his breath heaving in and out of his lungs.

"If you knew something about this, you need to tell me now, or this is going to get very ugly for you very quickly."

Aiden didn't let his stare waver as he crossed his arms. "Who killed Peyton Hoesch?"

Leaning back in his rickety chair, Nathaniel let his head loll back to fix his vacant stare on the ceiling. "Cameron killed Peyton Hoesch. He told me it was in self-defense."

Aiden strove to keep his voice calm. "Tell me everything."

"A couple weeks ago, Cameron left a flash drive in my office. It was a video, and he told me a few days later that he'd found it on the internet." He trailed off as he shook his head.

"A video of someone slitting a blonde woman's throat."

The man's face turned red, and his Adam's apple bobbed several times before he finally met Aiden's stare. "Yes."

36

First her father, and now her brother.

Noah couldn't help but feel a pang of sympathy for Maddie Arkwell, and he was almost reluctant to leave the interview room when Winter knocked on the door. He didn't make a habit of checking his phone while he was in an interview with a witness, but he was glad he'd answered when Winter called to tell him about Cameron Arkwell.

To his relief, Levi Brandt was with her when he opened the door. After a quick introduction, Noah felt more at ease knowing that Maddie and her aunt were in the victim specialist's capable hands.

As he and Winter set off down the hall, he glanced over to her. "Any word on Cameron Arkwell's whereabouts?"

Her face was grim as she shook her head. "Not yet. But a few people from the forensics team went with Bobby to search the Arkwells' lake house. I just got a message from him when they opened up the basement door. They found another locked room down there, and it was a perfect match to what we saw in the videos. They're going through it now, but there isn't much doubt left."

Noah lengthened his stride. "So, now we just have to find Cameron Arkwell. What's the status of Nathaniel's brother and his nieces?"

"We got word to the city police, and they're going to send a couple officers over to escort them here while we look for Cameron. They should be at the brother's house soon."

Noah blew out a quick sigh. "Well, I'll feel better once they're here. What about Nathaniel Arkwell? Is he still trying to claim that killing Peyton Hoesch was self-defense?"

Her blue eyes flicked to him as they rounded a corner. "No. About ten minutes ago, he told Aiden that Cameron was the one who killed Peyton. Nathaniel was upstairs when it happened so he didn't see anything, but he says that Cameron told him it was self-defense."

He pulled open a glass and metal door after they each swiped their work ID cards over a badge reader. Winter's strained expression wasn't just the result of the situation with Cameron Arkwell, but he knew better than to press the issue.

On some level, they'd both hoped that Aiden had been mistaken about the profile of their potential suspect. Profiling wasn't an exact science, and the knowledge that Parrish was fallible would have been enough to set Winter at ease regarding the SSA's grim outlook on Justin Black's fate.

But even though Noah was sure Aiden Parrish was indeed fallible, the man was good at what he did.

PULLING the license plates off my car had been a risky decision, but when I'd weighed it against driving through the city with a sign that immediately identified me to a curious cop, the choice seemed obvious. If Nathaniel had cracked and told the Feds about Peyton, then I was less likely to be pulled over for having no license plates than I was with my own plates.

I'd never cared much about cars, but I was glad for my four-door Mazda. The gunmetal color didn't stand out, and the make and model didn't set me apart from any other commuters that afternoon. There were hundreds, maybe even thousands of other gunmetal Mazda sedans on the streets of Richmond. I was just one in a veritable ocean. As long as I kept my seat belt fastened and obeyed traffic laws, I doubted any cop would even look twice.

Unless, of course, they'd put out an all-points bulletin. But even then, being nondescript gave me a distinct advantage. All I had to do was make it to my aunt and uncle's house, and from there, I could drive one of their cars out of the city.

As I slowed to an all-way stop sign, I glanced to the red blanket that covered the back seat. The rifle was locked and loaded, and I was only a couple blocks away from the house.

When I turned my attention to the rearview mirror, I tightened my grip on the steering wheel. The black car was still a couple blocks behind me, but I knew right away that it was a cop.

If they followed me to the house, then my plans would have to change drastically. I could abandon my task and flee the city right now, but I'd have to lose the unmarked car nipping at my heels. Though I still wasn't certain that they were after me, Nathaniel had always taught me to err on the side of paranoia.

Truth be told, I didn't *want* to abandon my task. Nathaniel had ratted me out, and I was about to deal him a blow from which he'd never recover.

With another quick look to the hidden rifle, I pulled away from the stop sign as quickly as I dared.

A few more blocks.

37

Autumn turned in her seat to regard the opening door. Though she was used to greeting her friends with a smile and a wave, Winter and Noah's grim expressions, coupled with the tension that crackled through the air like an electric current, kept the salutation off her lips altogether.

"Agent Dalton, Agent Black." Max Osbourne offered them a crisp nod.

As they took their seats for the impromptu briefing about the status of Cameron Arkwell, Autumn glanced around the room. Their ranks were thin.

Bobby Weyrick had gone with the crime scene unit to investigate a lakeside property owned by Nathaniel Arkwell while Agent Miguel Vasquez was at the Arkwells' house, and Agent Sun Ming had gone to the beach house in Newport News. They'd uncovered plenty of damning evidence so far, but they still needed to find their suspect.

Max Osbourne swept his gaze over the small gathering. "We don't have much time. There's an APB out on Cameron Arkwell and his car, but based on what we found at that lake house, and based on Dr. Trent's assessment, we've advised them to avoid engaging him if at all possible. If they spot him, they're expected to contact the bureau immediately."

To her side, Aiden nodded his agreement. "We don't know what he's armed with, but we're certain that he *is* armed."

Though the spark of indignation in Winter's eyes might have been a figment of Autumn's imagination, she could have sworn she saw her friend shoot an unsavory glance in Aiden's direction.

"What did they find at the lake house?" Noah asked.

The SAC ran a hand over his gray buzz cut. "The basement, which I'm sure Agent Black already told you about. And then the stockpile of ammunition. It looked like some of it was missing, but we don't know how much. There were a couple handguns and a rifle along with it, but again, we've got no way of knowing what was missing, if anything. But we're erring on the side of caution and assuming that Cameron Arkwell is armed to the teeth."

Aiden's pale eyes shifted from her to Winter and Noah. "He's going to try to kill his sister. He thinks she's at her aunt and uncle's house, so that's where he's headed."

Furrowing her brows, Winter shook her head slightly. "Why would he do that if he thinks we're on to him? Wouldn't he just leave the city?"

Before Aiden could make another comment, Autumn butted in. "He's a narcissist, but he's not naïve or delusional. If he suspects we're on to him, then he knows there won't be much he can do to get away, at least not in the long-term. He might consider trying to flee the country, but he ought to know that with airport security, he wouldn't get far unless he had a fake passport. Which is possible, but fake American passports are difficult to make, and it takes several weeks or months to get one. So, unless he planned ahead for a day such as this, it's just as likely that he doesn't have one."

As the irritability dissipated from Winter's eyes, Autumn realized the petulant glance hadn't been her imagination. There was a palpable tension between her and Aiden, but Autumn's curiosity would have to wait.

With an upraised hand, Max reached into his suit jacket to retrieve a smartphone. He stepped away from the table as he identified himself to the caller.

Autumn glanced from Winter to Noah and then back. "Cameron Arkwell is going to kill his family. He doesn't know for sure if he can get out of the country, but he does know that there's a chance he can make it to his aunt and uncle before we do."

Noah's mouth was a hard line as he nodded. "Maddie Arkwell and her aunt are both here. We just need to get to the uncle and his kids. Maddie said her cousins are twelve and fourteen. It's a Saturday, so it's likely they're all at home right now."

As she blew out a silent breath, they collectively turned their attention back to Max Osbourne.

The SAC pocketed his phone. "They found him."

Winter was on her feet in an instant. "Where is he?"

A shadow settled in over Max's face. "He's at Susanna and David Arkwell's house. The city police tried to intercept him, but he pulled up to the house and got out of the car with an AR in his hands. He pointed it at them but managed to get inside before the LEOs were close enough to take a shot."

"Shit," Noah spat.

Max gestured to the doorway. "The tactical team is geared up and ready to go, and we're going with them. From what the officer I just spoke with says, they're looking at the potential for a hostage situation."

Autumn pushed herself from her seat and casted a hurried glance over the four federal agents. "You can't negotiate with him. Not like you would with a normal person."

She could feel Aiden's eyes on the side of her face. "What do you mean?"

Pursing her lips, she met his curious stare. "He's not like a normal person. He's not doing this because he's panicked or because he legitimately thinks he'll be able to get out of there unscathed. Think of it this way." She held up her hands and looked to the other three agents. "It's like you're going to negotiate a hostage situation with Ted Bundy or Edmund Kemper. How do you think that would go? They want to save their own skin, sure, but they also want to retain control. The second they agree to your terms, they forfeit their control."

"Shit." This time, the utterance came from Max Osbourne. "Dr. Trent, you're coming with us."

The cold rush of adrenaline flooded Autumn's veins. As she opened her mouth to protest, to remind the SAC that she wasn't a federal agent, that this wasn't her job, she bit off the rebuttal. Mike Shadley, one of the two partners who ran Shadley and Latham, had told her two different stories about how he'd accompanied law enforcement to confront a volatile offender.

Whether she liked it or not, this *was* her job.

38

E ven in a residential neighborhood, snipers had the two-story house covered from three different angles. Winter and Max were crouched behind a squad car parked in the middle of the street in front of the house. Angled at the car's front and rear fenders were two more squad cars. Noah and a police sergeant were hunched behind the vehicle in front of the car she was behind, and Autumn was with Aiden behind the other.

More police officers stood or crouched behind a few other squad cars, including those that had been positioned to cover the back of the house. So far, Cameron Arkwell had only shouted for them to mind their own business and leave before he killed his three hostages.

Adrenaline had been a constant companion since Winter arrived at the scene, but she had learned to control the jittery movements and racing thoughts. Adrenaline was useful in a stressful situation, but stressful situations had changed over time. These days, humans weren't hunting wooly mammoths or saber-toothed cats. The tremor and panic that accompanied an adrenaline rush were no longer useful, at least not in a hostage situation.

As Winter adjusted the stock of the M4 Carbine against her shoulder, she clicked a button to speak into the microphone attached to her Kevlar vest. "Autumn, can you hear me?"

Static hissed in her ear before the connection cleared. "Yeah, I can."

Winter turned her head to Max and flashed him a thumbs-up. During her time with the FBI, Winter had become an adept investigator, but she suspected her knack for suspect interviews wouldn't translate to hostage negotiation. The city had trained hostage negotiators on staff, but Max Osbourne had reminded them that this was a federal case. And while the FBI also kept trained hostage negotiators on staff, none were currently available.

"Is this a full moon or something?" she muttered to herself.

Besides, Autumn had told them that Cameron Arkwell wasn't a normal hostage taker—if such a thing even existed. The techniques that most negotiators had been taught wouldn't necessarily apply to a dialogue with someone like Cameron.

She took in a steadying breath before she pressed the mic button again. She and Autumn were the only two on their frequency, so at least she didn't have to worry about maintaining formality when she addressed her friend. "Okay, I need to get him to start talking to me. Or to us, however you want to look at it."

After a click and a hiss, Autumn's voice buzzed in her ear. "Just be as straightforward as you can. He'll see through any attempts to placate him, so just come out and say what you mean. Ask him what he wants, and phrase it like that. Don't try to offer him anything until after he's answered."

Winter nodded to herself as she moved to kneel. She kept her head just below the side mirror of the cruiser—raised enough so she could see the house, but ducked down far enough to keep herself from becoming an easy target.

Her mouth had become a desert, and she swallowed in an effort to return some semblance of moisture to her tongue. "Cameron Arkwell!" The shout sounded hoarse, but she was just glad she'd actually been able to shout. "This is Special Agent Black with the Federal Bureau of Investigation. What do you want?"

The seconds ticked away, and she wondered whether or not he'd heard her. Before she could repeat her question, he finally spoke. "I don't want anything from you people."

The calm in his voice raised the hairs on the back of her neck. Autumn was right. This was like trying to negotiate with Ted Bundy.

Static hissed in her ear again before Autumn spoke. "I figured he'd say something like that. Tell him that's BS. Everyone wants something."

Winter inched a bit taller and dared another glance at the house. She hoped to see a red glow that would indicate which room he was in, but there was nothing. "I know that's not true. Everyone wants something, Cameron."

This time, his response was abrupt. "I'm not stupid. I know you people aren't going to give me what I want. I want you to leave, to mind your own damn business. This is *my* family, and you have no idea what you're dealing with!"

"The only thing that's going to motivate him at this point is the opportunity for him to stay alive," Autumn said. "He's here because he feels like he has an ax to grind with his father. He wants his father to suffer, so you can play up the felony murder rule and make it seem like Nathaniel's going to be in prison for the rest of his life. Ask him if he's willing to die right now just to slight his father, and then bring up the potential for Nathaniel's sentence."

Winter wasn't certified in hostage negotiations, but she was sure this wasn't how a typical case was handled. But she trusted Autumn.

As she peeked out to the house again, the area was still. Then, as she watched, the front window slid open a few inches, then a few inches more.

"We've got movement," Winter announced to the team.

The curtains were drawn, though, so it was impossible to tell who was lifting the window, but Winter thought she knew why. It was so that Cameron could shout through the screen to be heard by his audience. An audience of automatic rifles, edgy cops, and flashing red and blue lights.

Clearing her throat, she inched back to relative safety. "Is this really the hill you want to die on, Cameron? Because if this goes your way, that's exactly what's going to happen. There are snipers with itchy trigger fingers covering that house from every angle. Do you think you're going to come out here and fight your way through us after you kill them? You won't get two steps before someone blows off your head!"

WAS this the hill I wanted to die on?

Stepping away from the window, I turned to look into the eyes of my uncle and his two brats, and a renewed sense of rage shot through me.

This wasn't how it was supposed to end.

Sure, I could take out these three, but Nathaniel and Maddie would still be breathing in and out. They'd probably be featured in all the news. Hell, they might even be guests on the Dr. Phil show or something equally pathetic, where they could cry and talk about how they'd tried to help me. Protect me.

Fury was like acid in my stomach.

"I'm here because Nathaniel needs to pay for what he did!" I screamed at the woman who'd spoken to me. I wished I could see her. I wished I knew which one she was. But I didn't dare even peek through the curtains.

"He'll pay, Cameron," the woman said.

She was lying, though. Everyone lied.

"Who are you, again?"

There wasn't even a pause. "I'm Special Agent Winter Black with the Federal Bureau of Investigation. I've been talking to your father, Cameron. That's why I'm here. Because I know what he's done."

I walked toward the window again, desperate to take a peek. It was a trick. I didn't dare.

"What did he say?" I hated myself for wanting to know, but the question was out of my mouth before I could stuff it back.

"Nathaniel's going to prison for the rest of his life," the agent shot back. "You want him to suffer? Well, he's going to. Under the Felony Murder Rule, he's just as culpable for Peyton Hoesch's death as you are. He'll be tried for first degree murder."

I wracked my brain, trying to remember what the Felony Murder Rule was from my pre-law classes. Was the woman right? Or was it wishful thinking or yet another lie? Would the powers that be charge Nathaniel using the Felony Murder Rule? The man was a state supreme court judge, and his pockets were deep. A trial would be an uphill battle for the prosecution.

The silence dragged on as I considered all the options. After a few minutes had passed, the woman yelled, "Cameron, are you still there?"

"If you don't kill me today, then the government will just stick a needle in my arm a few years from now!" The anger had returned with a vengeance. Good. Anger was useful.

"Cameron?"

I whirled around at the sound of my uncle's voice. I'd almost forgotten that he and the brats were here. How could I have forgotten that? Was that part of the trick? Distraction?

"What?" I screamed and leveled the gun at the man. The girls at his side tried to scream, but the gags in their mouths kept the sounds at bay.

David Arkwell looked like he was about to shit his pants. "Keep me and let the girls go."

I rolled my eyes, the request doing nothing but making me angrier. But...he also had a point. I needed to give a little to get a little. I looked into my cousins' big blue eyes. Besides, this could be fun.

"Which one?"

My uncle blinked. "Wh-what do you mean?"

"I mean choose. You have to choose which girl to save."

My cousins began to cry harder, both of them hugging their father tighter, muffled words getting lost in the gags' material.

I laughed out loud, slapping my thigh at my uncle's expression. "Come on, David. Which of these little bitches is your favorite?"

David tried to hold his daughters closer, but the rope I'd bound him with limited the movements. In two long strides, I was on top of them, holding the gun at fourteen-year-old Pillar's head. The girl froze, a long whine issuing past the gag while her sister and father began screaming.

"Stop!" David yelled, and tried to actually kick at me.

This was fun.

"Not her?" I asked, yelling to be heard over the screams.

Even muffled, they were giving me a headache. I turned the gun on Paige. "How about this one?"

David kicked me again, and I brought the butt of the automatic rifle down on his knee, smiling as it gave a satisfying crack. The older man howled.

"Cameron! Cameron! What's going on?"

It was the FBI agent from outside. I ignored her. This was simply too much fun.

"Choose, you bastard!" I screamed, bringing the gun down again. "My daddy has a favorite and I'm sure you do too. Tell me. Tell them! They have a right to know!"

Red-hot pain ripped through my arm, and the gun almost dropped from my numb hand.

Crack. Crack. Crack.

More pain. This time in my shoulder and back. The impact spun me around until I was facing the window again and saw the bullet holes through the curtains.

I dropped to the floor, screaming from the pain.

It was chaos.

Girls screaming. David yelling. The lady from the FBI saying something I couldn't understand.

"Stop shooting," I cried over the madness, crawling over to hide behind a couch. "Stop!"

"Cameron! Tell me what's happening in there. I need to know what's happening, or my men are coming in and they will take you down." There was a pause, then, "It doesn't have to end like this."

There was blood everywhere. My blood.

The very sight of it made me sick, and although I thought I was ready to die a few minutes ago…I wasn't.

I just wasn't.

"I want my dad."

I hated myself the minute the words left my mouth.

❄

THE BREATH WAS BILLOWING in and out of Winter's lungs, even though her feet hadn't moved an inch. Things had gone to hell within a few moments, and she still wasn't sure what had gone so wrong.

They'd gotten a call from Susanna Arkwell, telling them about the nanny cams set up in most every room. She'd given them the passcode, and they were in. Then, within less than a minute, Winter and the team watched in horror as Cameron went from being reasonable to holding the automatic rifle to his young cousins' heads.

"Zulu," Max yelled, giving the snipers their code word to fire when ready.

And the snipers fired, using the video feed to locate the otherwise blind target.

Watching the screen, Winter witnessed Cameron take several rounds. Watched him slump to the floor and crawl behind a chair. There was blood, yes, but…

"He's wearing a vest."

Beside her, Max nodded, having already come to the same conclusion.

Winter waited for Max to order the team to breach the entrance, but he held them down. Winter understood why. Cameron's rifle was pointed at the girls and his uncle.

They'd only slowed him down, Winter feared. Made him madder. More desperate.

"Get him talking again," Max ordered.

Winter called Cameron's name. Tried to get his attention. Tried to reason with him, telling him that it didn't have to end like this.

Then Cameron Arkwell said something she never expected to hear from him. "I want my dad."

Winter finally let out a breath. She had him back, and she

also knew that he'd be pissed at himself for having said those words out loud.

"Ignore it," Autumn said through her earpiece, echoing her own thoughts. "It will only make it worse."

"Understood," Winter said.

"I think he'll try to negotiate next," Autumn said, her voice a bit breathless but calm. "I know we can't take the death penalty off the table, but the actual likelihood that he'd be given the death penalty *and* the likelihood that he wouldn't be able to appeal the sentence is really slim. The kid comes from money."

Though Autumn was out of Winter's field of vision, Winter nodded. "And there's always the potential for a plea deal. He confesses, and they take the death penalty off the table."

Max drew his eyebrows together. "Seems like we're getting a little ahead of ourselves, aren't we?"

Winter shook her head. "This is the only way. Offering him his life is the only bargaining chip we have."

The shadows casted by the blue and red lights shifted along Max's face as he nodded.

Readjusting her rifle, Winter leaned against the cruiser. "You can make a plea deal." Her throat was sore from shouting, and she regretted not snatching a bottle of water on her way out of the office. "You plead guilty, or no contest, and in exchange, the U.S. Attorney throws out the death penalty in sentencing."

Autumn's voice was back in her ear. "Tell him he doesn't have to die, but he has to be smart about what he's doing right now. But we know he's smart, right? It plays to his ego."

Winter didn't hesitate. "I know you're smart, Cameron. We wouldn't be here right now if you weren't. And if you keep playing this smart, then you don't have to die."

"Right, I can just spend the rest of my life in prison!

Because that's such an upgrade!" His tone bordered on outright hostile. If he was pushed much more, Winter was sure he would snap again. Snap worse. She didn't especially care about Cameron's fate, but there were three innocent civilians—including two children—in the house with him.

As Winter raised a hand to press her microphone, Autumn spoke again.

"His alternative is being dead," she said. "If he's dead, then people only hear Nathaniel's side of the story. No one ever hears *Cameron's* side. Nathaniel paints him in a light that makes him look like some kind of monster, and no one's around to question it."

Winter looked at the video feed, but Cameron hadn't moved from behind the chair. "If you're dead, Cameron, then you know who will tell your story, right? You know he'll be the only one left *to* tell it. How do you think he'll make you look? Do you think he'll take ownership over what he did wrong?"

Another lengthy silence. She could only hope he was truly considering the words.

"If you're alive," Winter continued, "then you control the narrative."

"How do I know one of your trigger-happy friends out there won't shoot me as soon as I walk outside?" To her relief, the rage had been subdued.

"If you come out here unarmed, no one will shoot you." Though Winter's voice was scratchy, her tone was calm and matter-of-fact.

Each second was agony. Whenever she poked her head out to make note of any movement, she expected the crack of gunshots to shatter the eerie quiet as Cameron unloaded the magazine of his rifle on his uncle and his cousins.

Her heart hammered against her chest, and she wouldn't let herself admit it but her hands were trembling.

Winter's stomach heaved.

At first, she couldn't place the reason for the sudden nausea when she thought that the tactical sniper team might shoot and kill Cameron Arkwell. But in the next breath, realization dawned.

What if he was Justin?

To Maddie, even to Nathaniel, Cameron *was* Justin. Cameron was the sweet little boy in the SpongeBob footie pajamas, but the years had turned him into something unrecognizable.

Cameron's shout cut through her racing thoughts. "Okay."

Had she missed something in the moments her mind was swept back in time? She cleared her throat. "Okay, what?"

"I'll come out. Unarmed. I'm setting the rifle down now."

She squinted at the window. "What about your uncle and your cousins?"

"They're fine." The plain statement was laced with bitterness.

With a quick glance to Max, Winter raised her weapon to rest the barrel along the hood of the squad car. She trained the red dot sight on the window but snapped the rifle to point at the door at the first sign of movement. The afternoon had become so still, she could hear the creak as the door slowly swung inward.

Cameron Arkwell's pale blue eyes fell on her as he took the first step onto the covered porch. With his blood-covered palms facing them, he raised his hands above his head and took another tentative step.

As soon as Cameron reached the sidewalk, a handful of police officers approached, each pointing a handgun or a rifle in Cameron's direction.

Winter's legs ached as she rose to stand. As she lowered her M4, she had to blink repeatedly to reassure herself that the scene unfolding was real. She turned her head to the side at the flicker of auburn hair in her periphery. Autumn had pinned her dark auburn hair back in a low ponytail, and block letters on the front of her Kevlar vest designated her as part of the FBI. With a slight smile, she raised a hand to flash Winter a thumbs-up.

They had gone into the negotiations with the hope that they'd manage to shoot and kill Cameron Arkwell before he turned his weapon on his uncle and cousins.

Instead, he was about to be hauled away in handcuffs.

39

W hen Autumn strolled into the offices of Shadley and Latham the Monday after Cameron Arkwell's arrest, she received a standing ovation. Though she hadn't watched the press conference about Cameron, she was told that the FBI credited her and Winter with the nonviolent arrest. After thanking the group of coworkers in the café of their ritzy building, she bowed a couple times, much to the amusement of Mike Shadley.

As she started toward her office, coffee energy drink in hand, her attention was soon drawn to a familiar voice at her back. A voice she hadn't wanted to hear today, but the second partner of Shadley and Latham was difficult to ignore.

Forcing a smile, she turned around to face him. "Good morning, Dr. Latham. How are you?"

As he extended a hand, her stomach lurched. With a chuckle, she held out her full hands and shrugged.

He grinned in response and mercifully retracted his hand. Autumn was mostly grateful for her sixth sense, but when the time came to touch Adam Latham, she avoided the gesture like the bubonic plague. She still didn't know the details, but she knew that Adam Latham was not a good man.

And every time she had the displeasure of shaking his hand, she became more and more certain that *she* was his newest infatuation. If she wasn't yet, she would be soon. She wasn't sure if she wanted to know what that would entail, and she'd even entertained the idea of searching for a different job.

Maybe I should have taken Aiden's offer to work at the FBI. At the thought of Aiden Parrish, her stomach dropped even lower. She thought they had become friends, but his demeanor around her the day before insisted otherwise. Her ability became diluted the more time she spent around someone, but she'd still been able to glean that Aiden was ambivalent toward her. She didn't know why he felt that way, but the sudden change had put a definitive damper on what should have otherwise been a good day.

And then, of course, there was Adam Latham. She would have rather run into Cameron Arkwell in the hallway. At least Cameron didn't have the authority to fire her if she made the wrong move in his presence. If the kid tried to come at her with a knife, she could break his arm in three places and knock him to the ground before he even knew what had happened.

Adam Latham was a different story. She couldn't beat him into submission, and she had no recourse for any unwanted advances he thought to make. Adam Latham had one thing Cameron Arkwell didn't. Adam Latham had power.

Autumn blinked a few times and shook herself out of the contemplation. "Sorry." She returned her attention to Adam. "I had a hard time sleeping last night, and I'm still a little tired. Hence this." She raised the coffee drink.

As he chuckled, there was the same unsettling glint in his eyes she'd spotted before. "No worries. I just wanted to catch up with you to congratulate you on a job well done. That was damn fine work, Dr. Trent."

She grinned, but the expression was entirely feigned. "Thank you, Dr. Latham. I appreciate it."

He held up an index finger.

Oh, shit. Here it comes. He's going to ask me out. Touch me. Something completely unwanted.

Her stomach churned as her pulse rushed in her ears.

He lowered his voice. "And I thought I'd come to you with this before anyone else."

The tentative creep of relief seeped into her tired muscles as she nodded. "Of course. What is it?"

"The FBI needs someone to conduct a clinical forensic evaluation of Cameron Arkwell. I've already recommended you for it, so they'll be reaching out to you sometime today."

She was so relieved that she didn't even care that he'd donned the same self-assured smile that made her skin crawl. "That sounds great. Thank you for that. I really appreciate it."

"No problem at all. I know you'll do an excellent job." Waving a hand at the hall from which Autumn had come, he shrugged. "Otherwise, I figured you deserved a day off. Go kick back and relax, and I'll talk to you soon."

Her smile was suddenly much easier to fake. "Thank you. Again, I appreciate it."

That, at least, wasn't a lie. She was grateful for any opportunity to relieve herself of Adam Latham's presence.

As soon as Autumn arrived home, she pulled off her five-inch heels and stripped out of her dressy slacks and button-down shirt. Once she was clad in a worn band t-shirt and a pair of capri sweats, she flopped down on the couch to check her phone.

With a chirp, the cat, Peach, leapt onto the cushion by her head and sniffed her hair. Autumn absentmindedly reached up to scratch the cat's chin as she unlocked her phone and Toad the dog snuggled in closer to her leg. There were a few new emails about her upcoming contract to evaluate Cameron Arkwell, but those weren't the messages that caught her attention.

She hadn't seen Dan Nguyen's name in her text message inbox in...how long had it been? More than six months, at least. She'd bought her new phone six months ago, and she hadn't hesitated to throw out their text message history along with the old device.

Sighing, she tapped the icon to pull up the new texts.

I saw the FBI press conference about Cameron Arkwell. I'm sure you've already heard it seven ways from Sunday, but I just wanted to tell you that you did a great job. Btw, I'm using your Halloween Xmas tree idea in my office. It gets me a lot of weird looks, but they crack me up. Other than eBay, where do you get your decorations? I think I need to spruce it up a little.

She'd started to chuckle by the end of the message. Dan had always been keen on eliciting looks of confusion from other people. Even though he dressed like a stockbroker on most days, he had an impressive collection of ridiculous Hawaiian shirts.

As she scanned the second message, her heartrate increased, and her mouth went dry.

Okay, well, I'll just come right out and ask, then. Would you be interested in meeting up for lunch or coffee or something? Just to catch up. Honestly, I'm really curious what it's like working at Shadley and Latham, plus all the work you've been doing with the FBI. If that's too weird, I totally understand.

Autumn pursed her lips and reread the message. Part of the reason for their split had been her desire to pursue a career rather than settle down to start a family right out of college. She hadn't dedicated her life to academia for eight years to earn the Ph.D. behind her name just to hang a plaque on the wall of her apartment.

Though she'd been mad at Dan at first, she had since realized that their age gap was to blame for the differing goals. Autumn had always liked the idea of a family, but she still wasn't sure if kids were realistic for her future. She couldn't conceive thanks to endometriosis, a tidbit that neither she nor Dan had known when they were together.

But maybe there was a chance they could still be friends. It would be a relief to have a friend around who she'd known for longer than a few months.

Before she could analyze the decision any further, her fingers flew over the virtual keyboard.

No, that's not weird. My boss gave me the day off if you're free. She didn't give herself time to second-guess the message before she hit send. *Oh, and I get the decorations at craft stores.*

Part of her was relieved that Dan didn't hate her, but part of her wasn't entirely sure of her motive for meeting up with him. But for the time being, she told herself she wanted to open the door for them to establish a friendship.

Plus, it wouldn't hurt to have an extra ally if Adam Latham proved to be as shifty as she thought.

40

W inter had called Maddie Arkwell the day before to ask if she could stop by to talk to her. Though she had no idea what she planned to say, Winter hadn't been able to shake the haunting similarities between the situation into which Maddie had been thrust and the situation Winter had faced down after her parents were murdered. Sure, Maddie's father and brother were still alive, but her brother would never walk the streets as a free man again.

Nathaniel Arkwell's arraignment was scheduled for later in the afternoon, and that was precisely why Winter had offered to stop by that morning. Though Maddie, Susanna, and David Arkwell might have viewed the bureau as protectors, Winter still wasn't sure how the judge viewed them anymore. Cameron might have been a sociopath, but to Nathaniel, the FBI were the people who had taken his son from him.

She swallowed against the sudden bout of uncertainty as she climbed the steps to the porch of the same house she'd stared down a couple days ago. The faint scent of blooming chrysanthemums and roses wafted up to greet her as she approached the door. She might not have known what to say to Maddie, but she knew she had to say *something* to the poor girl.

With a quiet sigh, Winter rapped her knuckles against the wooden door. A couple faint voices followed, and when the door creaked open, Winter offered a smile to Susanna Arkwell.

"Good morning, Agent Black." Susanna stepped aside as she shoved open the screen door.

Winter smiled. "Just Winter today." For emphasis, she brushed off the front of her gray canvas jacket.

Susanna smiled. "Winter, that's a pretty name. Maddie told us that you were going to stop by. I made some sweet tea, but I'll leave it up to Maddie to be a hostess."

From the corner of her eye, Winter spotted the young woman she'd come to visit. Like she had at the FBI office, Maddie had pinned her dark hair back in a ponytail, and a black headband held the wayward strands away from her face. Otherwise, the Nirvana t-shirt, flannel button-down, and skinny jeans reminded Winter of Autumn.

Winter gestured to Maddie's t-shirt. "You like Nirvana?"

With a slight smile, Maddie nodded. "Yeah. I like '90s music. It's way better than the stuff my classmates listen to."

Winter's smile came a little easier. "My...friend loves Nirvana and '90s music too." Friend? Was that still what she was supposed to call Noah?

She brushed aside the thought. She could contemplate Noah's title later.

Grinning, Winter held up a finger. "I also learned recently that Kurt Cobain and grunge music are what destroyed the popularity of '80s hair bands. I can't *stand* hair bands."

From the edge of the foyer, Susanna Arkwell chortled.

Even Maddie returned Winter's wide smile. "Aunt Susanna hates hair bands too."

Susanna spread her hands. "It's true. I was a kid when a lot of those stupid songs came out, and I couldn't stand them then, either. Maddie, honey, I made some sweet tea for you two. I'm going to go in the living room and read for a while. Let me know if you need anything."

"Thank you, Mrs. Arkwell." Winter lifted a hand as the woman disappeared around a corner.

Maddie gestured to a short hallway. "The kitchen's this way. We can sit outside if you want. It's really nice out today."

"Yeah, that sounds good."

Beneath Maddie's seemingly good spirit, a shadow lurked. Winter had seen the shadow before. She'd seen it in herself, and she'd seen it in Augusto Lopez.

That shadow was a toxic combination of betrayal and cynicism, of vengeance and despondency. It was the realization that nothing would ever be the same again, no matter how hard they tried to put the pieces together. Maddie had seen a side of humanity she could never un-see.

But as Winter watched Maddie pour them each a glass of sweet tea, she knew for certain she didn't want Maddie to end up like her. She didn't want every waking moment of the rest of the girl's life to be spent pining for revenge, or searching desperately for closure that didn't exist.

In silence, they made their way through a sliding glass door. The same welcoming scent of chrysanthemums and roses drifted along the stone patio. Maddie settled into a cushioned wicker chair beneath an awning, and Winter took a seat in the matching chair at her side.

As she sipped the sweet tea, Maddie's green eyes flicked over to Winter. "What did you want to talk about, Agent...I mean, Winter."

With a quick smile, Winter took a deep drink of her own tea. "I know you're going through a lot right now. You've lost your family, and I wanted to tell you that I know what that feels like."

Curiosity flashed along Maddie's face. "You do?"

Winter nodded. "When I was thirteen, a serial killer broke into my home. He murdered both my parents, and he took my little brother. I haven't seen him since."

"Oh my god." Maddie's eyes widened in a horror that was hard to look at. "I'm sorry. That must have been awful."

"So, as I said, I know how you feel, and I'm really sorry that you have to know how that feels." She offered the girl a wistful smile.

For the first time since she'd met Maddie a few days earlier, her face fell. Her gaze shifted down to the glass in her hand as she slowly nodded. "I feel like I'm stuck in a spider's web, you know. And that no matter how hard I fight to get lose, the more stuck I become."

Winter's web felt very much the same. Except that she could almost see the spider creeping up behind her, smiling as it strode in to make its kill.

Crossing her arms to control the shiver that raced through her body, Winter strove to remain calm in front of this girl. She needed to find her brother.

"I just miss my dad," Maddie continued. Her voice was hardly above a whisper. "And I guess I miss my brother too, even though I don't even know who he is anymore."

Winter's heart squeezed in her chest, making it hard to breathe. To her horror, emotion burned its way into her face. With all the willpower she possessed, she forced it away.

"Losing my parents and my brother, it's…" Winter paused to swallow against the new tightness in her throat. "It's made me who I am, and it's shaped absolutely everything about my life. I missed out on so much because all I could think about was revenge, and about what I lost. You never would've guessed it if you saw me, either. A lot like you today."

Maddie sniffled as she swiped a hand over her cheek. "It just feels like no one else cares like I do. I know my aunt and uncle are sad too, but not like I am. Their whole world didn't just fall apart over the course of twenty-four hours, you know? They don't know how that feels."

Winter met Maddie's forlorn stare and tapped herself with an index finger. "I know how that feels. I know how it feels for your world to grind to a halt while everything else goes on like nothing even happened. That's why I wanted to come visit you today. I wanted to make sure you know you're not alone."

Maddie brushed at her cheek again. "Did you ever find your brother?"

Shaking her head, Winter bit her tongue to keep the threat of tears at bay. "We're looking, but we haven't found him yet. He's out there, we just don't know where."

As they lapsed into silence, Winter wondered if she should keep her concern about Justin to herself. So far, the only person in whom she'd confided at any length was Noah.

This time, however, Winter hoped that Maddie could be the one to remind her that *she* wasn't alone.

Finally, she lifted her eyes from where they'd been fixed on the glass in her hand. "My friend thinks that my little brother is a sociopath."

Silence thickened between them before the girl nodded slightly. "Like Cameron."

"Yeah, like Cameron." Winter didn't see any reason to refute the statement. It was true, after all. Cameron Arkwell was a sociopath, and according to Aiden Parrish, Justin was too.

"There's nothing you could have done." Maddie's voice was gentle and quiet. "You were just a kid."

With a warm smile, Winter nodded. "I know. I want you to remember that too, okay? There's nothing you could've done that would have made any of this turn out differently. It might sound weird for me to say it, but none of this is your fault. Don't ever forget that."

"Okay." Maddie managed a small smile before she took another drink of her tea. "Can I ask you something? About my dad?"

"Of course." When Winter sipped at her tea, she realized for the first time how good the drink tasted.

Maddie's green eyes flicked back to her glass. "Is he going to go to prison?"

Winter pushed back a sigh and shrugged. "I'm not sure."

She had no idea if Arkwell's ties to other powerful aristocrats would save him from a trial and a jail sentence, or if a slick defense lawyer would get him out of the situation altogether. In the back of her mind, she suspected that Nathaniel Arkwell wouldn't be sent to prison, but she didn't want to give Maddie an answer if she wasn't sure.

For the first time, the thought that Nathaniel would make off with no jail time didn't come with a wave of ire. In some capacity, Winter understood why Nathaniel had tried to protect his son. She didn't agree with the decision, but she could put herself in Nathaniel's shoes.

"His arraignment is today, so you'll know more later on," Winter said. "Your dad's not a bad person. He made some bad decisions, but that doesn't mean he's a bad guy. Cameron is his son, and he was trying to protect him. Don't be too hard on him, okay?"

The shadows in Maddie's face lessened as she nodded again. "Okay."

The idea that Maddie's father might have harbored the same darkness as her brother was a war that the girl had undoubtedly waged with herself over the last couple days. Nathaniel Arkwell might have been an idiot, but he wasn't bad.

As Winter polished off the last of her drink, she reached into her jacket to produce a business card.

Maddie raised her eyebrows, but she wordlessly accepted the card.

"That's got my contact information on it. My email address and my phone number. Actually, hold on." Winter shuffled through her handbag for a pen. "Let me write my personal phone number on the back of it for you."

Eyes wide, Maddie handed the card back to Winter and watched quietly as she wrote out her number. "Wow, thank you."

Winter gave her another smile. "I'm going to head home, but I just want you to know that I'm here if you ever need me. If you just want to talk, even if it's about school or boys or whatever, you can call me. And if you ever need help, no matter what time it is, give me a call, okay?"

When Maddie nodded, the late morning sunlight caught the glassiness in her eyes. "Thank you," she managed.

Winter cleared the emotion from her throat as the girl's arms wrapped around her. She pressed her cheek into the girl's sweet-smelling hair and said a silent prayer that she be able to release the burden of her family's guilt.

Prayed that maybe, just maybe, Maddie would be different.

41

Though the digital clock told him that it was only a little past six in the evening, Noah was content with spending the rest of his night in bed. As his eyelids drooped, he tightened his grip around Winter's bare shoulders. The warmth of her body beside his was like a lull to sleep, in and of itself.

Her eyelashes tickled his neck as she traced her fingers up and down his forearm. "What am I supposed to call you?"

He blinked a few times and brushed the wayward hair from his forehead. "Um…how about Noah?"

With a quiet chuckle, she offered a playful punch to his chest. "Thanks, smartass."

Shifting in his position until he could see her eyes, he flashed her a grin. "Any time, darlin.'" He leaned down to kiss her forehead as she laughed. "I gather that's not what you mean, though, is it?"

She shook her head. "No. I already know your name, and unless you've been recently crowned a duke of some place, I don't think I need to worry about your title."

As he chuckled, he propped his elbow on the pillow to

rest his face in one hand. "I don't know. What do you *want* to call me?"

"Well, Duke Noah Dalton of Somewhere Around Dallas, Texas is a mouthful, so maybe we could shorten it. I don't think an acronym would work, so I'm open to suggestions."

Until he lapsed into a fit of laughter, her expression was so poised that she might have fooled an onlooker into thinking she was serious. When he was confident that the chuckling had passed, he nodded his agreement. "Yeah, that's a bit much. Maybe we could shorten it to something like 'boyfriend?'"

The corners of her eyes creased as she smiled. "You're not a boy, though. You're a man. Man-friend? No, that sounds weird."

He shrugged as he tried to keep himself from succumbing to another fit of laughter. "Maybe we just go with 'significant other,' or SO, as the kids say."

She nodded. "I like it. It's the proper level of sophistication for a couple people who work for the FBI."

Brushing a few strands of hair from her face, he leaned down for a light kiss. As she tucked her face in the crook of his neck, Noah wrapped an arm around her shoulders and pulled her as close as he could manage. A silence settled in over them, but the quiet was calm and comfortable.

The ability to enjoy a silence together was one of the many reasons he'd grown so fond of his and Winter's time together. To hear her confirm aloud that she wanted a term to make their relationship official brought a smile to his face.

"I went to visit Maddie Arkwell today," she said.

He kneaded his fingers against the base of her neck. "How'd it go?"

"I don't know. I think I got through to her. I hope I did." She scooted back and tilted her head to meet his gaze. "It's weird, but I think in some way, she helped me too."

He lifted his brows. "That's good."

Her lips curved into a wistful smile. "Sometimes it just helps to know that you aren't alone. That there are other people who know what you're going through."

"That's true. That's what helped me the most, I think. Chris, my stepdad, his father was a real jackass too. Him being there and being able to relate to me and Lucy helped us a lot."

The fleeting despondency lifted from her eyes. "I'm glad to hear that. He sounds like a great guy."

"One of the best."

"You know." As she rubbed his arm, her expression turned thoughtful. "I told Maddie this, but I don't think Nathaniel Arkwell is a bad person. I think he made some bad decisions, but he made them in the interest of trying to keep his kid safe."

"Yeah. I suppose that's true."

She scooted up to bring herself eye-level with him. Beside the hint of sadness, determination glinted in her bright eyes. "It made me think, and I don't want to do that. I don't want to make those same bad decisions. If we find my brother, and he's...like Cameron Arkwell, if he's *bad*. I don't want to make up excuses for him or do anything that might get another person hurt."

Sadness and respect and a dozen other emotions tore at Noah as he traced his fingertips along Winter's cheek. "You won't. I know you won't."

When she smiled this time, the expression wasn't sad or wistful. "Because you'll help me."

He pulled her until she tumbled across his chest, his hands on both sides of her face. "Because you're strong and wise and beautiful and good." He pressed his lips to the tip of her nose. "And because I'll help you."

As he pressed his lips to hers, she combed the fingers of

one hand through his hair. When they separated, the cadence of his breathing had picked up as the sense of anticipation worked its way through his body.

He could live to be a thousand, and he was sure he'd never get tired of the feeling he got when he was with Winter Black. His significant other.

SWALLOWING against the dryness in his mouth, Ryan O'Connelly straightened in his seat as Max Osbourne stepped through the doorway. Just behind him was a shorter man with a neatly trimmed goatee and dark brown hair. His tailored suit and shiny black dress shoes were a cut above the usual standard of dress around the FBI office. Before either of the two men spoke, Ryan knew who he was.

"Mr. O'Connelly." Max gestured to Ryan. "This is the U.S. Attorney who's handling your case, this is Ryan O'Connelly."

Ryan willed a smile to his lips as he rose to accept the lawyer's handshake. "Nice to finally meet you, Mr. Perez."

The corners of Perez's dark eyes creased, but the man's mouth barely moved. "It's a pleasure to meet you too, Mr. O'Connelly."

As they took their seats, Ryan clenched his hands together beneath the table. Though he'd been told by Max Osbourne that the U.S. Attorney had reached a reasonable decision, Ryan still wondered if his and Max's definitions of "reasonable" were the same.

Perez set his briefcase atop the circular table, and with a couple light clicks, he opened the top to retrieve a pile of papers. "SAC Osbourne told me about the help you gave the bureau during the investigation into Cameron Arkwell. If Arkwell's case goes to trial, you may have to testify. Would that be a problem for you, Mr. O'Connelly?"

Ryan shook his head. "Not at all."

Perez nodded and tapped a finger on a folder. "Good to hear. Now, I'll go over some of the high points I've drafted up, and then we can get into the specifics if you need more information."

All Ryan could do was nod. His heart knocked against his chest with the force of a hammer, and no matter how many times he tried to swallow, his mouth was as dry as a desert. Almost all of his cognitive energy was devoted to maintaining a neutral countenance, and he wondered how much longer he would be able to carry on the novel feat.

Perez gave him a hard look as he held up a finger. "First and foremost, the part I'm sure you've wondered about the most. If you follow all the details we've laid out in this agreement, you will serve no jail time."

Ryan had to fight from slumping over into a relieved heap. With a smile he hoped wasn't over the top, he nodded. "Thank you, Mr. Perez."

He didn't care if the FBI wanted him to jump through a series of flaming hoops like a tiger in a circus. If it meant he could avoid jail time, he would do just about anything.

Jason Perez's face turned amiable as he held up the next finger. "Second, you'll be on probation for the next five years. You'll be expected to remain in the state of Virginia until that time is over, and for the first year, you'll be wearing that nifty ankle monitor."

Ryan didn't care. He'd wear the damn thing for the rest of his life.

"Third." Perez raised another finger. "For the five years that you're on probation, you'll be working as an informant for the Federal Bureau of Investigation. Primarily in the White Collar and Cyber Crimes Divisions, but your help may also be requested elsewhere at times. You'll be paid for the work you do, of course."

With a nod, Ryan accepted the paperwork from the lawyer's outstretched hands.

Max Osbourne gestured to the papers. "The first task we're going to have you help with is tracking down the people who posted in the forum that Cameron Arkwell used."

I'd be half-inclined to do that for free. Ryan kept the thought to himself. "Of course. I'm looking forward to you guys finding some more of those bastards."

Jason Perez chuckled, and even Max cracked a smile at the candid response.

"Like I said, those are the highlights. Oh," Perez reopened his briefcase, "since you're not a fugitive anymore, this doesn't really apply, but we wanted to make sure you got it in writing. Your sister won't be charged with any crime related to your status as a fugitive."

This time, Ryan couldn't help but blow out a sigh of relief. "Thank god," he murmured to himself. "What about her ex-husband and the divorce?"

Max and the lawyer exchanged glances. As Max met Ryan's expectant stare, he nodded. "That's not in your agreement, but I'll help you with that, and I'll help make sure they can move to Virginia, if they so choose."

Any remaining tension fled from Ryan's muscles as he returned Max's nod. "Thank you both."

Shaking his head, Max chuckled. "Don't thank me yet. You've got a lot of work to do, O'Connelly."

Ryan's laugh sounded closer to a cough. "It's a labor of love."

LATER THAT NIGHT, Ryan sat at a workspace on the third floor. He'd been accompanied upstairs by an agent in the

Cyber Crimes Division named Ava Welford, and though her intent had merely been to show him where he would be working in the coming weeks, he'd taken the liberty of cracking open his FBI issued laptop.

He didn't have access to any of the confidential databases that the FBI agents used, and the majority of the information he provided would be gleaned through research he conducted on the dark web. Though the agents in Cyber Crimes had access to the dark web and the Marianas web, they weren't familiar with the forums in the same way Ryan was familiar with them.

Ryan knew phrases to use, phrases to avoid, warning signs, legitimate versus illegitimate forums. He'd been a patron of the internet's underbelly virtually since its inception. After all, the clients for whom he'd stolen priceless goods hadn't found him on Craigslist.

After a couple hours of absentminded perusal, Ryan perked up when he came across a familiar forum—a forum devoted to racist and extremist points of view. Unsurprisingly, the patrons of that particular site were enamored with people like Tyler Haldane and Kent Strickland.

He'd come across plenty of false positives in his search for their manifesto, but one of the newer posts on the site had already racked up dozens of comments. In the search for the killer of five young women, he'd neglected to check the forum for the past couple days.

According to the title of the original post, the poster had located a scanned hard copy of Tyler and Kent's manifesto. As he pulled up the document, Ryan fully expected the image to be a photo of an upraised middle finger or a picture of Rick Astley. He'd been Rick-rolled once already in his search.

Users of the dark web had a bizarre sense of humor, though Ryan assumed the so-called troll uploads had been intended to prank the Nazis and white supremacists who sought Tyler and Kent's manifesto. For that, Ryan couldn't find fault.

But this wasn't a picture of a middle finger with the words "Nazi punks, fuck off" written in block text behind it, nor was it a photo of the handsome singer.

This was text. Handwritten text.

Eyes wide, he rolled his chair backward and glanced to the doorway. "Agent Welford? Are you still here?"

Within moments, the agent stepped into the room. "I'm here. Do you need help with something?"

Ryan shook his head and pointed at the laptop screen. "No, but I found something I think you might want to see."

42

Though Winter arrived at the FBI office in good spirits the next day, a cloud of anxiety still seemed to follow her wherever she went. She suspected that, until she learned more about her brother's fate, the sense of trepidation would remain. But overall, she couldn't complain.

She'd slept for an entire ten hours. Ten hours of deep, restful sleep at the side of one of her favorite people. They'd both awoken refreshed before either of their alarms had started to buzz, and they had used the extra time to have sex in the shower. According to Noah, it was by far his favorite way to start the day.

On their way to work, they had stopped by a coffee shop for a morning treat. When the barista asked for Noah's name, Winter had been quick to interject.

With one hand on his upper arm, she had leaned in, looking perfectly serious. "He's Duke Noah Dalton of Somewhere Around Dallas, Texas."

The young man behind the counter was thoroughly confused by Winter's subsequent outburst of laughter, and Noah had raised a hand to cover his own chortle as he shook his head. "Just Noah," he had said. "Like the guy with the boat and all the animals. Noah."

His succinct description of the biblical figure had only renewed her amusement. On and off for the remainder of their trip to the office, she had chuckled to herself periodically.

It felt so good to laugh. She felt heady at the tension-releasing emotion.

By the time they arrived in the Violent Crimes Division, Winter had managed to don an air of professionalism. They had only just set their coffee and pastries on their desks when Max strode down the row of cubicles.

The SAC's gray eyes shifted from Winter to Noah. "Agent Dalton, Agent Black. Briefing room. Two minutes ago."

Their response was merely a couple silent nods. After shrugging at one another, they followed Max down the hall to the largest conference room in their section of the building. Though they used it for routine briefings, there were occasions when the space was utilized for training courses or meetings.

Sun Ming and Miguel Vasquez arrived shortly after Winter and Noah had taken their seats. Other than Max and Ava Welford, they were the only four occupants.

Worry and something close to dread settled on Winter as she casted another glance around the room. "Is this everyone?"

Shaking his head, Max gestured to the open doorway. "No, but now it is."

Bobby Weyrick nodded a greeting to them as he closed the door behind himself.

Max returned the nod. "Now, this is everyone. Parrish isn't here yet, so I'll give him the rundown when he gets in."

The feeling of dread grew. Aiden wasn't here yet? If she

hadn't seen his apartment for herself, she would have been convinced that the man *lived* at the FBI office.

"Agents."

Max's gravelly voice snapped her out of the contemplation.

"Last night, our newest informant, Mr. O'Connelly, came across Tyler Haldane and Kent Strickland's manifesto. Until now, it's only been rumored that it even exists. It's handwritten, and we've already matched the handwriting to samples of theirs that we have on file." Max's expression was as grim as Winter had ever seen. "It's a dead match. There's no doubt that this was written by them."

Winter's eyes widened for a split-second, but she promptly reined in the expression of surprise, even as she wondered where all this was leading.

Looking grim, Max crossed his arms. "That's not all of it."

Sometimes, Winter wondered if Max possessed the same ability to read people as Autumn.

He swept his intense stare over the room one more time. "There was a third person involved."

This time, Winter didn't bother to conceal her surprise. To the best of their knowledge thus far, the mass shooting that occurred on the same night Winter, Aiden, and Noah confronted Douglas Kilroy had been planned and carried out exclusively by Tyler Haldane and Kent Strickland. Neither man had mentioned a third person involved.

And why would they? They're loyal to one another.

"A third person?" Bobby Weyrick echoed. "Someone else helped them plan that? Did they do anything else?"

Jaw clenched, Max nodded. "They were at the Riverside Mall that night. We don't know where, but they were there to conduct reconnaissance for the two shooters."

And just like that, the web of killers grew bigger.

The End
To be continued...

Thank you for reading.
All of the Winter Black Series books can be found on Amazon.

ACKNOWLEDGMENTS

How does one properly thank everyone involved in taking a dream and making it a reality? Let me try.

In addition to my family, whose unending support provided the foundation for me to find the time and energy to put these thoughts on paper, I want to thank the editors who polished my words and made them shine.

Many thanks to my publisher for risking taking on a newbie and giving me the confidence to become a bona fide author.

More than anyone, I want to thank you, my reader, for clicking on a nobody and sharing your most important asset, your time, with this book. I hope with all my heart I made it worthwhile.

Much love,
Mary

ABOUT THE AUTHOR

Mary Stone lives among the majestic Blue Ridge Mountains of East Tennessee with her two dogs, four cats, a couple of energetic boys, and a very patient husband.

As a young girl, she would go to bed every night, wondering what type of creature might be lurking underneath. It wasn't until she was older that she learned that the creatures she needed to most fear were human.

Today, she creates vivid stories with courageous, strong heroines and dastardly villains. She invites you to enter her world of serial killers, FBI agents but never damsels in distress. Her female characters can handle themselves, going toe-to-toe with any male character, protagonist or antagonist.

Discover more about Mary Stone on her website.
www.authormarystone.com

facebook.com/authormarystone
goodreads.com/AuthorMaryStone
bookbub.com/profile/3378576590
pinterest.com/MaryStoneAuthor

Made in United States
North Haven, CT
10 June 2022

20059795R00170